Anni̶ who has ̶ orked ̶
and radio. She wa̶ also a rock 'n' roll DJ in America ̶ ̶ ̶ ̶ ̶ ̶ ̶.
She's a regular broadcaster on BBC Radio Ulster and RTE, and
more recently she has made her name writing plays for Irish radio
and BBC Radio 4. Annie McCartney is the author of *Desire Lines*
and *Your Cheatin' Heart*. *Two Doors Down* is her third book.

Also by Annie McCartney
Desire Lines
Your Cheatin' Heart

Two Doors Down

Annie McCartney

sphere

SPHERE

First published in Great Britain as a paperback original in 2007
by Sphere

Copyright © Annie McCartney 2007

A CIP catalogue record for this book
is available from the British Library.

ISBN 978-0-751-53594-5

Typeset in Bembo by Palimpsest Book Production Limited,
Grangemouth, Stirlingshire

Printed and bound in Great Britain by
Mackays of Chatham plc, Chatham, Kent

Papers used by Sphere are natural, recyclable products made from wood
grown in sustainable forests and certified in accordance with the rules of
the Forest Stewardship Council.

Sphere
An imprint of
Little, Brown Book Group
Brettenham House
Lancaster Place
London WC2E 7EN

Member of the Hachette Livre Group of Companies

www.littlebrown.co.uk

For Bernie

Acknowledgements

A huge thank you to my neighbours in Rugby Road for the inspiration, tea and sympathy – and the occasional glass of wine. I would also like to thank my long-suffering friends (they know who they are), my editors Louise Davies and Jo Dickinson, the great team at Little Brown, my agent Sheila Crawley, for her support, Judy Meg Kennedy and Naomi Leon from AP Watt. The Tyrone Guthrie Centre Monaghan for providing me with a haven of peace and, of course, Katy, Duncan and especially Iain. No thanks at all to the mad poglets.

1

At nine o'clock sharp on an unusually bright Monday morning, Sally O'Neill rode her shiny motorbike along Marlborough Road. She slowed down at the top of the street and with an expert swerve turned through a pair of high gates into a back lane, passing as she did so from urban grey to leafy greenery, and at this time of year, late May, through a profusion of blossom, birdsong and noisy children.

Marlborough Road, a wide, confident tree-lined street in south Belfast, sported on its odd-numbered side a fine example of a redbrick Victorian terrace. The row of tall houses stood proudly to attention, all but two of the neat front gardens framed by cast-iron railings. The brightly coloured front doors were a palette of yellows, blues and reds, with one a startlingly vivid purple. All sported polished knockers and letterboxes – three of them gleaming more brightly than the others, for Sally O'Neill knew how to clean brass. She cleaned three of the houses in Marlborough Road on a regular basis, and had at some time helped out in nearly every other house in the terrace, not only with the endless domestic chores, but with the endless domestic dramas too.

The terrace had the advantage of backing on to one of Belfast's finest parks. Those walking in the park might have noticed, had they been able to see clearly through the dense greenery, that a lane separated the houses from their back gardens, creating an enclosed world, a hidden little bit of Belfast. It was here that the residents played out their lives, rarely using their front doors, preferring to leave and enter by the back, enjoying the privacy the gates at the top of the lane afforded them.

In the summer months, the younger children rode their bikes up and down the lane, skilfully avoiding the occasional yapping dog, and roamed in packs from garden to garden with little to interrupt their fun but the odd tumble from the Nelsons' tree house or the wrath of Miss Edith Black when a muddy football struck her sparkling windows (plenty of vinegar in the rinsing water). All the comings and goings took place right here in the back lane. Endless visits to various kitchens, to chat or gossip, to drink lemon and ginger tea, to borrow milk or maybe beg something more exotic – a shoot of lemon grass, a pinch of cumin or a sprig of rosemary for a recipe. And strictly after six p.m., neighbours might also meet to indulge in a glass of wine or a refreshing gin and tonic. Sometimes, when an excuse could be found for celebration, a bottle of good champagne might even appear.

As she rode slowly down the lane, keeping a watchful eye out for children, Sally noticed that the McDonalds' wisteria had colonised at least two other houses, forming an arch of pale mauve blossom that stretched from number 25 to number 29 like a garland. Not for the first time, she thought how the back lane really came into its own in summer. The clematis Miss Black had planted five years ago had grown almost all the way up her lilac tree. At number 21, the McNamaras had inherited a large magnolia tree from the previous owners, and earlier that spring Sally had enjoyed the delicate pink flowers. Over the years she had gradually learnt the names of all the various flowers and shrubs from Miss Black, and knowing what the plants were added an extra layer to her pleasure.

She stopped outside the back door of the McDonalds' house and turned off the engine, then swung herself off the bike. She still felt a wee bit self-conscious about riding it, but each time she nearly lost her nerve she focused on how it had added a new dimension to her life. It made her feel different from the run-of-the-mill cleaning lady, and best of all, it gave the residents of Marlborough Road something to blatter on about. She smiled to herself as she imagined them saying, 'What noise? Oh, that. It's just my cleaning lady roaring off on her motorbike.'

She had won the bike in a competition. She'd filled out some form or other – *name three kinds of pasta and win a sexy Italian bike.* There was a time when she would only have known spaghetti and macaroni, but no longer: the kids in Marlborough Road seemed to eat nothing but fancy pasta, so she had simply opened Clare McDonald's cupboard, and written down *tagliatelli*, *papardelli* and *fusilli*, taking care to spell them properly. She hadn't expected to win, of course, but then ages afterwards, when had forgotten all about it, she'd got a phone call to say she'd won first prize. She simply couldn't believe her luck. At first she had fully intended selling the bike – it was a Piaggio, stylish, chic and worth quite a lot of money, something Sally didn't have much of – but when she saw it, she loved it so much she just decided to keep it. It was fire-engine red, with black swirly patterns on the petrol tank and plenty of sparkling chrome. She hadn't regretted keeping it for a minute. She stored it under a tarpaulin cover in her back garden, and every Saturday gave it a good wash and polish. Her heart filled with pleasure at the sight of it: it was hers, all hers. It conferred on her a sort of kudos that she'd never had before. Even now, after owning the bike for four months, she could recall perfectly the looks on the faces of Clare and the other women she cleaned for when she first turned up on it. For almost the first time in her life Sally had felt she measured up; she was exotic, special, like all of them in Marlborough Road with their iguanas, hamsters and macaws, and, of course, their free-range children.

'It's only me,' she called now as she entered. She took off her crash helmet, fluffed up her hair and straightened her clothes. Then she hung up her jacket and went to change into her slippers. She hoped Clare was upstairs at her desk, well out of the way. That meant she could make a good start on the kitchen before Clare came in looking for some camomile tea to calm her nerves. Awful-looking yellow stuff that tasted like hay, but it was too much to contemplate what Clare would be like without it. She drank gallons of it, but was still, in Sally's opinion, 'highly strung'.

Sally had answered an ad – *Lady wanted for light household duties* – nearly ten years ago and had been hired on the spot by Clare McDonald from number 25. 'Light household duties' was a bit of a misnomer, for there was nothing light about them. The place was totally disorganised and Sally had been welcomed into the chaos with utter relief.

Ten years ago Tony and Clare McDonald were just about thirty, a year younger than Sally herself. They had three children: Rory, eight, Evie, six, and the new baby, Anna. Their house, in the middle of the terrace, was roomy, tall (four storeys) and absolutely chock-a-block with stuff, all of it supposedly essential. At times the clutter nearly did Sally's head in. Each room was shelved from ceiling to floor, and the shelves were stacked full of books. She had never seen so many books outside a library, and she doubted anyone could live long enough to read them all. Still, apart from all the stuff, the house had a good feel to it.

Sally had grown up with the old adage 'a place for everything and everything in its place'. But then you could have fitted her small rented semi in west Belfast into the McDonalds' upstairs drawing room. Nonetheless, she slowly got used to the house and to the family, and gradually her original two hours once a week grew to two hours three days a week, and then three hours on a Friday, as Clare and the other women Sally cleaned for became more and more dependent on her.

As she put the kettle on, Sally surveyed the damage in the McDonalds' kitchen. They must have had a dinner party last night. Honest to God, you'd think Clare ran a restaurant. She seemed to entertain all the time, and although she could cook, she never used one dish when she could use ten. The dishwasher had been run, that was something, and the pots were steeping in soapy water. Sally would rush through the lot and reward herself with a cup of tea before she tackled the floor. That bloody dog had peed on it again. They had a sort of nappy thing they put down for it, but Sally thought that if someone would take the trouble to train the poor thing, or let it out at night, they could do away with the pads.

For some odd reason the dog adored Sally. It sat and looked at her with a soupy expression on its face while she bustled around it. She needed it out from under her feet now, though, if she was to tackle this mess. The dog gazed at her beseechingly.

'C'mon, you, out you go.' Sally opened the door and pointed. 'Go on. Out . . . get out!'

Lola went reluctantly. The residents all specialised in weird names for their pets, and used their surnames too, so Lola was known as Lola McDonald.

Sally's shouts had alerted Clare to her presence. Down she came. Sally handed over a cup of camomile; Clare sipped it gratefully, then moved to the bench near the kitchen window, yawning as she did so. She was still wearing her dressing gown, a worn-out blue towelling thing she'd had since Anna was a baby. Sally often wondered why she didn't buy a new one. But

5

then why would she? People like Clare could get away with wearing threadbare dressing gowns, not to mention old cardigans and shapeless tracksuit bottoms; you needed the confidence and the posh voice to carry it off.

Clare McDonald was a tall, slim, naturally elegant woman of around forty. She was pretty, with thick shoulder-length blonde hair that she mostly tied back. Her green eyes were striking and she had sharp, regular features, redeemed by a warm full mouth and lovely teeth. She had that particular ease of people who know they are attractive. She put little effort into her appearance, except when she was going out. Sally, on the other hand, fixed herself up every morning, even for just coming to work.

In the dining room the candles had all burnt down; it looked as if they had had a power cut. There were more candles than you'd see at a high mass, but this was par for the course. They were all very fond of candles in this terrace. Electric light seemed to unsettle them. Sally surveyed the damage. They had used those massive wine glasses again, like goldfish bowls on sticks; you could fit a bottle of wine in each. No wonder the bottles in the yard were piling up. All their back yards were stacked with empties for recycling. At home Sally put her bottles in the bin; she doubted that recycling her one wine bottle a week would save much of the planet anyway. She lifted the glasses gingerly; they had to be hand-washed as well, which was a pain. She was always terrified she'd break one. Not that Clare made much of a fuss about the occasional breakage, but Sally hated to be beholden to any of them.

Happy as she was in her job as cleaner and counsellor to the denizens of Marlborough Road, there was always a part of her that longed for something more challenging. But there was little chance of that; she had to live, didn't she? From time to time she thought of leaving, but they paid her well, and gave her holiday pay and birthday and Christmas presents, and since

6

she was qualified for nothing, it seemed as good as she could get. After all, she had a house to keep, and no husband. Not that she lost much sleep over that. Getting rid of Charlie had been one of the more positive things in her life. She didn't mention him to her employers; no one asked, they were all too preoccupied with their own lives. They just assumed that she was divorced, which suited her fine.

She had married Charlie O'Neill twenty years ago. He had had dark brown curls, a lithe figure, a great smile, and blue eyes that really twinkled, like bits of coloured glass. He had delivered bread every day to the Spar where Sally worked, and was great craic, just full of devilment. He would spend ages teasing and joking with the shop assistants, who were all mad about him and flirted with him like crazy. All except Sally. She was in love with him, but didn't join in because she didn't think she had the slightest chance of getting him. So when he asked her out, she could barely contain her joy. Of course she said yes, and that was it. In no time at all they were inseparable. Charlie seemed to adore her, and couldn't keep his hands off her. But Sally was a good girl, and Charlie had to set a date before he could get her to sleep with him. Not for Sally McManus a shotgun wedding. They would do things right and wait till they had somewhere to live before starting a family. She stuck to her guns, and they married the day after her twenty-first birthday. At first she thought it was so romantic to fall asleep every night and wake up every morning in Charlie's arms. She had yearned for a place of her own, growing up as she had as one of eight kids. But it wasn't long before she found out that there was more to life than romance.

Sally sighed and went back into the kitchen for a tray. She'd have the wine glasses washed in a few minutes, and then she'd tackle the ironing. She hated ironing, but it was part of the job description. She sensed Clare couldn't be pushed too far on this one, since she hated it too, so she suffered it, but Clare wasn't stupid and over the years had gradually whittled down the unruly pile so that now, instead of a huge crumpled mountain that just kept growing, Sally ironed only Tony's shirts and the children's school uniforms. She had been delighted when Rory, Clare's eldest, left school and went off to uni. At least Clare allowed her to use spray starch. Saffron McNamara, who lived at number 21, was convinced it was destroying the ozone layer, so Sally had to rely on steam there, and if anyone's shirts could have used a bit of starch it was Trevor's. God love him, he never quite looked the part of a successful solicitor. To make matters worse, Saffron had a habit of putting all the laundry in together at the wrong temperature. Very few things in the McNamara house stayed their original colour.

Sally set up the ironing board near the kitchen window; that way she could get a good view of the comings and goings in the lane. While she ironed, she listened to Gerry Anderson on Radio Ulster. She thought he was a scream, as sharp as a tack. He was so insulting to some of his listeners, but it didn't seem to bother them, or stop them ringing him up. If Clare was in the kitchen, Sally had to put up with *Woman's Hour*, and Jenni Murray talking about the problems of working mothers or obscure female medical conditions. Arranged marriages were a favourite topic. Sally had her own opinions about marriage, but she kept those to herself. Her troubles with Charlie had started after their daughter Bronagh was born. Charlie was not, to put it mildly, an ideal father. After he had worn out his lines about his little bundle of joy, he more or less left Sally to it. She had saved for years and had quit the Spar with the intention of having three children, but their second attempt ended in miscarriage so she resigned herself to having only the one. Charlie increasingly spent most of his time out with his mates, drinking heavily and hanging around in the bookie's. Every time Sally tried to talk to him about the lack of housekeeping money, or the loneliness of sitting in alone night after night, he would promise her faithfully that he was going to change. His eyes would light up as he shared his pipe dreams with her. He had plans for them, big plans. That was one of the reasons she had married him. She had truly believed him when he said he didn't see either of them spending their lives in a housing executive property in west Belfast. He had wanted them to move over to south Belfast, to a big roomy house. Well, Sally was in a big roomy house in south Belfast right now. The only problem was, she was cleaning it.

2

Wednesday was one of Sally's long days. After the morning spent at the McDonalds', she went to number 21, the McNamaras', for the afternoon. She had a quick sandwich at Clare's before she left. She didn't trust most of the things Saffron cooked. That vegetarian malarkey was all very well if you were a natural cook, but Saffron most definitely was not.

The colour purple sprang to mind immediately Sally thought of the McNamara home. She often joked that if she stayed still long enough, Saffron would spray her lilac to blend in with the background. Saffron loved the colour; she even had a purple toilet seat in the downstairs loo. Her house made the McDonalds seem like minimalists. Sally had overheard Evie saying this to her mum and thought it was right on the button. Saffron threw nothing out; she was much worse than Clare. Several of the children's grubby drawings were displayed about the place. Half-used candles were kept, elastic bands, string, unread copies of the *Guardian*, read copies of the *Guardian*, and all the children's birthday cards. Postcards from various exotic locations accumulated over the past ten years were stashed in piles here and there, or stuck to the fridge with magnets.

As for the drawers – well, there were no words to describe the state of the drawers. Sally daydreamed about holding a massive jumble sale and clearing out the entire contents of the house. In the meantime, she cleaned as best she could, but for all the hard work she put in, she felt she hardly made a dent in the place.

Saffron was sitting looking dishevelled, with Posy on her knee sucking away. Saffron gave a helpless shrug.

'Oh, Sally, thank goodness you're here. She won't stop feeding, and she had such a big lunch.'

'Saffron love, is it not time you stopped that? She's three years old. You know it's just for attention. C'mon, you,' she said to Posy, 'I'll get you a nice drink of juice.'

Posy came obediently. Sally glanced at Saffron's breast hanging there, looking abandoned.

'You need to get yourself some new underwear. Most of your stuff is in ribbons, and you've had that bra for years.'

Sally knew the state of the underwear of everyone in the terrace. Didn't she wash it often enough?

'You're right. Evie said she'd go with me to Marks any time. She says they have beautiful stuff there.'

'Well, the sooner the better.'

Unlike some of the women in the lane, Saffron didn't take good enough care of herself. For a start there was the vegetarian lark. Not a bad thing, Sally knew, but if there was anyone who looked as if they needed a good steak, it was Saffron. She spent hours cooking strange meals like mung bean stew, or couscous with aubergines, or stuffed vine leaves, all tasteless-looking concoctions made with vegetables Sally had never heard of. Now and then she relented and sent out for a pizza, but Sally was convinced there was no nourishment in most of the stuff she ate. She couldn't have weighed more than seven stone, and then she'd just sit for hours letting Posy suck the life out of her. Posy was getting all the goodness. She was a big, hefty

11

KK374410

child, more her father's build. It would have to stop. Sally was on a crusade.

She gave Posy a drink and turned to survey the state of the kitchen. Immediately she noticed two saucepans streaked with wax sitting on the draining board.

'Ach, Saffron, you haven't been making candles again?'

'Oh Sally, don't worry, I'll clear it up, I promise.' Saffron caught Sally's look. 'It's just that Edith is having her special barbecue and I thought it might be lovely to have some citronella candles. They keep the insects away without killing them, and of course we don't have to have all those awful sprays damaging our lungs.'

Saffron drove Sally bats with all this nonsense, but then she had the zeal of the convert, and Sally knew they were the worst. She had been brought up in east Belfast as a good wee Protestant girl named Enid, but had met some fellow who took her off to India, where she changed her name and became a vegetarian Buddhist. He eventually ran off on her, so she returned home and got a job temping as a legal secretary. One of her first placements was at McNamara & Son Solicitors. Even though he was some twenty years her senior, Trevor fell head over heels for this exotic waif, and within a month, much to everyone's surprise, had married her. Sally thought the marriage a good one. Trevor doted on Saffron, and that was how it should be, the man being the one beholden. Women got more attention that way. It was plain Saffron adored him too, though lately she seemed a bit too absorbed in the children. Treasure, she called him. When Sally first started working in this house she had found it all a bit strange, especially after the dynamism of number 25 and the austere peace of 29. This was like landing on another planet. Trevor had owned the house for years – his father had bought it for him while he was a student – but things had changed dramatically since 'the invasion', as he called it. His quiet bachelor residence, livened only by the discreet visits of lady friends, had turned into a family home teeming with children and animals. Within a year of their marriage, Simon was born. He was nine now. Posy came along six years later. Sally often wondered why it had taken Saffron so long to get pregnant again. She figured it had something to do with all that breastfeeding. She didn't like to ask what age Simon was when Saffron stopped.

Sally hadn't breastfed Bronagh; no one had suggested it. Everyone gave their babies bottles where she came from. You would have to be very sure of yourself to breastfeed. All the same, now she'd been around it so much and heard Clare and Saffron rave on about how good it was for the babies, she hoped Bronagh would do it when she had her own children. Clare had managed eight months with Anna – that was long enough – and Patricia Thompson from down the lane had stopped as soon as she got her figure back. But three years was far too long. Sally would have to have a word with Trevor. He needed to tell Saffron that enough was enough. Surely he didn't want her to waste away?

'Well, d'ye want me to do the kitchen?'

'As a matter of fact, I wondered if you could just do the children's rooms, mainly Simon's. I thought if his bed was changed he might get a good night's sleep. He has his Grade Two piano exam tomorrow.'

Sally hated cleaning Simon's room, or even changing his bed, because in order to do either she had to face his pet iguana. Saffron read this in her hesitation.

'Don't worry, Iggy is in the front room with Simon, and we've taken his cage out too.'

Sally nodded her approval and headed upstairs. In less than an hour she had the room spotless. She came back down to the kitchen to find Saffron stirring some vile-looking yellow gloop on the stove. It smelled like a curry. Saffron still had a yen for all things Indian. The house always reeked of incense, and she draped the lamps in scarves, and of course she dressed in that hippie gear as well.

Sally began to put the lids back on all the wee spice jars. She was halfway through when Evie McDonald came strolling in. Posy immediately ran to her, arms outstretched. Posy adored Evie, and the feeling was mutual. Sweet and Sour was Sally's private nickname for Evie. She was a delight outside her own home, but these last few years Clare had borne the brunt of all her vitriol, with Sally as an occasional witness.

'There was a phone call for you, Sally, to our house, someone with an American accent from a place called Maids to Order. She couldn't get you on your mobile.'

Saffron's ears pricked up, but she didn't say anything.

'How did they get *your* number?' asked Sally, inwardly cursing Bertha McClure.

Evie didn't know.

'Did she leave a message?'

'She would like you to call about a time for your appointment.' She handed Sally a piece of paper.

'Thanks, Evie, and just while you're here, when are you taking Saffron shopping for her new clothes?'

Sally needed to distract them. She didn't want them knowing her business, and she could sense Saffron was intrigued.

'Would you not take a wee run into town, Saffron?'

'I could go with you now,' said Evie. 'I'm not doing anything.'

'That sounds great. Why don't the two of yis get going? I'm here till five. I'll look after Posy and Simon. You could be back in two hours if it's only Marks you're going to.'

'But Sally, I wasn't even thinking of shopping. Good Lord, what about all this tidying?'

'To tell you the truth, I'd get more work done without you under my feet. Away you go, you've been threatening to go shopping for months.'

'Yes! C'mon, Saffron,' whooped Evie. 'I was born to shop!

14

I'll just tell Mum I'm off', and she was out the door like a bullet.

Reluctantly Saffron got up to get ready. She really needed to invest in some new clothes as well as underwear. Today she was wearing a purple kaftan sort of shirt with billowing sleeves and a bright lemon skirt covered with lots of wee mirrors. She had on a pair of industrial-looking sandals, and large gold hoop earrings, and she hadn't shaved her legs. She might as well be carrying a crystal ball, Sally thought. But she was a pretty girl, and with her beautiful creamy skin, dark brown eyes and thick curly hair, she could get away with dressing like someone daft. Besides, as Evie was fond of telling Sally, boho chic, whatever that was, was in.

'What is your appointment about, Sally? Anything exciting?'

'Ach no, nothing important.' Sally tried to sound casual.

'Why don't you use the phone? Go ahead.'

'No, I'll ring later, I have my mobile.'

Bertha McClure, a neighbour of Sally's, had recently been recruited by a new cleaning firm called Maids to Order. When she heard they needed an extra supervisor, Sally had sprung to mind. Bertha had been nagging at her to apply for over a month now. She knew that Sally would be an asset, and she thought she was starting to take the bait because Sally had humoured her and gone along to a meeting. Now it seemed that wasn't enough: Bertha had set up an appointment for her with Miss Maybeth Weston, the woman who ran Maids to Order.

Sally went quickly to her bag in the cloakroom, fished out her phone and dialled. She kept her voice low, for she didn't want Saffron to overhear.

Sally had formed her own opinion of Maybeth at the talk for potential recruits about a week ago. It wasn't really a favourable one. Maybeth reminded her of one of those evangelical TV preachers enlisting people into the army of the Lord.

But all the way home on the Piaggio, her bony fingers digging into Sally's back, Bertha had pleaded with her to just go and talk to Maybeth alone. Now Sally was wishing she hadn't agreed.

Knowing Saffron wouldn't be too long getting ready, Sally kept the call as brisk as possible. She agreed to go in and see Maybeth the following morning. She might as well find out exactly what she was being offered. It would do no harm. She wasn't committed to anything yet. And in truth she was flattered by Bertha's insistence that she could have the job if she wanted it. It was good to be in demand, and not just as a cleaner, but as a supervisor.

Evie was back within minutes, with Posy perched on her hip. The little girl was grinning with delight and carrying a DVD. Evie was never surly to Sally. She had inherited her mother's green eyes and blonde hair, and her height, with the bonus of her father's curls, warm smile and perfect teeth. Despite all this, she did everything in her power to make herself look unattractive, plastering her lovely clear skin with make-up, straightening her long curly hair and wearing clothes about four sizes too big.

'Straighten your shoulders, Evie, and stop slouching.'

'Oh Sally, you sound just like Mum!' Evie shot back, but she clearly didn't mind Sally telling her off. She regarded Sally as part of the family – well, almost; Sally was the cleaner after all. And despite the obvious attempts of the various families to make her feel part of them, Sally knew her place, though she didn't always like it. She tried not to dwell on the fact that she could have made much more of her life. She yearned to feel she mattered as much as her employers. She wanted to have the same self-confidence, the casual ease with which they took their place in society. She still felt intimidated by them. If she had had the support and background of these kids, there would have been no stopping her.

Evie settled Posy in front of the TV with her Pingu DVD.

16

'There, she can watch that for a while.'

Saffron severely limited her children's TV watching. She was convinced too much of it stunted their emotional development. Naturally Posy was gleeful at this rare treat. She loved Pingu. Sally could cope with cartoon penguins. They didn't leave foul waste everywhere like the awful Iggy.

Saffron came downstairs wearing violent purple eye shadow. She looked like a wee girl; she was so excited at going into town.

'Are you sure you don't mind, Sally?'

'Not at all. You need to get away more from this set-up, it'll do you good.'

'You're a darling. We'll be back by four thirty at the latest, and don't worry about the house, just watch Posy for me. Simon is in with Anna and the hamsters.'

'Just make sure you get some sexy underwear. Evie, don't let her buy anything too sensible. No more bras with flaps!'

'Don't worry, Sally, we'll do Ann Summers as well!'

'There's no call for that!'

'Chill pill, Sally, just a joke.'

And off they went, giggling like two teenagers. Sally got back to her work, and pushed all thoughts of Maids to Order out of her head. While she was finishing up scraping the wax off the pots, Edith Black popped her head round the door. She lived at number 29, and Sally did a few hours a week for her too. It was unlike her to drop in. She was looking frail, and Sally thought again that all those recent trips to visit her sister Ellen had certainly taken it out of her. Though a widow, Ellen, like Edith, was childless.

'Oh Sally, you're here! Ah yes, of course, it's Wednesday, isn't it? Do you know if Trevor is popping home for lunch?'

Sally looked at the pot of curried garbanzo and mung bean on the stove. She felt it would be safe to say that he wouldn't be.

17

'Saffron has gone into town with Evie to do some shopping, so I don't think so. Can I leave a note for him?'

'No, I wanted to talk to him about the barbecue. Don't worry, I'll see him this evening. Hmmm, interesting smell.' Her gaze swept the kitchen. 'Heavens, Sally, it's really terribly cluttered in here. Does Saffron ever throw anything out?'

'Not enough, if you ask me.'

'Yes, quite . . . Oh well, must dash.' And she whirled out as quickly as she had entered.

Sally watched Edith pass the kitchen window. She cut an unusual figure. She was a tall woman, big-boned, with broad shoulders, imposing and well built despite her recent weight loss. Her thick white hair was swept into a grand chignon – or a bun, as Sally would have been inclined to call it had she not been informed otherwise. Edith had few wrinkles for a woman of her age, having always avoided the sun. Her mode of dressing was old-fashioned; her clothes would have been in vogue thirty years ago. However, they were so out of date they were coming back in again, so much so that Evie was starting to take an interest in them. Sally had come to realise over the years that Edith's imperious manner was partly an act, although she was so in the habit of it now that she would have been hard pressed to find another mode of behaviour. The children mocked her a bit behind her back, but they were scared of her and behaved like little angels to her face.

In a couple of weeks' time, Edith was having a barbecue. She was not the sort of person you would naturally associate with outdoor activities of any sort other than gardening, but she had watched the barbecue culture develop in Marlborough Road over the last few summers, and oddly enough had found it exhilarating to dine alfresco. It reminded her of trips abroad. So she'd decided to have a barbecue built. She didn't favour those metal ones run by gas that the others had. They were much too common. Hers was a brick one, with a proper chimney. She had driven the unfortunate man trusted with the arduous task of building it – not to mention everyone in the lane – completely mad with all her attention to detail. Having decided that the Victorians had not specialised in barbecuing, she had gone for a rococo style, built entirely from old brick. She was looking forward to the evening. It was far and away the biggest event she had ever considered. She had her reasons for holding it. Firstly, she wanted it to be a showcase of sorts for Otis, one of her lodgers. He was the son of some close friends of Ellen, who had taught him English, and he was apparently a talented young man, despite his scruffy appearance. She also thought it would be an opportunity for people to meet Fintan Fanning, the well-known opera singer, and appreciate that she only took in the finest-quality lodgers. Perhaps he'd even treat them to a song. There was nothing more thrilling than the sound of a fine tenor voice soaring upwards in the clear air on a summer evening. She made a mental note to check the weather forecast as well. Sally had agreed to come along as a guest. She sometimes helped at these occasions, but Edith felt the time had come to include her on the guest list. After all, she was part of the Marlborough family.

Sally had accepted Edith's invite to the barbecue with some trepidation. She might be referred to as one of the family, but everyone knew that she was not their social equal. She hoped it would not be too much of an ordeal and that she would feel comfortable. She aimed to look casual, not overdressed, and she wanted above all to blend in. She had mentally run through her proposed outfit about a hundred times so far. She hoped she could manage it, especially now that Fintan would be there.

The phone rang, interrupting her thoughts.

'Is Trevor there?' A female voice; sounded like an English accent.

'No, he's at work. Who's speaking?'

'Oh, just a colleague of Trevor's. I saw Saffron in town and thought he might be home – not to worry.' The woman hung up abruptly.

Sally couldn't quite place the voice, but she was sure it was someone she knew; it sounded strangely familiar. Very odd that the caller hadn't given her name.

Sally was at the kitchen table trying to keep Posy occupied when she heard the front door open and Evie and Saffron came in laden with shopping bags. Evie had managed to persuade Saffron to buy not only lots of new underwear but a couple of lovely summer dresses and a jacket as well. Sally sat patiently through the impromptu fashion show, glad to see Saffron in such good form. Now that she thought about it, she hadn't been quite her usual self recently. Sally wondered why. There must be something up with her; Saffron was usually such a contented soul. Could it be anything to do with the mystery caller?

3

In west Belfast the eye is lifted from the urban sprawl to the familiar bright green shape of Divis Mountain, the highest in the ring of hills that surround Belfast. The legendary Hatchet Field, halfway up its gentle slopes, is well known and revered for the fact that it is home to the fairies. During the late fifties and early sixties, before television and cynicism claimed them, all children growing up here were well schooled in folklore. Sally's own childhood, pre-Troubles, was filled with visits to the Hatchet Field in vain attempts to see these fairies.

Nestling in the shade of Divis was the housing estate in which Sally lived. Practically all of her family, including her parents, lived within walking distance of her house. Hers was a small semi with a compact back garden, big enough for the odd few days of sunshine that Belfast caught throughout the summer months. Sally took pride in her garden; she kept it weed-free and had replaced the grass at the front with gravel. Over the last ten years she had slowly accumulated some plants from the garden centre, and had planted some wee bushes round the fringe. Miss Black had given her various cuttings, and Sally found to her satisfaction that she had green fingers. But for all her care, she didn't own her house. Many people in her neighbourhood were homeowners, and that remained Sally's dream; meanwhile she paid her rent on time and got on with things.

Some of her neighbours had really gone overboard with their gardens. Sally blamed Alan Titchmarsh for turning their heads. The gardens were littered with Davids, Venus de Milos and Cupids, and every second house had a water feature. The real gardeners grew flowers and impressive rose bushes, but many were content with trellises of fake roses in every shade including blue. Reality wasn't an issue. Sally knew better than to make her views known, for it would serve no purpose. Before she worked in Marlborough Road she had never really paid much attention to her neighbours' gardens, but now she often saw things through her employers' eyes. Miss Black, who had never ventured over this end of town, would have lost the run of herself entirely if she had seen these gardens. Mind you, her rococo barbecue would have been a big hit round here.

As for the inside of Sally's house, although she rarely invited the neighbours in, she kept it spotless. Over the years she had disposed of all the frills and fancy things. She went in for the plain, uncluttered look now; it suited the house. She had a couple of framed posters of flowers Clare had given her by an artist called Georgia O'Keefe, one in the living room and one in the hall. In the living room she had a copy of a William Conor she had bought in the Ulster Museum, and above the fireplace hung a painting of a bowl of fruit that Rory McDonald had done for his A level art. Clare had had that framed for her because she had liked it so much. They really brightened the place up. She would have loved to own a real painting, but unless she won the lottery, there'd be little hope of that.

Sally had only just got in from work and was getting the supper together when Bronagh breezed in the door. She had had her hair done pink and blonde this week. It had been deep red the week before with black underneath. Sally had given up worrying about it. She couldn't keep up with all the different colours these days. Bronagh had a pretty wee face and her father's blue eyes and could get away with it. She didn't make a lot of money at the hairdressing, but she worked for a fancy salon in town and she was getting well trained. One day a week she went to college, which meant she would have proper qualifications. She had big ideas of opening a hairdressing salon of her own, but she'd have a long wait. Sally just agreed with her when Bronagh told her of all her plans; she put Sally in mind of her daddy then.

'Mammy, I met Bertha McClure on the bus. She says she offered you a job as a supervisor for a new cleaning company.'

'She did. I told her I wasn't interested.'

'Maybe you should go along and check it out.'

'I might, but sure, one cleaning job's the same as the next, and I'm in a routine over there.'

'You'd be a supervisor, you wouldn't have to clean. Do you never get fed up cleaning?'

'Of course I do, but I'm used to Marlborough Road. They're good people really.'

'I think they're snobs.'

'What do you mean, snobs? Weren't they always very nice to you when you came over?'

That was true enough, they were always very nice to her, but Bronagh had still felt different. Sally had occasionally brought her along with her during the school summer holidays. She always wore her good clothes. The McDonalds ran around in grubby clothes she wouldn't be seen dead in, but they didn't seem to mind at all. It confused her; she thought rich people would be all dressed up. On one of her trips over there, she had worn the lovely new pink sandals she was so proud of, but Evie, who was wearing torn sneakers at the time, said 'You're wearing heels. That means your feet won't grow properly,' and Bronagh had suddenly hated her new sandals.

Bronagh had brought home some free vouchers for the salon. She was starting her hair-cutting; women's hair first, then men's.

'Mammy, would you do me a favour? Could you give these out to some of the ones over in Marlborough Road? Alan has been nagging us to get some new customers in.'

'I thought they were snobs? What about some of your chums? Couldn't they use them?'

'Alan says we aren't to give freebies to our mates. He wants people who might come back and pay. And none of my friends can afford our prices. He's put them up again. He just bought a Porsche.'

'Well give them to me then and I'll ask over there. Evie might like a haircut.'

'She probably wouldn't come.'

Ever since the remark about her shoes all those years ago, Bronagh had always felt intimidated by Evie. Sally was aware of this; she knew the feeling well. It was a class thing, of course, and Bronagh needed to get over it.

'I bet you she would be delighted to go. Her mammy's always giving out about how much her streaks cost.'

'These are just haircuts.'

'Well I'll take them over anyway. How many have you?'

'Six . . . they have to be used over the next six weeks. And they have to call first to make an appointment.'

Sally took the vouchers. Someone would use them, she felt sure. Maybe not Edith, for she just rolled her hair up into the bun thing, but she'd offer her one anyway. Clare loved a bargain, and definitely Trevor, he could do with a trim. His hair was a

24

mess. And she was sure Bronagh would do a good job. She took her work very seriously.

Bronagh helped her clear up and then they watched *EastEnders* together. Sally loved it when Bronagh stayed in and kept her company, though she was careful not to be too possessive; the child had to have her own life. She and Bronagh were close. She thought Bronagh was a great girl, very sensible, and there was none of the old nonsense from her that Clare had to take from Evie. Maybe it wasn't such a good thing to have all your needs catered for; it left you with nothing to strive towards.

Sally still fretted at times that she had deprived Bronagh of a father by leaving Charlie, but he had given her little choice, and technically *he* had left her. She thought back to all his promises; moving to south Belfast had been just one of his dreams. He often regaled her about all the foreign holidays they would take. In reality, Sally had only one holiday during her marriage. When Bronagh was four, she was lucky enough to get a week in a caravan in Port Ballintrae with her brother Liam and his wife. Charlie was to join them for the weekend; he didn't arrive, of course. Something came up. He was so repentant on her return, hugging her and Bronagh and telling them how much he loved them, that despite her misgivings Sally forgave him. She was to forgive him a lot over the years. Somehow she made it through by absorbing herself in her child, but bit by bit she found the love she had for Charlie dying in her. His easy charm finally wore thin. There were too many broken promises, too many nights alone in bed wondering where he was, listening for the sound of his key in the door and waiting for him to stumble upstairs looking for forgiveness yet again. But she was in no position to leave. Apart from the shame and the gossip, where on earth would she go? She had no qualifications. If she got a job, she would need to leave the baby somewhere, and all her family had plenty of kids of their own.

She found out the true extent of Charlie's gambling when she went to the credit union to get the money for Bronagh's First Communion dress. At first she thought they had made a mistake. She had had two thousand and forty-three pounds in there, her life savings, set aside for a deposit on a house of their own. The thought of it had buoyed her up during the endless rows and screaming matches with Charlie. But it was all gone; every last penny of it. Well, he had left two pounds in to keep the account open.

Sally didn't know which was worse: the hopelessness of losing her nest egg, or the pity in the woman's eyes when she told her there was no money left in the account. How had he found out about it? And why had she been so stupid as to open the account in both their names? She could barely make it home, her legs were so weak. She cried for hours, and by the time he came home that night, reeking of drink, she didn't even have the energy to argue with him. She just told him she would be borrowing a First Communion dress for Bronagh because they couldn't afford to buy one. And then she quietly asked him to leave. He didn't really believe she meant it. He moved out that night fully expecting to be reinstated in her good books when she calmed down. But his luck had run out this time. Sally stuck to her guns and ignored his charm offensive. She went back to work part time in the Spar and prayed fervently that she would never set eyes on Charlie O'Neill again. She did, of course; there were a few occasions when, full of the drink, he came round to the house promising he had changed and tried to get her back. But Sally was weary. She hardened her heart. She needed a better life for herself and her daughter. Then, out of the blue, Charlie was arrested and put away for armed robbery. For all his flaws, Sally couldn't believe he had had a gun. It was out of character, but she supposed it was a desperate attempt to pay off his gambling debts. She was shocked and embarrassed, feeling that Charlie's

26

actions reflected on her. How could she have been so stupid as to marry such a weak man?

A week later one of her sisters told her about the ad for a cleaning lady – and Sally's life turned the corner.

4

Sally struggled into her waterproof coat and trousers. It was Edith Black who had suggested she buy them. The first few wet days she had arrived on the moped she had looked like a drowned rat.

'Heavens above, Sally, you are drenched!' Edith had exclaimed. 'If you are going to keep that motor scooter you have to get kitted out properly. Otherwise you'll catch your death, and we can't have that.'

Edith was right: the weather here would put years on you. As likely as not it was raining either on the way there or on the way back. After a few soakings Sally gave in. She had got the jacket and trousers in a sale in the bicycle shop near Marlborough Road. They were very practical and well made; they'd never wear out. Mind you, they were far from flattering, so if there was the slightest chance it wouldn't rain she left them off, for she felt like a right eejit all geared up in them.

Arriving at Miss Black's, she struggled out of her wet-weather gear, hoping she wouldn't bump into the new lodger just yet. His name was Fintan Fanning, the well-known tenor. He'd arrived a few days ago. Sally had let him in and showed him his room. He was really friendly, not full of himself like some of them.

When Sally first started working for her, Miss Black had just retired from her job as secretary to the managing director of some important company or other. She spent a lot of time telling Sally how invaluable she'd been. Retiring had left her at a bit of a loose end. Sally found this understandable. After all, it couldn't be that easy for her to fill her days; there was a limit to the number of charity shops she could volunteer for, and Sally thought there was little point in her wandering round the house with her two arms the one length. Then out of the blue Miss Black was contacted by the Grand Opera House, and asked if she would put up a singer for six weeks. And so began her rebirth as landlady to the visiting talent, or at least some of it. She was very particular who she took in. Her lodgers were of a higher order altogether, people such as dancers from the ballet, opera singers, set designers; the more cultured types, of course. And Miss Edith Black enjoyed her bit of culture with a vengeance, there was no doubt about that. Last Christmas she had refused to take two of the dwarfs from *Snow White*, and there were mutterings from her more liberal neighbours about this being politically incorrect.

'It has nothing to do with their size. I never take pantomime performers,' Edith confided in Sally. 'Believe me, I wouldn't have taken Snow White herself. Now if they had been in the ballet or the opera it would have been a different matter.'

Sally suspected there weren't many operas that featured dwarfs, but you never knew.

Sally had worked for Miss Black for almost nine years. Having heard glowing reports from Clare, Miss Black had begged her for one day a week to do some 'light dusting'. By now Sally was wise to the true meaning of the word 'light', but she agreed anyway, and so on Tuesday and Thursday mornings she went to number 29.

She often marvelled at the variations in the interiors of the houses. From the front of the terrace it seemed the only difference was the colour of the doors. She liked the decor of number 25 best. Clare had a good eye, and obviously the money to indulge it. Sally loved the colour scheme. It was bright and airy, all yellows, pale blues and creams, and many of the windows had Roman blinds instead of curtains. The upstairs drawing room and the living room had big squishy linen sofas, and there were wooden floors throughout, except in the bedrooms. The house was full of real paintings, not prints from Boots or the like. Tony and Clare collected Irish art. New stuff too, some of it hard to make out, but colourful, and apart from one odd-looking painting of what appeared to be a nude man on a cow with two legs, Sally loved it all. Number 25 was a happy home. People tended to drop in a lot, and were always made to feel welcome.

Miss Black's house, on the other hand, was a wee bit too old-fashioned for Sally's taste. It was dark and quiet, carpeted throughout, with deep red walls downstairs and chintzy wallpaper in the bedrooms. The furniture was ancient, all antiques Sally supposed, which suited the house. These walls too were covered in paintings, though not modern ones like the McDonalds'; mainly rural scenes with gilt frames. There was a William Conor that Sally loved. It was a portrait of an urchin with a cheeky half-smile. In Edith's upstairs drawing room there was a very large painting that almost covered an entire wall. It featured a skinny, crabbit-looking man in a dress coat and top hat. Apparently he was some relative or other of Edith's. There was a brass lamp on the wall above it just to light that one painting, and of course that needed to be polished regularly. When Edith discovered how much Sally appreciated the paintings, she encouraged her to go to the museum, which was just across the park. So on her way home now and then Sally did go, just to look at the art collection. She knew that before she worked for Edith, the idea of traipsing round a museum would never have occurred to her.

Miss Black had two china cabinets full of crockery and lots of silver with twiddly bits, which were a bugger to clean. She insisted too on real Irish linen napkins, which she required to be starched and ironed. Her house retained a lot of the original Victorian features. She had been careful to let Sally know this, pointing out all the intricate carving round the cornice and the ceiling rose. More dust-gatherers, Sally thought, but then what would she know? She wasn't refined like Miss Edith Black. Mind you, her lack of refinement had been no barrier to a real warmth and understanding developing between the two women over the years. But Sally was still aware of her position, and didn't for a minute feel she was Edith's equal.

Fintan was sitting at the table having breakfast when Sally walked into the kitchen. He was a broad-shouldered, solid man, and would have put you in mind of that French film star Gérard something-or-other, although luckily he didn't have the big nose. Edith had only a small kitchen table, and somehow this accentuated Fintan's size.

He stood up when Sally came in and greeted her warmly. He was wearing a pair of fancy pyjamas; Sally felt immediately embarrassed but he had noticed her gaze.

'It's my karate suit,' he smiled. 'I wear it for t'ai chi.'

Sally nodded. She felt a bit wrong-footed, so she lifted his empty cereal dish and took it to the sink.

'Leave that, Sally, I'll do it. Can I pour you a cup of tea?'

She would have felt slightly uncomfortable just sitting down beside him at the table, especially were Edith to come in, so she thanked him and said she had a lot to get done, so she had better get started. All the same, it was nice of him to offer, she thought, as she went up to strip Miss Black's bed. She normally did the kitchen first, but she didn't like disturbing Fintan.

He was still sitting there with a music score in front of him when she came back down. She supposed she'd just have to work around him.

'I met Clare yesterday. Very nice woman, she's asked me to drop in for coffee any time.'

'Oh? I suppose she had you regaled with Maud.'

Clare lectured in Irish studies, and was writing a paper about Maud Gonne, some famous Irishwoman who was a great friend of Yeats. Sally still knew all the words to 'The Lake Isle of Innisfree'. Nearly twenty-five years ago her English teacher had offered a bar of chocolate to the first girl to learn it by heart, and Sally had won. She still thought of Miss Beckett with deep affection.

'Her thesis? Yes, she was indeed telling me about it. What an amusing title, "The pre-menstrual mood swings of Maud Gonne". I'm sure her tongue is very firmly in her cheek.'

Sally said nothing. She had an idea what the expression meant, but she didn't want to agree in case it gave him the impression that she was critical of Clare.

'I might call in tomorrow when you're there, how about that?'

'I'll be far too busy to stop for a chat. And I have to go somewhere from work.'

'Gosh, Sally, do you ever sit down?'

'Sure they don't pay me for sitting.'

Fintan laughed; he had a warm, throaty laugh.

'I suppose not. Well, I'd better not keep you back then.' He picked up his music and left.

After he'd gone, Sally felt sorry she hadn't had the tea, for wasn't he only trying to be friendly? But to tell the truth, she felt uncomfortable with some of Edith's lodgers. That other fellow, Otis Flaherty, the rock poet, she couldn't stand him. Fortunately he confined himself mostly to his room, but for some reason today he was downstairs. Sally gave the Hoover a vicious stab underneath his chair. She had asked him to move, but you'd have thought his arse was welded to the seat in front of the television. He was watching some loony daytime chat show: lots of shapeless, badly dressed people with big doughy faces. Miss Black was out, otherwise he'd have been up in his room smoking out the window and pretending he was writing a song for his band. Sally was on to him. She thought he was a leech. He had fooled Edith with his unctuous ways and all his chit-chat about poetry, but he hadn't fooled Sally O'Neill; she knew the type.

'Look, I'm watching this because I'm in the middle of like writing a song on the theme of daytime TV, so could you like clean someplace else?'

'Right then,' Sally said, 'I'll just leave Miss Black a note to say you were watching TV and didn't want to be disturbed – she'll want an explanation if I don't clean in here.'

She pushed her foot down on the button of the cleaner and watched the cord wind up with a snap. Then she lifted the Hoover and headed towards the door. Otis was up like a shot.

'Right, man, like take a chill pill, I'll go upstairs.'

Sally felt triumphant. Really, she had never met anyone so annoying in her life. Why didn't he get a place of his own?

Miss Black's lodgers stayed for differing periods of time. Some of them were performing for one week only. Others arrived for rehearsals and the performances, staying for as long as six weeks. Fintan would be here for ten, as his show was on for a month. Otis – a fake name if Sally had ever heard one – was supposedly writing a rock opera, so God knows how long that would take him.

Sally had begun to think that Edith should stop taking the lodgers; she believed it was all too much for her. She was worried about Edith's health.

Ellen, Edith's sister, had been ill for almost a year and was now in a hospice. Since Ellen lived in Portadown, this meant

Edith was driving back and forth three or more times a week. It was a long drive as well, almost an hour each way, longer given the speed Edith went at. It couldn't be good for her. She was losing weight and looked a bit peaky. Perhaps it was time Sally mentioned her concerns to Clare or Saffron. But she wasn't sure if it was her place to do that.

At times Sally felt like a therapist. You'd need a degree in psychology to cope with the lot of them, but Sally made do with common sense and lots of patience, and it got her by very nicely.

5

Sally was at the McDonalds' the following Monday when Clare spotted Fintan doing the t'ai chi thing in Edith's garden. She was out like a shot, and five minutes later was back with Fintan in tow. He was wearing his karate suit and looked slightly uncomfortable. However, Clare noticed none of this; after all, didn't she spend a lot of her time in the blue dressing gown?

'Put the kettle on, Sally, would you. I'll make some coffee.'

And away she went, grinding beans and chatting endlessly at the same time. The coffee would have her up to high doh in no time. She should stick to the camomile; she was hyper enough on that.

'Oh, I forgot, excuse me. Fintan, this is Sally; Sally, meet Fintan Fanning.'

'Oh, Sally and I have already met,' Fintan said with a smile. Clare looked surprised, then collected herself.

'Of course you have, at Edith's, silly of me. We're all desperately dependent on Sally over here. She keeps us in order, don't you, Sally?'

Clare gave her flirtatious laugh, which meant she wanted Fintan to fancy her. She did this without thinking; Sally had watched it often enough. Of course once he showed the slightest interest she would start talking about Tony, or the children, or her thesis. Then whoever the man was would start feeling uncomfortable until he got over his initial misapprehension and appreciated her amazing mind and her domestic goddess qualities simultaneously.

But Fintan was talking to Sally, his lovely blue eyes attentive. He really was a very handsome man. Sally reckoned him to be in his early forties.

'How many houses do you work in?'

'Just the three: here, Miss Black's and the McNamaras' at number twenty-one.'

'And all very different inside?'

'Yes, that's right.'

He looked around appreciatively.

'They are really lovely big houses. You'd pay a fortune for one like this in London. Edith tells me they are listed buildings.'

'Yes,' Clare chipped in, 'we all love it here, and it's such a great place for children to grow up, what with the back lane to play in.'

'Yes,' said Fintan wryly, 'there do seem to be quite a number of children.'

'Oh, Edith thinks they are all monsters, doesn't she, Sally?'

'I wouldn't say that. She just thinks they are allowed to get away with far too much. And she could be right.'

Clare nodded vigorously.

'She has a point. We are all too soft on them.'

She poured the coffee; you couldn't see through it.

'Sally?'

'No thanks, I'm all right. I'll do your study now while you're down here.'

Sally left them chatting. She was beginning to find Fintan a bit disconcerting. She couldn't remember the last time she had felt so attracted to a man. He was so open and friendly, but maybe all famous people had that ease with them. That was why people liked them so much. Just because he looked at her when he spoke didn't mean he fancied her. Once upstairs, she took a deep breath. Clare's study was always a challenge, and it was good to get her out of the way when she tackled it. That way she could chuck more out. What was the point of Clare having a computer if she filled her study with papers? It was a good job no one smoked in this house; one spark and it'd all be up in flames.

Sally worked steadily and had the study in a semblance of order when she heard the sound of raised voices. She rushed downstairs. Evie was standing in the middle of the kitchen holding a glass of water. She was pale, bleary-eyed and wearing only a long crumpled T-shirt. She'd obviously just got out of bed.

'Evie, answer me! Why aren't you at school?'

Clare was shouting accusingly at Evie. Fintan was sitting looking distinctly uncomfortable. Sally felt sorry for him. He was trapped.

'I feel sick. Doh! I texted you earlier, Mum. I was up all night throwing up,' Evie shrieked back even louder.

'You texted me? From your bedroom? Honestly, Evie, you redefine the word lazy!'

'You see? I knew you would throw a psych if I told you in person, and I was right.'

'I am not throwing a psych; you're not sick! You've a hang-over, and little wonder, going out on a Sunday with that layabout and getting up to God knows what.'

'Mikey is not a layabout. You're a snob, and *you* can talk about drinking – just look at the yard, it's full of empty bottles. You'd think this was a home for alcoholics.'

'Evie, we were entertaining last night, and I certainly don't need to explain to you why there are bottles in the yard.'

'Anyway we only have history this morning and it's of no use to anyone.'

'History – no use?'

'Yes, taught by that saddo who thinks she knows everything.'

'She certainly knows more than you ever will at this rate.'

'You should never have had children; you have no maternal instincts.'

The voices rose even higher.

'Will you two stop for a second, please?' Sally broke in. 'How am I to get my work done with all this screaming? Evie, why don't you go and get ready for school? I'm sure your mammy will write you a wee note to say you weren't very well this morning. Would you be in time for your next class if you left now?'

Evie's school was just a ten-minute walk from Marlborough Road.

'Yes, I suppose so.' Evie looked sheepishly at Sally, then turned to go back upstairs.

'And Clare, you have a cup of camomile tea and calm yourself. You and Evie can have a chat later.'

'Yes, you're right. Sorry,' Clare added, noticing Fintan.

'Oh, don't mind me, I have work to do. I'd better go.' Fintan got up to leave, glad of a chance to escape.

'I'm sorry. That was very rude of me, but Evie is driving me crazy at the moment.' Clare fixed her face in a rueful smile, expecting forgiveness. 'Poor Sally, I'm sure we drive her nuts with all this bickering. I know I should try to stay calmer with Evie, but she is so provoking.'

Fintan still looked a bit shell-shocked.

'Aren't you lucky you have Sally to sort things out for you?' He moved quickly to the door. 'Maybe I'll see you tomorrow, Sally – you're at Edith's then?'

'Yes, in the morning.'

Sally felt embarrassed that he had asked her in front of Clare;

she hoped Clare wouldn't think she had been making up to him. But Clare said goodbye to him as if nothing had happened. Sally would have been mortified in her position.

'Oh, Sally, she's dreadful, isn't she?' Clare shook her head sorrowfully.

'Sure they're all the same at that age. She'll grow out of it, they all do.'

'I hope you're right. Well, Fintan's not the only one with work to do.' Clare sounded a bit uncomfortable, as if she had suddenly realised that all the screaming in front of Fintan had been a bit too much. She made her way up to her newly cleaned study.

Clare and Evie did have a difficult relationship. Clare flew off the handle too quickly with her. But then she had little or no support from Tony. In Sally's opinion Clare's husband spent far too much time at work. Even now, ten years on, she still wasn't quite sure what Tony did, except rush off to work with a bulging briefcase looking stressed. He was something high up in the Civil Service, and knew a lot of important types who kept coming to dinner. He was very friendly to Sally, though, and always looked pleased to see her. Sally suspected she eased his conscience a bit. He probably felt guilty that he left all the domestic matters to Clare, so he willingly paid for Sally.

Sally's own daughter, Bronagh, two years older than Evie, had gone through this rebellious stage too, but then Sally was used to being a single parent and had learned to handle her alone. She didn't go in for shrieking. She'd found out the hard way that it didn't work. All the yelling and screaming at Charlie had just ended in heartbreak.

6

Sally's appointment with Maybeth was at ten a.m. She was prompt; it wasn't in Sally's nature to be late for anything. Maybeth ushered her into her office. No secretary, Sally noticed as she sat down. The office looked as if it had been quickly cobbled together. Sally had developed an eye for quality in her years of working for the Marlborough Road gang. In her own home she had learned to go for plainer looks: no patterns, and nice toning colours. This office was a clash of peach and turquoise, with really tacky curtains. The carpet was synthetic; she felt the static as she walked across it. Maybeth obviously had no taste – that is, if she had been the one responsible for it. Maybeth came straight to the point.

'Can I ask your present salary?'

Sally had it worked out precisely. She was unsure whether to tell Maybeth the exact figure. She wasn't paying tax on it. However, she took the chance, stressing the fact that it was tax free.

'And your hours?'

Sally told her.

'Well,' Maybeth said, 'that seems an extremely generous

amount.' She made a note on a pad. 'That is more like US wages, but I'm sure we can match it. Bertha – who as you know is a dynamo – seems to think that you will be worth every penny.'

Bertha a dynamo? From what Sally understood, dynamos were lively, sparky people who moved fast, not fat dour grumps like Bertha McClure. The only muscle Bertha moved with any regularity was her tongue. Sally wondered briefly if Bertha had told Maybeth she was a dynamo, or whether Maybeth had decided that herself. If the latter, then there was more wrong with Maybeth than her taste in decor.

Sally sat and rearranged her face in a smile and listened to Maybeth chitter on about the number of hygiene technicians she would be hiring and the impressive advertising campaign she had planned. She told Sally that they would be getting a photographer in to photograph Bertha and Sally dressed in their gear for billboards all over the town.

'Gear? What gear?'

'Well, you'll just love these.'

Maybeth opened a cupboard, and with a flourish pulled out a peach-coloured polyester jumpsuit with the logo 'Maids to Order' embroidered on the left-hand pocket. It was vile; Clare would have had a taste blackout on the spot.

'Surely if I'm not cleaning I won't have to wear those?'

'Well, we would like all our hygiene technicians to be instantly recognisable, so yes.'

'But Bertha told me I would be driving round just supervising all the other cleaners; I could hardly wear that on my bike.'

'I know, but there would be times when, say, another hygiene technician did not make an appearance, and then I guess we would hope – in the spirit of company congeniality – that you would fill in for him or her. So we would issue you with two pairs of regulation cleansing apparel.'

41

'Him or her?'

'Why yes, we are hoping to recruit both sexes.'

Sally snorted with derision; she couldn't help herself. Most of the men she had had anything to do with were totally useless in the home, and that included the ones she worked for. When she was married to Charlie, he seemed to think that every little bit of domestic nonsense was her job. He even used to boast to his mates that he never lifted a hand in the house – it was women's work. And as for Tony, Trevor and the likes, well they just paid up and shut up. Now and then Sally would watch Trevor as he walked aimlessly round the kitchen trying to work out which handle to pull down to find the dishwasher. When Posy was born he was next to useless, at one stage flooding the living room as he blundered into the birthing pool while Saffron was mid-contraction. Tony allegedly could cook, but then he was never there, and in Sally's opinion, hurling steaks or chops on to a barbecue was hardly cooking. If Maybeth was looking for male cleaners, she'd have a long look.

'Would you not have to change the name if yis had men?'

'Why Sally, we haven't considered that just yet. But that indeed is a point. Now, when would you be available for the photo shoot?'

'I'm not sure I want to take part in that. I'll need time to think it over, and of course I'd have to wait until the residents could get replacements.'

Maybeth's mouth tightened, but she smiled; well, it was a sort of smile.

'Why Sally, I do declare you are playing hard to get! Listen, why don't you let me know by next Monday? We would like you to start by the beginning of next month.'

Sally was already feeling sure she wasn't going to take the job, but somehow the words wouldn't come out to say no. Instead she thanked Maybeth and left. On her way out she turned and asked, 'Oh, who decorated the office?'

'Why, I did it all by myself. Don't you just love those colours?'

Sally nodded. That wasn't a lie: the colours were fine, only not there and not in that order.

Normally Sally was up and showered and on her way out the door by eight o'clock. Today was a rare day off, so she took her time over breakfast, even allowing herself the luxury of a boiled egg. She was at the kitchen table, finishing a piece of toast and reading a magazine, when her sister Eileen's face appeared at the window.

Sally's heart sank. She got up to open the door. Eileen only called round when she was after something.

'Hi, what's up? What do you want?'

'What's eating you? I don't want anything. Did you get out of the wrong side of the bed this morning?'

'No, but how did you know I was here? I don't normally have Fridays off.'

'I phoned the McDonalds and they told me.'

'Eileen, you have no right . . .'

'Well you should turn your mobile on then.' She paused dramatically. 'I just thought you should know – Charlie O'Neill got out yesterday.'

For a minute Sally thought she was going to faint.

'How do you know?'

'He was in Milligan's last night. He's put on a ton, and he's lost most of his hair. His waves have waved him goodbye.' Eileen related these facts with relish, as if in some way they would be compensation for the fact that Charlie was out of prison.

'Oh God, what am I going to do?'

The almost forgotten rush of dread hit her. What would happen now, with Charlie out of jail? What if Clare – or even worse, Edith – found out? Although Sally had implied to Edith that she was separated, and had been the one to instigate it,

43

she had left out the detail that Charlie was in jail. She had been afraid that in some way this revelation would contaminate her; make Edith think less of her for being foolish enough to marry Charlie in the first place. Edith frequently complimented Sally on her good judgement and common sense. If she knew about Charlie she would revise her opinion, and Sally couldn't bear the thought of that.

'Well? What *are* you going to do?' Eileen looked at her, patently excited by the whole thing. Eileen's life was dull. She was the youngest of the McManus clan, still in her early thirties, and was married to a loser whom she avoided by spending lots of nights out on the town with her mates. They had no kids. Sally thought she should get a life and leave him. But Eileen wouldn't have thanked her for her opinion so she said nothing. She couldn't be bothered getting in the middle of it all.

Sally's overwhelming feeling now was panic. During the last ten years she had successfully banished Charlie from her life and thoughts. All that the Marlborough Road lot knew were the simple facts. She was separated; he was away. They didn't ask where and she never told. The very idea of him being free was sickening. She would have to let Bronagh know. She couldn't take the risk of him showing up at the house. Bronagh was going out with her mates tonight directly from work; she'd phone her at lunchtime.

After a while, having delivered her bombshell and not getting the response she'd hoped for from Sally, Eileen left. Sally's plan of taking a wee run into the town didn't seem enticing any more. She tried to busy herself round the house, but ended up sitting watching daytime TV – something she never did. She was half-heartedly looking at *Richard and Judy*, and feeling sorry for herself, when her phone rang. She thought she might as well take the call. Her day was ruined now anyway. It was Bertha McClure, sounding delighted with herself. She was outside Sally's house. Eileen had told her Sally was off today.

Sally opened the door to Bertha with bad grace. Bertha barged in and plonked her big fat arse on the sofa, barely able to contain her delight.

'Oh Sally, wait till you hear. Maybeth just loved you. She thinks you – hang on a wee sec, I wrote it down.' Pulling a piece of paper from her pocket, she read out:

'"Radiate efficiency". She'll be writing you a letter offering you the job. Isn't that brilliant?'

'Look, Bertha, I am not sure about the job. You told me that going along to see her didn't commit me to anything. I mean, I haven't made up my mind if I even want to leave Marlborough Road. And even if I was going to, I'd have to give in my notice.'

'Notice, whaddya mean, notice? How much notice?'

'I'm not sure, maybe a month. I couldn't just leave them all in the lurch.'

'A month? I don't think so! She wants you to start as soon as you can.'

Then Bertha's eyes narrowed, she looked like a snake, or even worse, like Iggy McNamara. Sally felt like punching her in the mouth. She said nothing. A sleekit grin spread over Bertha's big ugly face.

'Here, Sally, is it true that Charlie is out?'

'Who told you? I don't know anything about him.'

'I heard he was in Milligan's last night. I thought you'd better know. I wouldn't think all them snobs in Marlborough Road would like it if they knew you were married to a jailbird.'

'I'm not married to him any more. We are officially separated, and anyway they wouldn't be interested.'

'Sure if you left now and took Maybeth's offer, they would never have to know about him at all.'

Sally had a sickening feeling in the pit of her stomach. Maybe Bertha was right. If she handed in her notice before anyone in Marlborough Road learned about Charlie, she could leave with her head high.

Bronagh arrived home directly from work to see how her mother was. She had appeared to take the news calmly when Sally had called earlier to tell her about her father being out of jail, but then she had been in work.

'I just wanted to check on you before I went out. Have you seen him?'

'No, but our Eileen has, she came round this morning to tell me.'

'Leave it to Eileen, can't wait to spread the bad news.'

'I'll understand if you want to see him; after all, he's still your father.'

'I'm not ready to see him. I hate what he's done to us, to you.'

'You never said . . .'

'Sure why would I? You had enough to cope with and I didn't want to make it worse for you.'

Sally could hardly swallow. The lump crept up her throat. She nodded her emotion and Bronagh squeezed her hand.

'I spent years in school with people telling me my da was a jailbird. If he'd been in the RA or something it would've been cool, but he was just a rotten oul' criminal. It was shite. I hate him.'

But Sally knew that she didn't mean that; perhaps she was saying it out of loyalty to Sally, or more likely because the news confused her. Nonetheless, she was grateful for Bronagh's apparent desire not to get in touch with Charlie right now.

7

Sally was on eggs all weekend. Every time the door creaked or the phone rang she got tense. She hardly slept a wink, and eating was out of the question – she couldn't chew, her mouth didn't seem to function – but thankfully there was no sign of Charlie. She refused Eileen's offer to go out with the girls to Milligan's on Saturday night. It was a ridiculous idea, being the last place Charlie had been sighted. No, she thought, avoidance tactics were best. She put herself under house arrest for the rest of the weekend, afraid she would bump into him on the street or at the shops. Her ex-in-laws lived nearby, as did two of Charlie's sisters. By Monday she was so worn out that she wondered if it was worth calling Clare and saying she was unwell. They could hardly complain; she rarely missed work – maybe twice in ten years – struggling in with colds and sniffles rather than let them down. But prudently she realised that staying at home would achieve nothing, so she got on her bike, so to speak, and by nine o'clock was in Clare's kitchen wading through a stack of pots.

About eleven o'clock, she was just about to have her cup of tea when a tentative knock on the back door startled her. It was Fintan Fanning.

She felt odd seeing him after the weekend she had just had. She was sure she looked as wrecked as she felt.

'Clare's out,' she told him.

'Oh well, never mind that. I came to see you. I saw the bike.' He indicated the kettle. 'Am I just in time for tea?'

'What kind?'

'Real tea, of course.' And he sat down quite naturally at the table.

Sally wasn't sure what to say, but Fintan had no such qualms.

'Well, Sally, I hope you had a restful weekend.'

'Ach, I was just futtering about, didn't do much. Have you no rehearsals today?'

'No, just a costume fitting this afternoon.'

Sally told herself to get a grip and act normally, but she felt paralysed. The events of the weekend had stunned her, and she didn't have Fintan's ease of conversation in the first place. She had been glad this morning that Clare was rushing off to the library and a lecture. Just herself in the house, unless you counted Lola, who was in her basket in the corner of the kitchen, her worshipful eyes trained on Sally.

'You seem a bit distracted, Sally. Is everything all right?' His blue eyes were fixed on her, compelling her to confide in him.

'Well, I've been offered another job.' Best to tell some of the truth, she felt. 'It's a new cleaning service and I'd be a supervisor, you know, have more responsibility.'

Fintan laughed. 'Good Lord, Sally, you couldn't possibly have more responsibility than you have around here. Heaven knows how they'd manage without you.'

'I wouldn't just be a cleaner.' The words were out before she could help it.

Fintan looked at her thoughtfully.

'Is this what you really want? I mean, are you fed up with Marlborough Road?'

'It's hard to be sure. No, I don't think I'm fed up with

Marlborough Road so much as I'm fed up just being a cleaner. I mean, I always thought I'd be . . .'

Sally trailed off. What did she think she would be? Realistically, what else *could* she be? She had quit school just before she was due to sit her O levels, so she'd left without a single qualification. As the eldest of her family she was expected to contribute financially as soon as she could. The money was needed, with so many children to feed. It wasn't that she was stupid – she'd always been in the top half of the class – but absolutely no one from her street went on after leaving age. Plenty of the neighbours thought Sally's parents had given her notions of herself by allowing her to go to the grammar school in the first place. Sure didn't the uniform alone cost a fortune?

Fintan interrupted her musings.

'Yes? You thought you would be . . . ?'

'Well, not a cleaner. I mean, I worked as a manager of a shop when I first left school. I only took the cleaning job because it allowed me to work fewer hours for more money.'

'What has changed?'

'I suppose housework is so . . .'

'Repetitive?'

'Yes, and I sometimes feel like I'm a servant.'

'I understand, but they do respect you, Sally, and they love you. Anyone can see that. And they are very dependent on you.'

'Ach, don't worry about me, Fintan, I'll get over it. Maybe I'm getting ideas above myself.'

'Well, let's think,' said Fintan. 'There might be other options open to you, you know? How many hours a week do you work?'

'Three days here, that's nine hours, two mornings at Edith's and two afternoons at Saffron's. Although sometimes I do extra hours if they're stuck.'

'So you would have time to go to classes?'

49

'Classes?'

'Yes, Sally – classes. Get some qualifications and you'll be able to get a better job. You know everyone here would support you. I'm sure they would all love for you to further your education. Don't you think?'

'I don't know. I suppose Clare is always banging on about the benefits of education. And I didn't even take my O levels.'

'Why not think about doing some GCSEs? The basic ones first.' He smiled at her. 'A few at a time, see how you get on.'

'I've never thought of that. Maybe I could.'

After Fintan had left, Sally thought over what he had said. He was probably right, but it would take some effort on her part. It was years since she had done any studying, but doing some course or other might be a good idea. Maybe she would pick up a syllabus from the tech. As for the other job, well, she wouldn't say yes or no . . . not just yet. She had almost told Fintan about Charlie, but something made her hold back. There was no reason for anyone over here to know. Unless, God forbid, Charlie O'Neill reared his ugly mug and they found out about him. There was no way she could stay on if that happened.

'Sally, do you think Trevor still loves me?' Saffron asked later that day.

'Ach, Saffron, of course he does. Why on earth would you think that?'

'He's just different these days. He doesn't come home for lunch any more and he seems to criticise everything I cook. And I'm sure he's been eating meat on the sly. I found a receipt for a lunch and it was for two people and two steaks.' Saffron looked on the verge of tears.

'Well that hardly means he's stopped loving you. He's never made much of a secret of the fact he finds it hard being a vegetarian. If he didn't love you, he'd never even have tried.'

Now that Sally thought about it, Trevor had been in odd form this last while back, but he was working extra hard, and Saffron didn't make things easy with her incessant pandering to the children. Sally had watched him fidget while Saffron spent an hour nursing Posy. It wouldn't have surprised her if Trevor felt a wee bit neglected now and again, but she didn't say this to Saffron.

'I'm so tired these days, Sally, I have no energy.'

'Saffron love, you worry far too much. Why don't you have a nice bath and light one of your aromatherapy candles? I'll take Posy down to the McDonalds'. I've got to do an extra hour there, and there's no one in today. She can watch a DVD.'

'I was going to read her French storybook to her.'

'Well sure isn't Pingu French? She can watch him instead.'

And before Saffron could protest, Sally took Posy's hand and led her out. She knew Saffron needed the break and would be a lot calmer when she brought Posy back.

Saffron was indeed in much chirpier form on Sally's return. She asked if Sally would take a suit of Trevor's to the dry cleaner's. Sally had hung it up earlier whilst tidying the bedroom. It had been lying crumpled on the floor. She nipped up and got it, promising Saffron she'd drop it in on her way home. She put the suit in her pannier and closed it, and was starting up her bike, thinking she couldn't wait to get home to put her feet up, when she was startled by a tap on the shoulder. It was Fintan.

'Are you going through the town, Sally?'

'Yes, I am.'

'I don't suppose I could have a lift?'

Sally was speechless. 'I haven't got an extra crash helmet,' she stammered eventually.

'Oh, I'll take my chances, I've always fancied a ride on one of these.' And he climbed up behind her and wrapped his arms around her waist as if it was nothing at all.

Sally dropped him outside the opera house. He gave her a cheery wave and shouted, 'See you tomorrow!' and she rode off feeling distinctly light-hearted. It was amazing what a bit of attention from a good-looking man could do. It was only when she arrived home that she remembered she had forgotten to stop at the dry cleaner's.

8

Sally finally remembered to call in at the dry cleaner's with Trevor's suit on her way to work. The assistant was a young girl who could hardly be bothered looking up at her. After searching the pockets aimlessly, she handed Sally a few pieces of paper.

'Here,' she said, 'are these any use?'

There were a couple of old receipts and a note with a message: *Can't wait to see you. I'll be outside if the weather's good.*

Now what was that about? Sally crumpled it with the receipts and threw them all in the litter bin outside. The note made her feel uneasy. The writing looked familiar; she'd seen it before, but it wasn't Saffron's. Then she had a thought. The call, the note, Trevor's odd ways – could he be involved with someone else? She told herself she was imagining things, put the thought out of her head, and set off for Marlborough Road.

Sally always made more headway in any of the houses she cleaned when she had the place to herself – no chat and no interference. She was a fast worker, and normally didn't even sit down for her cup of tea. Today she was taking advantage of Clare being at work to give the McDonalds' fridge a good clear-out. Finally a chance to bin all the stuff that was past its 'use by' date. Why on earth anybody needed five different jars of mint sauce was beyond her – especially when they made such a big deal of making the real thing from a garden overrun with fresh mint.

She was manoeuvring the glass shelf back in, trying not to break it and not quite getting it straight, when a voice said, 'Here, let me do that for you.'

She was so startled she almost dropped it. It was Tony, home from work in the middle of the afternoon. Now that was a rare sight indeed.

'Tony? What's up? Did you lose your job?'

Tony laughed good-naturedly. 'I know, Sally, I'm a terrible case. I had a meeting this end of town and decided to drop in. Is Clare here? '

'No, I'd say she'll be back shortly. Would you like some tea?'

'No, don't let me interrupt. I'll get it myself – would you like one?'

Sally refused, and just as Tony was sitting down to drink his, Clare arrived through the back door.

'What's happened, Tony? Did the office burn down?'

'There's no need to be sarcastic, Clare. I had a meeting end earlier than I thought, so I came home.'

'Really? Well I hope you manage to finish that tea before you remember something of vital importance and rush off.'

'I've a favour to ask, love.'

'Oh, I knew you wouldn't be here for the good of your health.'

Sally felt uneasy stuck in the middle of this sniping, but all the various jars of mayonnaise and God knows how many out-of-date cranberry sauces were on the counter, so she felt she couldn't just walk out and leave the mess. On the other hand, she didn't feel she should hear whatever it was Tony had to say. She excused herself and made to leave the kitchen, but the pleading look on Tony's face told her he needed a witness.

'No, Sally, don't go, really it's nothing important. Clare love, I've invited Harvey McLeod to dinner.'

Harvey McLeod was Tony's boss, a junior minister in the Northern Ireland Office.

'Ah Tony, you're not serious! You've invited the minister to dinner? Here? In this house?'

'Yes, we've had people from the office before.'

'Yes, but not the minister.'

'He's a really decent fellow. He was saying he was fed up with eating out in restaurants night after night, so I thought it might be a nice gesture.'

'When have you asked him for?'

Tony looked uncomfortable. 'He said he was free on Thursday night.'

'Thursday? But that's tomorrow.'

'I know. I'm sorry, love, I wasn't expecting him to be free so quickly. I thought maybe we could just throw some steaks on the barbecue.'

'Hardly – I thought you told me he loved his food?'

'I'm sure he'll appreciate whatever you cook.'

'Thursday night . . . no one goes out on a Thursday. Who will I ask, or is it just *en famille*?'

'What about Shane from the office?'

'God, no! I'll ask a few of the neighbours. Now I'll have to spend tomorrow trawling through the cookbooks. But don't worry. I have nothing else to do all day.'

'Listen, love, don't put yourself out, anything would be great . . . I mean, anything you cook usually is. I'll sort the wine out. I know he likes Fleurie. And I'll try to get home early.'

'Brilliant, I can't wait.'

'Erm . . . He'll have two minders with him.'

'Ah Jaysus, do I have to feed them as well?'

'I'm not sure. Maybe they just wait in the car.'

'Well *do* they wait in the car? Or do I feed them?'

'I'd better call and check.'

'Oh honestly, Tony!' wailed Clare. 'Talk about being dumped on.' She turned to Sally, who knew instantly what was coming.

'Sally, is there any chance you could come tomorrow instead of Friday? I'll need you here if I'm going to be cooking all day.'

Sally felt a brief stab of resentment. It was typical of Clare to do this, ask her with Tony looking at her beseechingly as well. No doubt she'd overpay her, but Sally had been looking forward to seeing Fintan tomorrow and she needed a bit of peace – far more likely at Edith's than in the chaos of number 25.

'I suppose if you can sort it out with Edith – if she doesn't mind me coming to her on Friday.'

Clare beamed delightedly. 'Oh thank you, Sally. I'm sure she won't mind and we can always ask her along to dinner.'

'Do we have to?' Tony said. 'I mean, she could bore for Britain.'

'Given his position, I'm sure Harvey McLeod is well poised to cope with the occasional bore. He must meet loads of them at work. Had you given me advance warning, I could have trotted out some interesting people. But it's a Thursday night and I have had one day's notice. So unless you want to send for a carry-out, shut up. Plus Edith will be doing us a favour letting us have Sally.'

Sally thought there was something ridiculous about that idea, Edith allowing Clare to have her. It was almost like she was a vacuum cleaner or something. But she knew Clare didn't mean it like that.

'I think Edith might appreciate a night out, Tony,' Sally said gently.

'Her sister is very ill and she doesn't look great herself with all the running up and down to Portadown. I've been worried about her.'

'You're right, Sally – that was a bit unkind of me. It's just that she can be an awful snob and she can rattle on a bit. Doesn't she know someone Harvey's related to?'

'I think she used to work for his uncle.'

'Is there any chance of your staying on a bit longer to help with the wines, Sally?' Tony and Clare both looked at her hopefully. 'Help with the wines' was code for clearing up all the dishes.

'Well I suppose I could manage it this once. Bronagh has a late night at the salon on Thursdays.' After all, she figured, she only had to do these extra nights about twice a year, and she usually enjoyed them. She didn't mention that she was glad of an excuse to get out of the house in case Charlie O'Neill came calling.

Clare and Tony both looked relieved.

'Oh, Sally, you're an angel. I may start looking through the cookery books for a pudding.' Clare was fuming inwardly at the whole deal, but she didn't want to start on Tony now in front of Sally.

'What about that lemony chicken thing you make? That's very nice.'

'You're right, Sally. Maybe I will make the Moroccan chicken; let me see if I have all the ingredients.'

'I can take you to the supermarket, sweetheart.' Tony was anxious to please now that Clare had calmed down.

'Well let me check what I have first.'

'In that case I'll just nip upstairs first. I've a few calls to make. Give me a shout if you need me.'

As Tony left the kitchen, Clare started to rummage through various cupboards. Sally hoped she hadn't just binned a vital ingredient. She was finishing off the fridge when Fintan strolled past the back window.

'Oh, there's Fintan Fanning,' Clare said. 'I must ask him if he'd like to come tomorrow night.'

She went running out the back door and called down the lane. Fintan came walking in after her, looking slightly trapped.

'Now you will have a cup of tea?' She indicated all the cookery books on the kitchen table. 'I'll just move these. Fintan, this is awfully short notice, but would you like to join us for dinner tomorrow night? About half seven? Tony has rather landed me in the middle of things by inviting his boss, and I need some interesting guests.' She beamed at him. 'I'm asking Edith as well,' she added hastily.

'That's very kind of you, Clare. I'd like that. I do have a rehearsal tomorrow, but I would be finished by then.'

As he made to leave, Anna came rushing in from school with Simon in tow.

'Mum, can I go to Simon's, please? He's going to help me with my maths.'

'Anna, where are your manners? Fintan, this is Anna, our youngest, and Simon McNamara, her friend. Fintan is an opera singer, you two, isn't that wonderful? He is staying with Miss Black.'

'Oh?' Simon's earnest little face perked up. 'Mum is taking me to *Tosca* at the opera house. We are reading the libretto.'

'Really?' Fintan seemed impressed. 'I am playing Cavaradossi.'

'Does that mean you are a tenor?'

'It does indeed.'

'I'd like to be Scarpia, he's an evil villain.'

'Would you now?'

Fintan and Clare exchanged amused looks. Wasn't it well for them, Sally thought, knowing all about opera? She had been to an opera, years ago, while she was still at school. Sister Maura, the nun who taught music, had asked if there were any girls keen to go on a trip to the opera house to see *La Bohème*. They had listened to it in class and Sally thought it the saddest story ever and the singing just wonderful. She brought in all her pocket money to buy a ticket. There were only twenty places.

She had left something behind in the music room, and as she rushed back to get it she overheard two of the nuns talking. She caught her name and her breath and waited outside the room. Apparently twenty-one people had brought in the money and they were deciding who shouldn't go.

'What about Sally McManus, Sister Maura? You could leave her off the list. Why on earth would she want to go? No background whatsoever.'

Sally's heart was in her mouth, but Sister Maura had stood her ground.

'Well I have to disagree with you there, Sister Agnes,' she said. 'Sally has followed the libretto avidly and produced the most wonderful work on the opera. If she hadn't managed the ticket money I would have used the school funds and taken her myself. Now Suzanne Savage pays no attention in class and wouldn't be at the school if her father didn't give so generously to the building fund. I'll suggest to her that she go with her parents. Lord knows, a bit of culture might do them good.'

Sally couldn't do enough for Sister Maura after that, but the phrase *no background* had stuck with her ever since. She knew what it meant – poor, not the right accent, second class.

On the way out the door, having refused a cup of tea, Fintan turned to Sally.

'Oh Sally, in case I don't see you tomorrow, I was going to mention that I get some complimentary tickets for the run. I thought perhaps you would like a pair.'

'Oh, I'd love to go to the opera. We've been meaning to book,' Clare said eagerly. Fintan looked a bit taken aback. Really, thought Sally, the nerve of her. She could obviously afford the price of a couple of tickets.

'Well if they offer us any more, I'll certainly get you some.'

59

He turned back to Sally. 'I thought you might want to wait till near the end of the run. Till we find our feet, as it were.'

Clare was looking at Sally intently, probably hoping she'd say no. Sally quickly made up her mind, rather pleased that Fintan had chosen her over Clare – it was like the time with Sister Maura all over again!

'That's very nice of you, Fintan, I'd love to go.'

'Good, we can sort out which night later on.'

And off he went. Really, Sally thought, as she put the last of the jars back in the now gleaming fridge, the effect that man was having on her, she must be losing the run of herself entirely. He was hardly George Clooney. Clare, looking slightly miffed, went off to talk to Tony. Anna came into the room. She had changed out of her uniform to go to Simon's.

'Oh Sally, guess what? When I was coming home from school I saw Evie in the park. AND a boy was lying completely on top of her.'

'If he was completely on top of her, how do you know it was Evie?'

'Oh Sally, you know what I mean. They were snogging, like in the movies. You know, all soppy like. It's so embarrassing. Everybody knows she's my sister. And he has purple hair! I saw them.'

Clare came rushing into the kitchen.

'What did you say, Anna? You saw Evie with a boy on top of her? In broad daylight? What were they doing?'

'Nothing, Mum, I was just joking.' Anna had thought Clare was safely out of the way.

'Oh my God! Sally – call Tony. He needs to go and get her out of the park.'

Sally felt another situation coming on. She headed for the kettle.

'Clare, calm down, she's sixteen. I'm sure they were just having a cuddle.'

At that moment, Evie, who, despite being engaged in her romantic gymnastics, had seen Anna peering at her, stormed through the back door and grabbed her sister by the arm.

'Well, you grotty wee spy. Have you told everyone, then?'

'Mum, she's hurting me.' Anna began to wail loudly.

'Honestly, Evie, could you not curtail your behaviour in public — and in your school uniform too.'

'You know, Mum, it's really perfectly normal behaviour for teenagers. At least it wasn't a girl. So you can be glad I'm not a lesbian. Especially since Anna is probably one.'

'And he has purple hair.'

Evie pushed Anna aside contemptuously.

'The colour is aubergine, you little saddo.'

'Does the school allow him to have hair that colour?'

Clare was pitching for a fight; Sally could hear it in her voice.

'He doesn't go to school. He's left.'

'Oh my God, how old is he?'

Anna, bored with it all now, left with Simon in her wake, and Sally began to fold the laundry. It was relentless, this endless sparring between Clare and Evie.

'He's nineteen — maybe twenty. I don't know and I don't care, and before you start getting all snobbish about him, he's in a band and he works at a bar in town and there's nothing wrong with people who don't go to university. Isn't that right, Sally?'

'Leave me out of this one, Evie. I'm just putting the laundry away before I go'.

But the noise had brought Tony downstairs, and as Sally excused herself and left, she could hear him trying to calm Clare down, with Evie now in floods of tears.

'Clare, for heaven's sake! Why do you always have to make an adversary of her?' Tony sounded exasperated.

'I do not — you don't know the half of it. You are never

61

here. You're only home now because you needed a favour! She's not studying at all for these exams. She has a forged ID, she's drinking, and I don't know who this boy is – or where he's from.'

'He's lovely, just because he's not a snob like you. Dad would like him.'

Sally left quietly. This row would go on for a while. She was glad to get on her bike and home. Sometimes Marlborough Road would wear you out.

When Sally arrived home, Bronagh was in the kitchen and had put the dinner on. She had just poured one of those jars of sauce over some chicken and cooked some rice. Nonetheless, Sally was delighted.

'Well this is fantastic, love, just what I needed.'

She went upstairs to get changed. The dinner was on the table when she came back down.

'Evie McDonald is coming in to the salon next Wednesday to get her hair cut.'

'Is she? That's great. I told you she was delighted with the free voucher.' Sally had done as Bronagh asked and distributed the vouchers round the three houses. Everyone had been pleased. It didn't seem to matter how much money people had; they all liked getting something for nothing.

Sally tucked into her meal. Things tasted great when someone else had gone to the bother of cooking.

'Clare's asked me to help out tomorrow night. She's having some fancy dinner party. Would you do my hair for me?'

'Aye, no problem. Who are they having this time?'

For all her sour opinions on them, Bronagh loved the tales of the famous people who visited the houses in Marlborough Road, even if they were just minor celebs.

'Harvey McLeod, the politician, some of the ones in the lane, and Fintan Fanning the opera singer.'

62

'Oh, nobody cool then?'

'No, unless you count Fintan.'

'But you said he was an opera singer.'

'Well he is, but he's lovely. Very polite and thoughtful.' Sally hoped she wasn't blushing. 'I'm just doing it for the extra money, and you'll be out.'

'Why not? You spend too much time in this house alone.'

They ate quietly for a few minutes, and then Bronagh put her fork down.

'I saw my daddy in the town today. He was waiting for me outside the salon at lunchtime. He said he'd like to see you.'

Sally felt her knees turn to jelly. She suddenly had no appetite for her meal.

'You would still know it was him, but he's awful quiet-spoken, and he looked really sad.'

'I don't want to see him. I wouldn't care if I never set eyes on him again.'

'I know that, Mammy; he said Eileen told him that. But if you change your mind, she has his mobile number. He's staying with Carmel.' Carmel was Charlie's sister. 'He said he might be getting a job in London.'

'I hope to hell he does!'

Sally got up to clear away. She was shaking. On the one hand she could understand Bronagh being curious about her father, and she hated herself for sounding so bitter. But even after all these years, Charlie's betrayal still hurt. She just wasn't ready to let him back into her life in any shape or form. He had done enough damage in the past. All the same, that was no reason to keep Bronagh from seeing him. Sally had always felt guilty about depriving her of a father.

Bronagh had moved into the living room to watch TV. Sally followed her and sat down beside her.

'Bronagh love,' she said gently, 'I told you before, I don't mind if *you* see him. He's your father.'

'I know that, Mammy, and I'm going to think about it, but I haven't made any arrangements.'

And they left it at that.

9

Total chaos reigned when she arrived at the McDonalds' the following day. Clare was wailing round the house like a banshee. Evie was sitting listening to her iPod whilst painting her toenails a sort of metallic green and sticking wee diamonds on each finished one. There was glue on the table, and about ten saucepans, some full, some empty and dirty, strewn around the kitchen. Hamlet the hamster's cage was on the draining board. He had forsaken his afternoon nap for a whirl on the wheel. Radio 4 was on full blast. Classical music was wafting from the front room, the TV was on somewhere, and from upstairs the strains of that rap music Evie liked drifted down. Anna and Simon were on the kitchen floor with Ophelia the other hamster and about six little pink bald creatures on a towel. Sally took a deep breath. Clare saw her and smiled with utter relief.

'Oh Sally, thank God you're here. It's crazy today.'

'So what's new?'

'Sally, Sally, come and see! Ophelia has had six wee babies!' Anna was ecstatic.

'Would you like to hold one?' Simon asked, cupping one of the little things in his hand.

'Ugh, no, I certainly would not. Now put them all back in the cage or they'll die. You're not supposed to handle them.' The children obediently did as Sally told them. 'Now take them up to Anna's room and keep them there. They probably need a nap, and I have a kitchen to clean.'

Sally surveyed the scene. Clare was in Nigel Slater mode, or should that be Nigella Lawson? Nigel and Nigella, honestly you couldn't make it up, Sally thought. One thing was for sure, those TV chefs must have an army to clean up the mess they made. Unfortunately for Sally, she was Clare's army.

'I'm doing the Moroccan chicken as you suggested, Sally. It's always popular and I have all the ingredients.'

Sally filled the sink and started on the pots. It was going to be a trying afternoon, and to think she had agreed to stay on and help this evening. While Clare thanked her lucky stars, Sally wondered if she had any.

Usually the residents of the lane kept their social lives and their neighbourly life fairly well separated. But in emergencies they tended to call on each other. So Bill and Laura Nelson from number 31 had been asked, Patricia Thompson from the last house on the terrace, with her partner Dave, and of course Edith and Fintan. Despite several heavy hints, Clare had resolutely refused to ask Edith's other lodger, the ghastly Otis. She didn't like what she knew of him. All he seemed to do was spend a lot of time smoking out in the back lane – and by the smell of it, not always tobacco.

When Harvey McLeod had been appointed as junior minister for Northern Ireland, the local press made quite a thing about his Northern Irish connections. This had especially delighted Edith, since one of the directors of the firm she had worked for was an uncle of Harvey's. She appreciated the fact that she was finally getting to meet him. She had phoned Sally last night and told her not to worry about coming on Friday, because she would be away from Saturday till Tuesday.

'Somewhere relaxing, I hope?'

'Oh, just to my sister. I'll see you next week as usual.'

Trevor and Saffron were going to drop in for a drink later, after everyone had eaten. Clare couldn't cope with a veggie meal as well. By six o'clock things were almost under control. Laura Nelson brought round a large raspberry pavlova, assuring Clare and Sally that they were 'all the thing' again. How desserts could be in and out of fashion was a puzzle to Sally, but it looked amazing. She put it well out of the way; she didn't want Evie or Anna to poke at it or pick the raspberries off. Clare would have a fit.

Tony and Clare were using the dining room tonight. Sally looked at the table appreciatively; it was beautifully set, with flowers, candlesticks and all the best wine glasses. Clare had a real flair for that sort of thing. Evie and Anna were eating first in the kitchen, though their parents encouraged them to mingle with the guests and chat to them. Sally supposed that that was how they built up their confidence. She couldn't have imagined Bronagh being able to chat to a government minister at ten years old; even now, at eighteen, she would have found it difficult. No doubt about it, it was a different world entirely. Sally had spent a lot of time at evenings like this just observing. She found that provided she kept in the background and just got on with her job, no one really took any notice of her, which suited her just fine. Perhaps she had a slight inferiority complex. She found it hard to chat to people she had just met.

Her sister Eileen had no such qualms. In the past she had come with Sally to help out on a night like this. She had been a great success because of her chat and the way she flirted with the men and teased the women. But Sally had always felt a bit ashamed of her. She couldn't really pinpoint why, exactly. Maybe it was Eileen's 'working class and proud of it' demeanour. Her sister didn't feel the ones over here had anything more going for them than luck, and accident of birth. She was right, of course, and Sally wished she could feel like that, but she couldn't; perhaps her ten years working for them had made her more keenly aware of the disparity in their lives.

Eileen hadn't been remotely intimidated by any of them; she was very free with the chat and too free as well in helping herself to the drink. Later that same evening, when she was supposed to be clearing up, Sally had found her deep in conversation with Saffron. Alarm bells rang when she caught the word 'Charlie' and saw Saffron's eager little eyes fixed on Eileen, waiting for some crumbs of gossip. Sally grabbed Eileen firmly by the shoulder and marched her into the kitchen. Fortunately it was empty.

'Don't you be gossiping about me to any of them!' she said furiously. 'I don't want them knowing my business.'

'I wasn't gossiping,' Eileen said feebly, but Sally could see she was lying.

'What have you told her?'

'Nothing,' Eileen said sullenly. 'Sure you pulled me away before I could get a word out.'

'I heard you mention Charlie.'

'She mentioned him; she asked how long you had been separated from him.'

'And?'

'I told you, I didn't get a chance to say anything.'

'Good, it's got nothing to do with her.'

'She's nice, Saffron; she said I could drop in to see her any time.'

'Well I don't want you dropping in; she's my employer, and you can't mix work and pleasure.'

And that had been the last time Eileen had been over in Marlborough Road. Sally saw to that.

68

Harvey McLeod was an amiable sort of a fellow and very low key for a government minister. He couldn't have been more than his late forties; in fact Sally had some recollection of reading his age in one of the papers and being surprised, for he had that settled look about him that made him seem older. He also had the self-confident manner of someone who was used to giving orders. He was unmarried, supposedly gay. Clare loved gay men; the way she behaved with her friend Padraig was shameless. She took their sexual preferences as a sign that she could flirt safely all night long, a chance to prac-tise the wiles and cute looks that the years of marriage had dulled.

The dining room with its high ceiling looked imposing in the dying sunlight. Clare had just lit the candles. There was a large gilt mirror that sat above the fireplace; it stretched almost to the ceiling. Sally had a full view of the table and could see herself reflected; standing by the door, looking a bit ill at ease, whilst the dinner guests, now well oiled by wine, gesticulated and laughed loudly and confidently. Fintan was talking animat-edly to Patricia Thompson, who seemed to be hanging on his every word. Sally felt a wave of jealousy, followed immediately by an inner voice telling her to get a grip. After all, he was a single man, and he would hardly be looking for someone like her – a cleaner – to rescue him from his bachelor state. She smiled at him and moved quickly round the table, lifted some nearly empty dishes and went back into the kitchen. Trevor and Saffron were just arriving as she entered. Evie had agreed to sit with Posy whilst they were here. Simon was upstairs with Anna and the brood of hamsters.

Trevor was in good form; there was nothing like an evening away from the children to cheer him up. Saffron, on the other hand, looked a wee bit lost. Sally poured her a drink at once; she could see there was something troubling her, though she had worn her new outfit and looked well, and Evie had been up earlier to do her make-up. Trevor, needing no coaxing, was emptying a bottle of red wine into a glass he had lifted from the counter top.

'Have they finished eating?'

'No, I'm just about to bring this in.' Sally indicated the raspberry pavlova.

'Ah, great stuff, just in time for pudding, then.'

He took a gulp out of his glass and led the way into the dining room. Sally busied herself in the kitchen. She would leave after the last dishes were cleared.

Her mind ran busily as she washed up. She needed to find something to give her some self-worth. Cleaning other people's kitchens wasn't going to do it any more. Earlier on, when Edith and Fintan had arrived, Anna had asked Sally, 'What is your cleaner called, Sally?'

'She's called Sally O'Neill.'

'Is she? The very same name as you? That is really funny.'

Clare interrupted. 'Anna, off you go if you've finished your meal. Sorry, Sally, I'm sure she didn't mean any harm.'

'Don't be silly, Clare. Sure all the kids round here think that houses come with cleaners attached,' she joked.

Maybe that was the only way to go: think big. If you expected that someone else would come and clean your house then perhaps you would be likely to marry someone who could afford to pay for it. Thinking of Anna, she remembered it was time the child went to bed. She went into the TV room to tell her. As she did, she noticed that the front door was slightly ajar and went to close it. In the nick of time she realised that Laura Nelson and Trevor were standing outside. Laura was having a cigarette. Trevor must be keeping her company; he sometimes smoked cigars. They were huddled close together, and something about the look of them gave Sally a feeling of unease. Then she saw Trevor lean towards Laura and kiss her on the ear.

70

'Don't worry,' he said, 'it'll all work out.'

It suddenly hit Sally like a thunderbolt. That voice on the phone – it had been Laura, of course; the English accent gave her away. Why hadn't she realised? And the note; that was why Sally recognised the writing. On the few occasions she had bailed Laura out, she had left her a list of things to do. Oh dear, poor Saffron. Sally's heart went out to her. That was all she needed.

Sally backed away, not wanting to be seen. Clare called her, asking where the cream was, and Sally didn't have time to think about Trevor and Laura as the rest of the evening passed in a torrent of dishes. She didn't leave till the kitchen was sparkling and the guests were settling down to brandies. Tony had offered her a drink, but she refused, protesting that it would make her fall off the motorbike.

She had got to the top of the lane before she noticed somebody standing at the gate. He was a small bald fellow, and she didn't recognise him, but he was barring her way so she stopped the bike.

'Sally? I just wanted a wee word with you.'

Her heart stopped. Oh, he was changed, there was no doubt about that. The last ten years hadn't been kind to him. He was grey and bald and worn-looking, an air of defeat hanging about him like a shroud, but she'd have known those eyes anywhere. It was Charlie O'Neill.

'How did you find out where I worked?'

'I met Bertha in Milligan's.'

'Bertha? Oh God, just wait till I see her. How dare she?'

'Don't get mad, Sally. I made her tell me. I didn't like to go to the house. Look, I just want a wee chat for old times' sake.'

'Old times' sake? I'd rather forget the old times if you don't mind.'

'Please, Sally. Sure did Bronagh not tell you I was going away for good?'

71

'I have nothing to say to you, Charlie. Now would you please move?'

And she started up the bike and rode off, leaving him standing with his mouth open.

10

Bronagh was apprehensive about Evie McDonald coming in to get her hair done. What if she made a mess of it? Aside from the idea of giving Evie something to complain about, Bronagh took her job very seriously. She wanted to be a good hairdresser and she knew from her limited experience that the good cutters got all the clients. Alan, the owner, had really pissed her off by insisting she find some fancy new clients. How could she manage that? But she was hardly in a position to complain. The problem was, she didn't know any rich people. The Marlborough Road ones were as close to rich as she could come up with, but Alan's idea of wealthy was people who drove Porsches, wore Ebel watches and dressed like Posh and Becks. She was raging that Kelsey, another trainee, had told Alan that Bronagh's mum worked in millionaire homes, although she supposed she had sort of exaggerated Sally's job a bit to Kelsey on their day release to the tech.

Some other fellow had rung up for the free haircut as well, a Mr Flaherty. He was coming in for her last appointment today. She vaguely remembered that her mother found him irritating, so she wondered why Sally had given him the voucher. She hoped he didn't have a wire about himself.

Just then, Evie walked in. She turned heads. The thing was, she didn't seem to notice the effect she had. Bronagh watched Joe, the only male trainee, gaze in open admiration at her.

'D'ye want me to shampoo for you, Bronagh?'

He smiled sickeningly at her as if he liked her; he was a nasty wee shite really, full of himself. Usually Bronagh had to fight with him to get him to shampoo her clients, though he was her junior so he'd no choice on that one. He'd only been at the salon for six months.

Evie was all smiles and chat, and obviously delighted to let Bronagh loose on her hair. Bronagh began to relax. Maybe Evie wasn't so bad after all. And she sort of looked rich; she was tanned and confident. She had a posh voice. Even Alan looked over approvingly.

Bronagh wasn't sure what to say to Evie at first, but she was really easy to talk to. She had picked up a magazine with yet another article on Posh and Becks and so they started to chat about David Beckham's tattoos. Evie wondered if he would have room for the names of any more children he might have. She didn't approve of tattoos. Then they got into a mild disagreement about Kate Moss. Was she gorgeous or not? Evie thought yes, but she wasn't Bronagh's type. They then discovered they both had the same handbag (from Topshop), so the time flew.

It was obvious Evie was well satisfied with her haircut; she even let Bronagh persuade her to have a fringe. As she was getting ready to leave, having thanked Bronagh profusely a million times for cutting her hair so well, Bronagh said to her:

'Someone else from Marlborough Road is coming in to have his hair cut today. A Mr Flaherty.'

'You are kidding me?'

'No, do you know him?'

'Not really. He stays at Miss Black's. He's a rock poet or

something. My boyfriend Mikey sort of knows him. He's quite old, like about thirty something.'

'Does he have hair?'

'Yes, absolutely loads of it.'

'Well that's all that matters.'

'But ...' Evie paused dramatically, 'it's bright red. He's a ginger minger!'

They both burst into uncontrollable giggles. It took Bronagh a few minutes to stop. Evie McDonald was a laugh. She offered to put Evie's name down to have her highlights done in two weeks' time. You could get them done at the training night for a tenner. Evie left a £3 tip, hoping it was enough, and suggested to Bronagh that she come to Edith's barbecue with her mum, though they both knew she wouldn't.

The minute Otis Flaherty walked in the door, Bronagh knew it was her client. They didn't get many like him. What a wild-looking guy. Evie certainly hadn't lied about the hair; he was a real carrot top, like Ronald McDonald. He was, as Evie had said, older – about thirty at least – and not a bit attractive; still, he had loads of hair, which he wore the Bob Geldof way, a bit unkempt and looking like he needed a shampoo. She couldn't wait to cut it off.

Otis surprised her by being very chatty and pleasant. Bronagh didn't say who she was, and obviously Sally hadn't said anything to him about her, so they just chatted generally. He did have a bit of a wire about himself, though. He told her he was an Ulster Scots poet as if it was some kind of big deal. He said he recited his poems with the backing of a rock band. Bronagh had never met a poet, at least not to her knowledge. But she'd heard somewhere that Belfast was full of them, so she'd probably walked past a few dozen in town without knowing it. It wasn't as if you could exactly pick one out in a crowd. Still, there was a part of her that thought it a romantic profession. Otis was currently writing a book of poems all about love. She

75

was the kind of girl, he said, that poets would find inspiration in.

'You have beautiful blues eyes,' he said, 'like limpid pools.'

She felt a bit offended at that. All she knew about limpets was that they were sea creatures and clingy, but he had nice thick hair so she concentrated on that. It was a good head to train on. She just smiled and chopped away.

He wanted to look good for next week, he told her. He had a gig at the Empire. 'I can leave your name on the door if you like. It should be good craic.'

'I'm not sure it's my scene, but thanks anyway.'

'How do you know if you don't check it out? You can bring a friend if you like. I'll put plus guest.'

'Okay then. I'll see if Tiffany will come with me.'

She thought about it after he had left. Perhaps she would go. It would be something different; she got fed up going out to the same clubs every week. And he was a poet after all. She'd phone Tiffany when she got home. She decided not to tell her mum, though, especially since Sally had said Otis got on her nerves.

11

Miss Black was in the kitchen in a bit of a flap when Sally came in to work on Tuesday morning.

'Ah, Sally, good to see you. I have been looking for the voucher you so kindly gave me. It's good for six weeks, is it not? I thought I would have a trim at some stage. It is very good for the hair, you know, to trim the ends every now and again. My late mother, God rest her, used to singe the split ends of our hair as well to keep it strong, and if I may say so it really worked. Both Ellen and myself have a good head of hair. Don't you agree, Sally?'

Sally did indeed agree; who was she to argue? So she admired Miss Black's thick tresses and told her she'd have a look for the voucher and if she couldn't find it she would talk to Bronagh and see if she could give her a replacement. Reassured, Miss Black left for her charity shop. Sally hung up her coat and listened. The place seemed to be empty. She was glad. She wasn't in form for either a chat with Fintan or a run-in with Otis, and if by any crazy chance Charlie came to the door, at least she would be able to deal with him without an audience.

Of the three houses she cleaned, Edith's was the only one

with drawers that remained in a semblance of order. Her cutlery was neatly in the appointed drawer, though not the good stuff of course, the family silver. To her eternal delight, Edith had inherited that. Her sister Ellen hadn't been interested. She had gone for the more contemporary look, which meant she and her husband Derek actually had stainless-steel cutlery, designer of course, but stainless steel nonetheless. It vexed Edith, but as she told Sally, it had turned out lucky for her. Not so lucky for Sally, though, who had to clean the silver and put it all back carefully in the walnut box with individual little drawers.

Sally pulled open one of the drawers in the kitchen dresser. She had given the salon voucher to Edith in the kitchen; perhaps she had put it away here. She carefully sorted through the contents. Bits of tidily rolled string, paper napkins – Edith disapproved of them, but used them from time to time in an emergency – cocktail sticks, and the warranties for all the electrical goods. It was also full of cards for plumbers, electricians and various services, even though Edith always used the same people, and the occasional flier for a Chinese restaurant or the local Indian, as well as the napkin rings of course, the everyday ones made of African walnut. The silver ones were kept in the dining room sideboard.

Sally's eye was caught by a hospital appointment card. It was for Miss Edith Black and gave the name of the consultant, Mr Brian Smedley, Department of Oncology, and the date, two weeks away. Oncology? Sally couldn't quite remember what that was, but she had a feeling it wasn't a cheerful department. She could hardly ask Edith what it was about, but she hoped for her sake it wasn't anything serious. She had enough to contend with. Sally tried to dismiss it, and rummaged in the other drawer, but there was still no sign of the voucher.

She was polishing the mirror when it came to her, shockingly. Of course! Her sister Sheila had had breast cancer, and she was attending the oncology department. Oh no, surely Miss Black couldn't have cancer? Sally thought about it. Maybe the word meant something else; she'd look it up. Miss Black kept a large two-volume dictionary, complete with magnifying glass, on the shelf in the den. She used it sometimes when she got stuck on the *Times* crossword. Sally got it down, opened it, and checked. Yes, there it was – oncology . . . that part of medical science that relates to tumours. How bland it looked, the definition. Her heart froze. Surely not? Maybe it was just a scare . . . it frequently was.

'Is everything okay, Sally? You look like you've seen a ghost.'

Sally dropped the book.

'Ach, Fintan, I didn't hear you come in.'

'I came down the back. I'm thinking of phoning the police, actually. There's a dodgy-looking character at the top of the lane; he's been there all morning. I asked him what he wanted and he said he was waiting for someone, but . . . Hey, are you okay? Is something up?'

Sally had gone pale. Was it Charlie out there again? She made a fuss of putting the dictionary back.

'Here, let me do that. Goodness, this is heavy. Have you been doing the crossword?'

'No, I've been looking up the meaning of the word oncology,' she blurted out, shaken by her suspicions about Charlie.

A flash of alarm crossed Fintan's face.

'And you know what it means?'

'Yes, I had figured it out, but I wanted to be sure.'

'Do you want to talk about it, Sally. Have you had bad news?'

Sally shook her head. 'No, not me, it's this.'

She went to the drawer in the kitchen; Fintan followed her. She took out the card and handed it to him.

'Edith?'

'Yes, I was looking for her free voucher for the hairdresser's and I found this.' She didn't want Fintan to think she was a snoop.

'The hairdressing voucher?'

Sally nodded.

'I still have mine, but the other was sitting on the table last week. I think I saw Otis lift it.'

So that was that mystery solved, she should have thought of that. Still, he mustn't have used it. Bronagh hadn't mentioned anything. Fintan moved to put the kettle on.

'Can you take five minutes to have a cup of tea?'

Sally nodded and sat down. She felt quite shocked.

'Perhaps it is something simple, like a mole, or a smear test.'

He wasn't even embarrassed saying that to her, she noticed.

'No, I have had both of those and you just go to the outpatient departments.'

'Well let's hope it isn't anything serious. I'm sure she would have said.' He poured two cups of tea. 'I wonder should we say anything to her? She's such a private person.'

Sally didn't think they should. If Edith had wanted anyone to know, she would have mentioned it. They'd just have to keep an eye out for her.

They were sitting drinking their tea when Evie came in through Miss Black's door, knocking carefully. Edith was adamant that no one should just barge in. Her back door was kept closed most of the time.

'Hi.' Evie said, smiling winningly at Fintan. 'I'm selling ballot tickets, only a pound each. Are you interested?'

'Sure I couldn't win an argument.'

'Don't forget your gorgeous motorbike, Sally.'

'That was a competition, but I'm happy to buy a ticket.'

'I've sold twenty so far. Isn't that good?'

'How many have you left?'

'Just five. It's for breast cancer research. It's very important work. This cancer affects everyone, even Kylie.' She held up a multicoloured wrist. 'Look, I'm wearing a pink band for it as well.'

'I'll take the last five,' Sally said impulsively.

'Are you sure?'

'Yes, why not?'

She exchanged a look with Fintan. It seemed such a co-incidence for Evie to have come in just at this moment.

'What's the prize?'

'A holiday for two in Crete.'

'Crete?'

'Yes, we've been there, to a villa, last year, don't you remember? It's lovely. Dad thought it was too hot, though.'

'Well I could use a bit of heat; the weather here would put your head away. If we have one more rainy day, I'm selling the bike.'

'No, Sally, the bike is cool. Good for your image.'

'I'd like to buy one as well, Evie,' Fintan said. Hang on. Let me get my wallet.' He went out of the kitchen.

Evie looked after him.

'Gosh, he's dead good-looking, Sally, isn't he? I mean for someone old.'

'I wouldn't know.'

'Well he is. Mum wants us all to go to the opera to see him, but I'm not really the opera type, y'know.'

Fintan came back in waving a fiver.

'Here, Sally, let me treat you.'

'Don't be daft.'

Sally took out her purse and tried to get Evie to take her fiver.

'Here, Evie, I'll treat Fintan.'

Fintan pressed his own fiver on Evie.

'I'll have three; Sally, you have two.'

Evie laughed. 'Okay okay, don't fight over it. Look, I know

what. Each of you have two in your own name and one joint one. I'll put both your names on one of the tickets.'

And negotiations over, she left. She was off school at the moment and obviously had got fed up revising. This way she could go in and out of all the houses and see what the vibes were.

Fintan looked at Sally.

'Oh Sally, I hope Edith is okay. It's very worrying. I've got so fond of her over these last few weeks.'

What a nice man he was, Sally reflected. He fitted in so well in Marlborough Road. She finished her work, bade him a cheery goodbye and went up the lane to number 21. She had a good look for the strange man Fintan had mentioned, but thankfully there was no sign of him.

12

Sally let herself in the back door of the McNamaras' with a cheerful smile on her face and a bright hello, Charlie and her troubles pushed firmly to the back of her mind. She came upon Saffron, sitting woebegone in the kitchen. Posy was perched on the long kitchen table painting eggshells. Saffron was a quare one for the mosaic collages, ever since she had done a children's art course last year that featured them heavily. The house was practically papered with them. Beside Posy was a pot of wallpaper paste, sheets of paper, several brushes and a mess that suggested that the excitable three-year-old had spent quite some time mashing the lot together. The cauldron was bubbling away on the Aga, some foul smell wafting upwards, and the iguana was sitting motionless on the shelf above it.

Jesus, you couldn't make this up, Sally thought. Iggy stared at her through his heavy-lidded eyes, and shifted his long tail as if he knew she had it in mind to kill him. With a bit of luck he'd fall into the curry gloop when no one was looking.

'Well, Saffron, are yis nearly finished with this?' Sally indicated the mess with a fixed smile.

'Oh Sally, I'm so sorry, it's just been hard to occupy her. I'm not feeling in the best of form these days.' Saffron sighed heavily in case Sally thought she was insincere.

'Is Simon here?'

'Yes, he's upstairs in his room.'

Sally marched purposefully to the bottom of the stairs and shouted at the top of her voice: 'Simon, you come down here this minute.'

Simon came running down the stairs two at a time. He always paid attention to Sally, even though poor old Saffron could be screeching like a banshee for him to come down all day long with little result.

'Yes, Sally?'

'That Iggy McNamara one is sitting on the shelf on top of the Aga. Now if you want me to go out that back door and never come back again, you can leave him there.'

'Oh, Sally, I'm very sorry. I forgot all about him. You see, being an arboreal lizard he likes to sit in trees, so I thought he could sit up there and watch Posy painting, and as a matter of fact, he rather likes the heat.'

Simon had a precise, clipped little voice, like he had swallowed a dictionary and it was coming up in chapters, Sally thought.

'Well he gives me the heebie-jeebies, so if you don't mind, I'd like him to go upstairs and watch you instead. That's higher up, isn't it?'

Simon lifted the thing off the shelf and carted it upstairs. It glared at Sally on the way past. She didn't meet its gaze. It would turn your stomach just to look at it.

It took Sally about twenty minutes to clear the table, put all the mess away and make Saffron a cup of herbal tea. Then she brought Posy upstairs and ran her a bath. Posy looked as if she hadn't seen water for a week. Sally bathed and dried the child and went to find something to dress her in; that done, she plonked her in front of the TV with the Pingu DVD. It would do her no harm to watch it again and it kept her quiet. She went back down to the kitchen and found Saffron still sitting immobile at the table, flicking listlessly though a book. Sally just got on with her work. She figured Saffron would talk when she was ready.

Eventually, when the kitchen was clean and tidy, the dishwasher going and a load of clothes on, Saffron spoke.

'Oh Sally, what on earth am I going to do?'

'About what, Saffron?' Sally didn't think there was anything particularly different about today, except that Saffron's usually upbeat mood had been replaced by this air of doom.

'I know Trevor has stopped loving me.'

'Ach, Saffron love, you said that last week and I told you it's nonsense. Of course he loves you.'

'Do you think he could be having an affair?'

Sally's heart sank. She thought back to what she'd seen at the McDonalds' the other night. Could there be anything serious going on between Trevor and Laura Nelson? No matter if there was; Sally wasn't going to be the bearer of bad news, and besides, it was probably nothing. Laura and Trevor were both lawyers and saw each other professionally, and Trevor doted on Saffron; they had been married over ten years. Sally always thought it a good match.

'Why would you think something like that, Saffron?'

'Oh, I told you he's stopped coming home for lunch almost completely, and then when he does come home in the evening he's taken to popping out for drinks to any house in the lane that'll have him, and he was so rude this morning when I mentioned the barbecue . . . he said he didn't care what I marinated, I could grill Iggy for all he cared. I'm glad Simon was still upstairs.'

Sally thought of the pot bubbling on the stove. The smell would have knocked you out of the house. Many a man would have left for better cooking.

'Well, Saffron, maybe things aren't going too well at work. He does seem a bit distracted. Have you tried to have a chat with him?'

'No . . . and there's something else. Sally, I think I might be pregnant again.'

'Think? Have you had a test?'

'No, but I haven't had a period in about four months and I feel really queasy in the mornings.'

'Mother of God, Saffron, that sounds fairly convincing.'

'But I have an IUD in.'

'Sure two of my sisters got pregnant with an IUD in; in our Nora's case the baby was born with it on its head. It was okay, though. A healthy wee boy.'

'Gosh, Sally!' Saffron looked horrified.

'You need to get them checked regularly; they can work loose. Would you like me to go round to the chemist on the bike and get you a test thing?'

'Oh Sally, if you don't mind, that sounds like a good idea.'

Saffron was indeed pregnant. Sally couldn't believe she hadn't realised it sooner. She was surprised Evie hadn't noticed it when they were out shopping. Sally looked closely at her; she was more bosomy than usual and her tummy was quite pronounced, definitely a few months at least. On anyone else it would have been obvious before now, but Saffron was so thin and wore all those shapeless kaftans. Sally got her to call the doctor and make an appointment, which she did without protest, glad to have someone else take charge.

'How am I going to cope?' Saffron started crying.

'You'll have to take it easy for a while. Maybe you'd think of putting the children into school in September; stop teaching them at home.'

'Perhaps you're right; it'll be hard to manage a third. I'll talk it over with Trevor tonight, though he has a late meeting.'

She stopped and swallowed hard. Sally felt sorry for her; she looked utterly miserable.

'I hope Trevor doesn't mind my being pregnant.'

'I'm sure he'll be delighted.'

But both of them wondered if indeed that would be the case.

When Trevor finally got home, late again, Saffron had dinner ready. She'd made a vegetable curry – it was one of her better efforts – and she had also opened a bottle of wine, real wine, not the organic vinegar they usually had. A feeling of alarm washed over him. He gulped heavily on his glass. The place seemed quiet, ominous. There were just the two of them, either ends of the kitchen table. The children had already eaten and were over with Anna.

'So what is it, my pet? You have something to tell me?'

'Treasure, darling . . .' Saffron looked tense. 'I don't know quite how to say this.'

'Give me a clue . . . Is it about the children?'

'No . . . Have you noticed anything different about me recently?'

Trevor thought rapidly. Was this a trick question?

'Different in what way?'

'Well, we haven't been making love much recently, and so you might not have noticed that I am a little plumper—'

'Haven't we?' he interrupted. 'I'm sorry, my pet, I suppose I've had a heavier than average workload, and you've been somewhat distracted . . .'

'Yes, I know, darling, I'm not complaining. I haven't been feeling well, but now I know what is causing it.'

Oh Christ, she wasn't going to tell him she was ill, was she? She was dying, and he was being punished . . . Oh no, and he really did love her. The curry rose in his throat. He felt sick.

'What *is* causing it?'

87

'I'm pregnant.' She looked at him almost pleadingly.

'What? Surely not? Haven't you got a coil thingy fitted?'

'Yes, but they sometimes can work loose, I think.'

Trevor couldn't quite get his voice to work. This was the last thing on earth he had expected, and the timing couldn't have been worse as far as he was concerned. But Saffron expected him to be pleased, so he tried to smile. It was okay for her, she had had all day to think about it and she had accepted it, and anyway, she had always wanted a large family. Trevor couldn't believe he had got away so far with only two. Oh God, what a nightmare. He finished his glass of wine and poured another, then looked at her. She was sitting there quietly, the tears about to flow. He got up and went round to her and took her in his arms. He did love her really; it was just so hard being married all the time.

'Don't worry, make an appointment with Dr Jones and I'll come with you.'

'Oh thank you, Treasure. I have already phoned. I'm seeing him tomorrow. I knew you'd understand.'

Somehow they made it through to bedtime without Saffron bursting into tears again.

Trevor lay in bed tossing and turning and hoping that it wasn't true – Saffron, pregnant, he couldn't believe it! Perhaps when they went to see Dr Jones tomorrow they would find out she wasn't. This was all he needed; his life was complicated enough.

Saffron liked Dr Jones a lot. He was a lovely man and had been very supportive of her when she had decided to go for a home birth with Posy. Trevor sat nervously reading the paper while she went into the consulting room. After the doctor had examined her and questioned her about her last period, he reassured her that the coil was well and truly missing but that all looked fine. Then he did a scan, and there clear as anything were two little babies, wriggling round top to toe inside her.

'Aha!' he said with a big beam. 'Well, well, well. Two of them. That's a big surprise, eh?'

And he sent the nurse out to get Trevor, who came in looking distinctly uncomfortable. Saffron felt sick. She was apprehensive of Trevor's reaction; something in her waters made her feel he would not be delirious with happiness. Even the idea of a third child had seemed to plunge him into gloom. And she was right.

'Twins?' he squeaked at Dr Jones in disbelief. 'Are you sure? Surely she can't be having twins?'

13

Bronagh took a lot of time over Sally's hair, wanting her to look her best. Her mother needed a good night out. The whole business with Charlie had been upsetting for her. She wasn't going to dress up too much because she was sure everyone but Edith would be casual. Despite having already decided what to wear she tried on about three different outfits before she settled on a pair of turquoise linen trousers she had bought in the sale and a pale cream cotton sweater. She decided against dangly earrings and just went for the little pearl ones Bronagh had bought her for Christmas. She wasn't taking the bike. She wanted to have a glass of wine and you couldn't be too careful these days. Drink went straight to her head anyway. She called a taxi and waited outside the door in case the driver missed the house. He was there on the dot of seven.

Sally arrived at Edith's front door and wondered whether to ring or let herself in, but she was a guest tonight after all, so she chose the former. They would all be out the back; maybe she should have walked down the lane. But no, she heard footsteps coming down the hall. Someone was in. Fintan opened the door and smiled at her. He was wearing a blue polo shirt tonight. It matched his eyes. He seemed very relaxed.

'We're all out the back. We weren't sure if you would come down the lane or not, so I said I'd wait.' His gaze swept her appreciatively. 'You look great, Sally.'

'Oh, I clean up well,' she said with a smile. But she was delighted with his compliment.

They walked through to the kitchen, where Edith was finishing off a pasta salad.

'Ah, Sally, how nice to see you. We're almost ready, I've just a few more things to bring out.'

'Let me give you a hand, Miss Black.'

Edith paused, about to hand her the bowl, and then said, 'No, not at all, Sally, I can manage. After all, you are our guest of honour.'

Sally hoped as she followed Fintan out the back that Edith hadn't overcooked the pasta. It would be just like her.

Many's the barbecue in these isles that has been ruined by bad weather, but tonight both luck and sunshine shone on Marlborough Road. Edith's garden had a full profusion of summer flowers at the moment and looked delightful. Saffron's citronella candles, some a little lopsided, provided extra perfume. There were three large wooden tables placed together and an assortment of chairs. A selection of bowls containing various salads were already sitting out, covered for the time being in clingfilm. Sally noticed they were mainly using plastic glasses, though Edith had also wine glasses laid out. Not her best ones, of course.

Tony had managed to make it home in time for once. Just as well, because he was the designated chef for the evening. He and Bill Nelson were currently bent over the barbecue sipping beers and turning steaks and chicken fillets. Patricia Thompson was talking animatedly to them, dressed in shorts and a backless top. Trevor was lurking behind, also drinking a beer, looking as if he was afraid to get too close to the meat in case he went wild and grabbed it all in a frenzy. On a separate gas barbecue Saffron's organic vegetarian offerings were cooking accusingly.

Everyone was indeed casually dressed. Clare was wearing an outfit not dissimilar to Sally's own, but you could tell her linen trousers were expensive, and her sweater was most definitely not Marks and Spencer. Fintan led Sally over to one of the wooden chairs and found her a cushion. She was relieved to see there was no sign of Otis. Laura Nelson wasn't there either; she would be along later. It seemed she had some important meeting or other.

'Now, Sally, you're not to lift a hand tonight.' Fintan smiled at her, making her melt. God, he was gorgeous. 'Let everyone look after you for once.'

A drink was placed in her hand, a glass of sangria, which was red wine and lemonade and tasted quite pleasant. Edith came back out and was chattering away, filling glasses. Saffron sat quietly, not saying much, with Posy clamped to her as usual. Sally had noticed as soon as she arrived that Saffron's down-in-the-dumps mood didn't seem to have lifted at all. She wondered how the doctor's appointment had gone, and if all the others had been told yet. As Edith reached her with the jug, Saffron refused a glass.

'Oh Saffron, *do* have some, dear. This sangria is wonderful, very refreshing, my own recipe, although I myself love Pimm's at this time of year.'

Saffron shook her head. 'No thanks, Edith, I'm fine, really. I have some juice here.'

Clare, overhearing, brought over another large glass jug filled with sangria and fruit.

'Here, Saffie, have some of this, it's very weak. I made it. It'll only give you a slight buzz.' She leaned over conspiratorially. 'Avoid Edith's. I think she's put a ton of gin in it.'

Saffron bit her lip and looked into Clare's face.

'I can't have anything to drink, Clare. I'm four months pregnant.'

'You're not serious?'

'Yes, I'm afraid so.'

She looked towards Sally for moral support. Sally smiled at her reassuringly. She had been hoping for Saffron's sake that the 'do it yourself' kit might have been wrong. She moved and sat on the garden seat beside Saffron. She wanted to hug her, but instead patted her on the arm. Saffron seemed on the verge of tears. Clare, open-mouthed at the news, plonked the sangria on the table and herself on the bench beside them.

'My God, Saffron! Gosh, you sly old thing! You never said a word. Are you delighted?'

She gave her a hug, and Saffron smiled wanly.

'I only found out for sure today. Sally got me a kit. I mean, I've suspected since last week, and I was sort of coming round to the idea. I've always wanted three, I could have coped with that, but it looks like I'm having twins.'

'Looks like?'

'No, it's definite. There were two on the ultrasound.'

Twins? Poor Saffron. That was the last thing she needed; a frail wee thing like her. Sally nearly choked on her drink.

'Twins? Gosh!' Clare rolled her eyes.

'Yes, twins,' Saffron echoed miserably.

'But it'll be fun. You'll have to talk to Laura when she gets here.'

Sally thought of Jack and Eric, the Nelson twins. With luck Saffron would have girls.

'When are you due?' asked Clare.

'November. I have to go for a second scan next week. I think poor Treasure is still in shock. Aren't you, darling?'

Trevor looked over. He was standing with Bill and Tony, looking distracted, but he had heard.

'Yes, we're pleased of course, but it was unexpected,' he ventured lamely.

Bill Nelson smiled encouragingly at him.

'Twins are great, good company for each other.'

His two were now seven-year-old monsters who had managed to see off about four au pairs in the last two years. Sally thought it was just as well they had each other – no one else could put up with them.

As the party went on around her, Saffron thought of the scene in the doctor's office. She sipped her juice quietly and watched her husband, remembering his horror when the doctor said it was twins. Trevor was darting looks here and there. His mind seemed elsewhere.

Bill Nelson called one of the twins to go and see if his mother was back yet. All the food was ready. The children lined up to be served. Simon dutifully took his quorn kebab, then announced to the assembled company:

'We must be expecting one more person. There's an extra steak, even counting Mrs Nelson.'

'You should work for MI5, Simon,' quipped Sally.

'Actually, Sally, I am considering it as a career option.'

'I've been half starved all year at uni, Simon, and I'm having two steaks, so there.' Rory McDonald, who had just arrived home today from university, was obviously in on the plot. Sally saw immediately what was up. The steak was for Trevor. Maybe that was why he was acting so shifty. At least she hoped that was the reason.

'You do realise that you are increasing your chances of CJD – aside from murdering a defenceless animal, of course.'

'Thank you for the info, Simon, I appreciate your concern.'

Rory patted Simon on the head and laughed good-naturedly, and the matter was dropped. Sally had a few more glasses of the sangria. They were pouring it out like there was no tomorrow. She was starting to feel relaxed. Evie arrived with

Mikey, who aside from the famous purple hair seemed to have pierced several parts of his face at random. She had got permission to go out with him later on, provided she endured the barbecue first and brought him along so Clare and Tony could meet him. Sally could tell Clare found him outrageous but was trying, for Evie's sake, to play down her disapproval. Tony, who had made a face when Mikey's back was turned, was keeping quiet. Mikey seemed uncomfortable; he was doing that shifting thing, swallowing too much and smiling too brightly. Sally's heart went out to him. These people were great, but they had no idea how off-putting they could be to outsiders.

Eventually all the children were fed, and dispersed to charge up and down the lane and annoy the rest of the inhabitants. Other residents had been asked to join the gathering later on for drinks. Sally thought that Edith was in good form, positively sparkling, and flirting outrageously with Fintan, who seemed to take it all in his stride. She thought back to the hospital appointment card she'd found in Edith's kitchen. Perhaps there was nothing wrong with her. After all, anyone could have a bit of a scare.

The idea of having the barbecue on Midsummer's Day had been Edith's. And she had to be given credit for choosing well. On the longest day of the year it simply didn't get dark in Belfast, particularly on a warm night with a clear blue sky such as this. It was almost nine and the sun was still shining. It would be light almost till midnight. As Edith pointed out to Evie and Mikey, who were sitting listening (a captured rather than captive audience), the reason for this was that Belfast was situated at fifty-four and a half degrees latitude north.

'Oh yes, we are very far north and no doubt would not have our lovely cool temperate oceanic climate were it not for the happy fact that the Gulf Stream wraps itself round the island of Ireland and prevents the worst excesses of winter.'

Sally didn't want to argue about the worst excesses of winter

95

bit, but she didn't think the Gulf Stream helped much when she was battling though icy rain on the bike summer and winter alike.

'Oh yes, remarkable, don't you think?'

Miss Black smiled brightly whilst gazing roughly in the direction of Mikey's pierced eyebrow. Evie had a glazed smile fixed and Mikey just looked baffled. Sally suspected that the Cokes they were drinking were at least fifty per cent vodka. She thought the sangria had certainly loosened Edith up. She was in magnificent form. She had missed her vocation; she should have been a teacher.

Her lesson was interrupted by the arrival of Laura Nelson, looking trim and tanned and glamorous in a lime-green linen dress. She sat down, accepted the proffered glass of sangria, and waited while Bill got her a steak and a plate of salad. Sally watched Trevor; she was interested to see how he would handle this, but he used Laura's arrival as a distraction to sneak off into the McDonalds' kitchen for his large sirloin steak. He had watched Rory carry it inside on a plate, saying he'd have it later. He hadn't intended the meat issue to become such a major one, but he just couldn't resist every now and then. He felt guilty; he felt like he was always cheating on Saffron – in more ways than one.

When he returned from the kitchen, Saffron stood up to excuse herself; all the excitement had been a bit much for one night.

'I think in view of my condition I can leave early. Trevor, would you round up Posy and Simon, darling?' And off she went.

'What condition?' Laura had turned to Trevor, who appeared not to hear her question. 'Trevor, did you hear me? What condition? Is Saffron okay?'

'Oh, you missed the announcement earlier, Laura.' Clare laughed. 'Saffron is pregnant and expecting twins!'

'Yes, I think poor Trevor is still in shock.' Tony patted Trevor on the back jovially.

Laura placed her drink on the table, faced Trevor and said in an icily cold voice, 'How on earth could she be pregnant?'

Tony leaned smilingly over to Laura – all the men flirted with her a little, thought Clare.

'I guess Trevor must have been misbehaving himself!'

Trevor stood there frozen, like a little boy about to be slapped.

'Yes, I suppose you must have been misbehaving, Trevor. It seems you are somewhat of an expert on that.' Laura almost spat the words out at him. Then she reached over and patted him on the head. 'Well congratulations *are* in order then, aren't they? You clever old thing. And with twins – a double whammy! I'm sure you're thrilled to bits. Imagine you becoming a daddy again, and at what? Fifty-two? No, almost fifty-three. That'll make you seventy-one when they go to college. Gosh, what a big challenge for you. I wonder if you are up to it. I doubt it very much.' And to everyone's astonishment she slammed her drink down and stormed off.

14

Bronagh had listened to Tiffany nagging all the way over in the taxi to the Empire. She had already necked a half-bottle of vodka before they left the house and sounded like a parrot on speed.

'Why are we going here? What is a rock poet? I've never heard of one before. I bet you the drinks will be twice the price.'

All this whingeing was unsettling Bronagh. She wasn't exactly sure what a rock poet was either, but she certainly didn't want Tiffany to know that. So she explained patiently for the tenth time that they could always leave early if it was no good, and offered to buy the first two rounds just to shut her up. She had her fingers crossed that their names were actually on the list. She could imagine Tiffany's reaction if they had to pay in. But they were there, right at the top: *Bronagh plus one*. She relaxed a bit. That was one less thing for Tiffany to bitch about.

It was really stuffy in the bar, and smoky as hell. The band weren't on yet. The crowd was weird – lots of Goths and student types. All the tables were full. Bronagh pushed her way up to the bar and tried in vain to catch the eye of a barman.

Tiffany stood beside her, arms folded and a venomous look on her face. Bronagh was having no luck, and was about to change her mind and go when she saw Otis in the crowd. He caught her eye and waved, then worked his way effortlessly through the crowd.

'You made it.'

'Yes.'

'We're on at ten.' That was an hour away. He leaned over and caught the barman by the sleeve. 'Put this drink on our tab, will you, Declan? Cheers. I have to go and get ready. Catch you later, doll. Okay?' And he gave her a big cheesy grin.

Bronagh felt pleased he had bothered to come over. She ordered the drinks – double vodkas with cranberry juice – and handed one to Tiffany.

'That's the fella whose hair you cut.'

'I know.'

'That's how you got the free tickets,' Tiffany said accusingly.

'Yes, so what?'

'He's dead old; he must be at least thirty. Here, do you fancy him?'

'No I do not! I just thought it would make a change to see a live band.'

Bronagh suddenly saw a free table. She pushed her way over and sat down, keeping the other seat for Tiffany. They'd stay for the first half anyway; it might be okay.

Back in Edith's garden, Laura's outburst had been forgotten and Clare's pudding – 'something wonderful with plums' – was being served for the adults, the children having had ice creams. A few of the other neighbours had joined them, and the wine was flowing. Sally was glad she had come. She was enjoying herself, and Fintan was sitting by her side acting as if she was the most beautiful woman there. She was almost starting to believe it herself.

Suddenly the children came running en masse into Edith's garden, babbling about the strange man who had climbed into the Nelsons' tree house and right now was spying on everyone.

'A strange man! Where? Show me – what strange man?' Clare was up like a shot, shrieking down the lane. The others followed in a straggle. The children were delighted they had created such a rumpus.

The Nelsons' tree house was about eight feet from the ground. Bill had built it a few years back into the largest tree in his garden, which was a horse chestnut. It was in full bloom now, the candles pointing upwards and the leaves thick and green. The children loved it in summer for the shelter it gave them, and of course in autumn for its rich harvest of conkers.

Before the residents and Sally reached the garden, they could hear someone giving an extremely loud and drunken rendition of Van Morrison's 'Brown-Eyed Girl'. A rather dishevelled balding man was sitting precariously on the edge of the platform, clinging on with one arm and fortifying himself with sips from a can of beer between lines. To Sally's mortification and horror, the singer was none other than Charlie O'Neill.

Several pairs of eyes gazed up at him. Charlie immediately spotted Sally, and carolled drunkenly at her in a loud voice: 'Yew ma brown-eyed gurl . . . Sally, oh Sally, why did you leave me? I loved you, so ah did, I loved you, Sally.'

All eyes swivelled in unison to Sally. She felt her head swim, and stood rooted to the spot as he continued to address her.

'Why will you not even talk to me, Sally? All those years I thought about you, all those wasted years. You're the only woman I ever loved. What God has put together, let no man pull asunder.' And with this pronouncement he fell backwards into the tree house and passed out.

There was a kind of stunned silence, and then everyone began to talk at once. Patricia Thompson was looking at Sally as if she had a bomb under her arm and was about to detonate it.

'Who on earth is he? What is he doing here? How does he know your name, Sally?'

Sally shook her head. She had totally lost her voice.

Fintan moved protectively to her side.

'I've seen him before. He's been standing at the top of the lane a few times recently. I told him to move off.'

'Do you know him, Sally?' asked Clare, eyebrows arched.

'I . . . No, I don't know him . . . I used to know him,' Sally whispered, almost in tears. She couldn't bring herself to say he was her estranged husband.

'Shall we call the police?' Edith assumed her headmistress voice.

'No, don't be ridiculous. We'll just ask him to leave, unless of course he's been bothering you. Has he, Sally?' Tony asked.

Without replying, Sally turned on her heel and ran down the lane. She went straight into Edith's garden and picked up her handbag, then made her way through the house and out of the front door. As fast as she could, she ran out of Marlborough Road and on to the main road to get a taxi home. She would never be able to face any of them again. Her whole body was trembling violently. The bastard, the stupid bloody bastard! Hadn't he done enough to ruin her life years ago? It was sickening, his turning up and making her look like a total eejit in front of everyone. She would call Maids to Order first thing on Monday and accept Maybeth's offer. They'd hardly want her back here after this scene. She could still plainly picture Patricia Thompson's sneering face. She would take a week's leave and start the following week in her new job. She was distraught. Why tonight? And just when she was relaxed and getting on so well with Fintan. It was all ruined now.

She got to the taxi rank and there was a cab sitting waiting.

She gave him her address and sat back in the seat. The Friday-night rush hadn't started yet, and the streets were full of young ones out enjoying the good weather. The taxi had her home in no time. The house was empty. Bronagh would be out till late. She went in and plonked herself down on the living room sofa, and then, unable to hold out any longer, allowed herself to cry. She thought she wouldn't be able to stop. When finally she calmed down, she knew sleep was out of the question. The sight of Charlie serenading her from the tree house was playing over and over like a clip from a ghastly newsreel in her mind's eye. Each time it scrolled past, her humiliation deepened. She felt as if her entire body was blushing. Why could he not just leave things well alone and let her get on with her life?

The band had been going for nearly an hour. Bronagh, on her third drink now, was beginning to chill out. Tiffany, on the other hand, was getting surlier by the minute.

Otis was at the microphone, wailing like a demon. The band was playing softly behind him, gazing expressionlessly at the crowd. Bronagh listened carefully; you could make out the words despite the noise of the crowd.

'Your love curls round me, ties me, chokes me, it spins me. I am left reeling. It sets me free, makes me dizzy.'

Otis began whirling around. The drumming intensified.

'God, he makes me dizzy. No wonder they're called The Reelers,' Tiffany said sourly to Bronagh.

Privately Bronagh thought the poems were nonsense, but she wasn't going to admit that to Tiffany. The band was good, though.

'What would you know about poetry?' she sniffed.

'Nothing, but I know that's shite. Anyway, he looks like Mick Hucknall.'

Tiffany had a point. Perhaps, Bronagh thought, they'd do better to cut their losses and go. She was about to suggest this,

102

but just as they were finishing their drinks, Evie McDonald walked in with a fella with purple hair. She spotted Bronagh and waved.

'Hiya, Bronagh, great crowd, isn't it? This is Mikey.'

Bronagh introduced Tiffany, who affected nonchalance.

'Yeah, Bronagh said you came to the salon; you had the free coupon.'

Bronagh was mortified, but Evie laughed.

'Too right. Let me know if you get any more. Mikey needs to get his hair back to normal if he's going to get back in our door.'

Mikey looked at Evie adoringly and nodded.

'I don't think they liked me round there.'

'Is it still going on?'

'Yes, we left early; some madman started singing in the Nelsons' tree house, so we legged it and left them all to it.'

Bronagh hoped Sally had had a good time at the barbecue, but she had no intention of asking in front of Tiffany, who was on the defensive now that Evie had joined the company.

The band stopped and Otis came over to them. Bronagh noticed a lot of the girls nudging each other and looking at him. Honestly, the way people behaved if you put yourself forward at all. You'd have thought he was Robbie Williams; sadly Bronagh figured Tiffany's assessment of his talent was closer to the truth. Bronagh was distracted by Evie's presence. Throughout her life, all she'd heard from Sally was Evie McDonald this, Rory McDonald that, and then the wee one, Anna; what a pet she was, and how clever. Sometimes she felt jealous of them; they seemed to have it all. Good looks, brains, a daddy with an important job; plus *her* mother around to slave for them. She knew the real reason Tiffany was grumpy was that she felt out of her depth. Bronagh didn't feel entirely comfortable either, but she was determined not to show it. Evie was treating her like a mate. She joined in the banter and

103

said she'd probably wait around for the second half. In reality she planned to leave and put Tiffany out of her misery, but she would choose the moment.

As soon as the band started and Otis began another of his poetic raps, she whispered to Evie that she was leaving. She nodded towards Tiffany and mimed as if to say her friend was about to be sick. Evie waved goodbye and the two girls went outside. It was still light, so they decided to walk into town. They might go for a few at the club all their mates favoured. Bronagh relaxed. She was glad they'd left. At least she could be herself now.

'You were talking all posh in there,' Tiffany said accusingly.

'Don't be ridiculous. I was just making myself heard above the crowd. Our English teacher Miss Walsh used to say to us, "Don't mumble, girls, enunciate!" Well that's what I was doing.'

'Hmm, it looked like showing off to me.'

When Bronagh arrived home a few hours later and a little the worse for wear, she noticed the light on in her mother's bedroom. She didn't go in. She answered Sally's 'Is that you, Bronagh love?' with 'Yes, Mum. Night night, see you in the morning.'

It was just as well, because she would have seen at once that Sally's soft brown eyes were red and swollen from crying.

Sally spent the entire weekend in a limbo of indecision and upset. She had turned her mobile off and unplugged the phone. Extreme she knew, but she wasn't ready to face any of her employers. There was no way she could go back to Marlborough Road now. Friday night had been the last straw, for she had no guarantee Charlie would stay away. She had to leave her job; she couldn't cope with Clare, Saffron and Edith thinking badly of her. They would wonder why she hadn't come clean about Charlie earlier, and if they heard that he'd been in jail, they probably wouldn't want her anyway. It was unbearable to think about it. Eventually she decided it would be best if she wrote rather than phoned. She found a notepaper and envelope set that Edith had given her last Christmas, and wasted three pages before she was finally able to compose something that satisfied her, aware of her grammar, her spelling and her handwriting. In the end she wrote:

Dear Clare,

I am addressing this to you since I have worked for you the longest. I am sorry after all this time to have to tell you that I have got a new job and will be starting it next week, so I won't be coming back. It is nothing personal. I enjoyed working for all of you in Marlborough Road. I hope this will not put you out too much. I am sorry not to give you more notice, but there are plenty of cleaners out there. I would be glad if you could please tell Saffron and Miss Black.

Yours truly,
Sally

That was the best she could do. She'd post the letter first thing on Monday, right after she'd called Maybeth and accepted the job with Maids to Order.

15

Monday morning at nine o'clock, Clare shrugged herself into her blue dressing gown and yawned. What a weekend. No wonder she wasn't feeling at all rested. Friday night had ended in chaos. It had taken four men all of half an hour to wake Charlie and get him down the ladder. They had sent him packing but the party was over. Sally's disappearance and Laura's outburst had put a dampener on the evening, and Edith had suggested everyone head home. Fittingly, it had rained all of Saturday and Sunday.

Clare had a paper to prepare, but first she needed a strong cup of tea and a piece of toast. She went downstairs, glancing into the TV room on her way to the kitchen. Honestly, the place was a tip. Rory and Evie just took so much for granted. She noted the discarded cans and juice cartons piled in the wastepaper basket, the empty cereal bowls and spoons on the floor. She would have to tell them both to shape up. She wasn't having a summer like last year, with two big lumps dossing around eating her out of house and home, up all night and sleeping away the days. Rory was home for the rest of the summer now and he needed to find work soon. Tony was firm that there was to be no more freeloading. And for that matter Evie needed to get a job; the end of term was about a week away and she couldn't live on the money she made from babysitting Posy. As for Mikey, pierced and tattooed Mikey, well she hadn't the energy to even go there. Evie had been in at some ungodly hour on Friday, but since Rory was just home and Tony was around for most of the weekend, Clare had decided in the interests of family harmony not to make an issue of it.

The kitchen was another disaster area, so she decided to do a bunk upstairs before Sally came – if she came at all. Clare dismissed the uneasy feeling she had about Sally running off on Friday night. Too much drink had been taken, she reasoned. So what if some old tramp had taken a fancy to Sally? Still, poor Sally had been totally overwhelmed by the incident. Clare had had no luck calling her over the weekend. She was crossing her fingers Sally would show up as if nothing had happened, but she was late, and that was most unlike her. She had kept great time since winning the motorbike.

The *Guardian* was on the table; Clare lifted it and tucked it under her arm. She'd just have a quick flick though it while she ate her toast. Then she'd shower and begin her work.

In a very tidy kitchen on the other side of town, Sally O'Neill sat feeling dejected. She had posted the letter earlier with a first-class stamp, but of course it wouldn't arrive until tomorrow so she was awaiting with trepidation the inevitable phone call from Clare. She had been rehearsing the words in her head all weekend. Her tea had gone cold; she got up and rinsed the cup. It was almost ten o'clock. Maybe she'd take herself out of the house, but somehow she felt unable to move.

Predictably, at ten thirty, the phone rang. It was Clare, of course.

'Ah, Sally, you ran off on Friday, we couldn't believe you'd gone. We got rid of the drunk; he left with no bother at all. Fintan said he's been hanging round before, but he's been told in no uncertain terms . . .' Clare trailed off. 'Sorry for rabbiting on. Are you okay? Are you not coming in?'

'No, I won't be in today.'

'Oh Sally, you're not sick, are you? Don't worry, Rory can just pull his weight. Sure we'll see you on Wednesday. Do you need anything? Is it a tummy bug?'

Clare knew it was nothing of the sort, but she hoped that maybe by going through these formalities she was giving Sally a chance to opt out of a final decision.

'I don't feel myself, Clare.' That was true enough, she didn't. 'I've written you a note.'

'A note? About what?'

Sally didn't answer; there was nothing she could think of to say. She felt wrung out, quite unable to explain.

'You'll get it tomorrow. Sorry, Clare, I have to go.'

She put down the phone dejectedly and decided to take herself into town; there was little point in staying about the house, for she knew she would find it hard to put in the day. Her heart was too heavy.

In the end it was a sort of lost day. She couldn't get her mood up at all. So after a half-hearted wander round the shops, she came back home. Bronagh was lying on the sofa watching daytime TV, *Big Brother* or something. What a waste of time, lying around doing nothing watching other people lying around doing nothing. It couldn't be good for you.

'You're home early.'

Sally nodded agreement.

'Bertha called, she said she'd drop round later.'

'Great, I can't wait. Are you just going to lie there all day?'

'It's my day off; I'm not doing any harm. What's eating you?' Bronagh felt a brief stab of alarm. Maybe Sally had found out about Friday night and Otis. From the little Sally had said

108

had always been thus. There were other issues, such as Lola and Iggy, and Chutney, the Nelsons' macaw, but she had always seemed relaxed if abusive about these pets.

Friday night seemed to hold the key. Who was the drunk?

'Could it have been a workman from number thirty-nine?' Clare suggested. (Patricia Thompson was having her kitchen redone.)

'He seemed to know Sally; he certainly knew her name,' added Tony.

'Maybe it was her ex-husband?' Saffron suggested. 'Sally's sister Eileen told me a few years ago that he was fond of the drink.'

'I thought he lived in England?' Edith said this as if living in England was the equivalent of living in Tierra del Fuego.

'There is fairly free travel between England and here, Edith.' Tony tried to sound good-humoured, but this whole thing was pissing him off. How had they let themselves get so dependent on one person? He liked Sally a lot, and he knew she kept Clare under control – well, relatively – but for that kind of money, surely they could get anyone? He suggested this tentatively. Clare almost exploded at him.

'No, we can't get anyone else. How could we? We trust Sally, you can leave anything lying around; she's discreet; she knows the houses, the children, even the pets, and it would take ages to get someone else into her routine.'

'Maybe if we struggle through the summer, get the two big ones to help a bit more . . .' Tony knew immediately that this sounded limp, and he was right. Clare's voice shot up about twenty decibels.

'I have agreed to an extra class next year because Anna will be at big school. At least with Sally I know that two and some-times three mornings a week the house will be manageable.'

'Your house is always lovely, Clare. I mean, compared to mine,' Saffron volunteered, feeling sorry for Tony.

But Clare was off on a tangent. 'This is what happens, I suppose, when we take on too much and need other women to help us out.'

'Clare, your mother has had domestic help all her life.' Tony couldn't ever understand Clare's issues. The way he saw it was Sally did a job, they paid her, end of story.

'Yes, but my father was a GP, she had to have help. She needed to be available to answer the phone.'

'Precisely! That is why you are more entitled to domestic help than your mother.' Edith sounded brisk. 'I don't think we have time to agonise over the philosophical aspects, Clare, just the reality of the situation. We need to get Sally back.'

But Clare was in self-flagellation mode. 'Maybe I should have been friendlier to Sally, treated her more as an equal, but that's so unrealistic; in the final analysis, I'm her employer. Although I do have issues about another woman working for me, I can't just stop work. Aside from the money being useful, I couldn't stand being at home all day. I mean, when Anna was small, I thought I would be found suffocated in a pot of home-made playdoh.'

'I quite enjoy making playdoh,' Saffron chipped in, 'although Sally hates the way it sticks to the pots.'

'Ladies, could we forget about the playdoh and get back to the business in hand?' Working for the Civil Service as he did, Tony had got fed up with meetings rambling on for hours with no conclusion.

'Yes, we really need to get her back again. Even with the two older ones at school, it's going to be hard.'

Edith hadn't pleaded her own circumstances – her house was more ordered than the other two – but she felt that at this particular juncture in her life, she should be doing less not more. If Sally left, she would have to stop the lodgers, and then what would there be to do? The house was far too big for one. And there was the other matter of her health, though she was staying positive on that. It would be very lonely without Sally. Her neighbours were lovely, but they all had such busy lives and such big families.

Tony surveyed them all.

'I think a delegation over to her house is in order. No point in sitting here chatting.'

'Don't be ridiculous, Tony. We can't just barge over there and demand an explanation.'

'She seems very fond of Fintan; perhaps we could ask him to contact her,' Edith suggested. She thought Clare was very snappy with Tony; all he had done was made a suggestion.

'Good idea, Edith.' Trevor nodded enthusiastically, and downed a second glass of Tony's wine, even though the others were all pointedly on tea.

Edith had thought things over carefully. She had seen Sally develop a thing about Fintan over the past few weeks. It seemed an unlikely match, an opera singer and a cleaner, but Sally had a quick mind; she didn't have to stay a cleaner. Edith Black suddenly saw herself in the role of fairy godmother, but she wouldn't rush things. She would bide her time.

The consensus was to leave things for a week; they could blunder on without her. There was always the hope that she would hate her new job – or even miss them. All fingers were crossed.

16

Evie had just a few days to hand in her history project. It would form a large part of her mark. She needed one further interview for her Blitz on Belfast section. Clare had suggested Miss Black, who was apparently a small child during the Blitz and therefore qualified as an 'actual witness'. Hundreds of people had been killed then, because of the Harland and Wolff shipyard, which the Germans were trying to bomb. Evie was bored with it all; why didn't people just get over it? It seemed to keep them permanently annoyed. Mikey had the right idea, leaving school and working in a bar. Her own parents were obsessed with education. Clare was even doing a PhD. Imagine, Evie thought, at *her* age. It was totally ridiculous. What was the point of knowing loads of stuff about Yeats and Maud Gonne? Who cared?

She went downstairs and into the kitchen. Clare was in there, sighing a lot and cleaning in a way she hoped everyone would notice. She'd been in a foul mood since Sally left. Evie was really sorry Sally wasn't coming back. Sally was like part of the family, she'd been coming here so long. Evie hoped she might change her mind. She would ask Bronagh when she went in to get her highlights done.

'Mum, would you ask Miss Black if she would tell me what it was like living in the Blitz?'

'Honestly, Evie!' Clare snapped. 'I thought that project was meant to be handed in months ago!'

'Yes it was, but I got an extension.'

'On what grounds? That you were too busy going out drinking to do it?'

'God, Mum, you are so tuned to Moan FM these days.'

'What?'

'Just moaning twenty-four seven.'

'Well maybe if I had someone to help out in the house a bit more, and your father paid us an occasional visit instead of living in that bloody office of his, I might not have quite so much to moan about.'

'Whatever. Are you going to ask Miss Black for me?'

'No, go and ask her yourself! I'm busy cleaning this filthy house.'

Evie stormed out of the back door.

One didn't just stroll into Miss Black's; her back door wasn't always open anyway. Evie was about to go round the front, but then she noticed Miss Black in her garden. She was kneeling on a little pad, weeding. Her garden was easily the nicest in the lane. It had neat flowerbeds either side of the lawn and they were a riot of colour at the moment. There were clusters of tiny deep blue flowers planted along the border, and taller flowers of different colours, and beautiful velvet crimson roses like something off a chocolate box. A little path made from hexagonal stones ran down the middle of the lawn. The small conservatory was furnished with iron garden furniture and of course the famous rococo barbecue was tucked away in a corner at the back. It was the only garden the children avoided; that was why it still looked good, Evie thought as she tiptoed up the paving stones.

'The flowers look absolutely gorgeous, Miss Black.'

'Ah, Evie! Thank you so much. I am glad you appreciate them. They are a joy at this time of year. It's such hard work keeping them weed-free. Now, can I do something for you?' Edith knew Evie was hardly there to talk about flowers.

'I'm doing a project on the Second World War, on the Blitz on Belfast, and Mum thought you might have some stories I could write down.'

Edith put down her trowel and regarded Evie.

'I was only a babe in arms then, Evie, you understand.'

'Oh I know that, Miss Black, it's just our teacher told us we'd get more marks for reality stories. Mum's Auntie Mary told me some things, but she's way older than you, almost eighty.'

'I see. I'll bring some lemon barley out to the conservatory and we can talk there. You have a pen and paper? Good.'

To Evie's satisfaction, Edith Black told her a long story about being carried up Divis Mountain as a small child to escape the air raids and how she was dressed in a little suit called a siren suit. She also told how her father had had a cousin killed and his body had been laid out in the Falls Baths with hundreds of others. Edith's father had to go along to identify him. She seemed to enjoy talking about it all and Evie didn't have to pretend to be interested. It was a great story. She wrote it down verbatim. Maybe history didn't have to be boring after all.

When Miss Black had finished, Evie carried the tray back into the kitchen for her. Otis was there, sitting at the table. Even with all his wild-looking red hair cut off, he was still a minger; a ginger minger. Evie smiled at the idea.

'Oh, hullo, Evie,' he said, mistaking her smile for a friendly one. 'Great craic on Friday, sorry you couldn't stay till the end.'

'No, I had to be home, my mum throws a psych if I'm back late.'

116

'I see your wee friend Bronagh left early.'

Evie could tell Otis was trying to sound dead casual. He obviously fancied Bronagh, though he was really old. He could be her da, or not far off it.

'Oh yes, the other girl, Tiffany, was feeling sick. She had to go.'

He looked pleased at that.

'Well if you see her, tell her we might be opening for some of the big bands at Oxegen. She might like to come.'

Evie was impressed. Oxegen was a great rock gig, held each year outside Dublin in Kildare. She wondered if he was really going to open for a big name or if he was only boasting. She had wanted to go but her mum had said she couldn't go to a concert away from home unless she was with Rory. Maybe her mum might let her go with Bronagh. *She* was eighteen, after all.

'I'll let her know. I may be seeing her next week.'

'You wouldn't have her mobile number, would you?'

'Sorry, no. You could always call her at work.'

Bertha rapped on Sally's window about six o'clock while Sally was finishing her meal. Bronagh had bolted hers down and was upstairs getting ready to go out. Sally opened the back door with a heavy heart.

'Well, Sally, only a few days now till you are a Maid to Order.' Bertha beamed at her with satisfaction.

'I thought the whole point was that I'd not be a maid, I'd be a supervisor.'

'No, you are deputy supervisor, I'm the chief supervisor.'

'There's no cleaning involved, is there? Have you been cleaning?'

'Ach, a wee bit, you know. Maybeth says it's just till we have the full quota of staff. But you needn't worry. You go to a different house every day, and the people aren't even there.'

117

'Maybeth told me I'd be driving round inspecting the cleaners and making sure they finish the typed lists.' Maids to Order had job sheets that itemised the various tasks required in each household.

'You don't seem to be looking forward to it much,' Bertha ventured.

'No, I'm not. I wish to God I hadn't agreed to take the job.'

'Well you can hardly back out now. I mean, how would that look for me? After me getting you the job, doing you the favour.'

Sally didn't rise to the bait; you could never win an argument with Bertha anyway. She was far too thick. There was no point in changing her mind now and going back to Marlborough Road. What was done was done, and she'd have to live with it.

Miss Black had not had an opportunity to talk to Fintan about Sally till now. Fintan had been preoccupied. *Tosca* had opened on Tuesday, to extremely flattering reviews in his case. He had three performances this week. Possibly he hadn't even realised that Sally had not been in to work.

Edith waited up especially for him; she was sure he would oblige and use his winsome charm on Sally. It was almost midnight when he got in. He was surprised to see her.

'Ah, Edith, you're up late.'

'Yes, I wanted a chat, and besides, I haven't been sleeping well recently so there's no point in my going to bed to toss and turn. How did the show go tonight?'

'We had a great audience, very appreciative, gave us a standing ovation. It should be in good shape by next week.'

Edith planned to go the following week. Her friend Isabelle was going to accompany her. Fintan sat down on the chair opposite her.

'So what did you want to chat about?' He forced himself

to sound bright. He hoped it wasn't anything to do with the hospital appointment card. He was tired. 'Is something wrong?'

'I'm afraid Sally is not coming back.'

'Oh no! I had a feeling that would be the case. How awful for everyone. I have tried to phone her. Are you quite sure?'

'Yes indeed, she wrote a letter to Clare – well, a note really – to say that she has another job.'

'Has anyone tried to talk her out of leaving?'

'Well that's why I wanted to talk to you, Fintan.' Edith stood up and moved to the sideboard. 'I was just going to have a small whisky. Would you join me?'

She poured two malt whiskies and sat down again. She looked at Fintan intently.

'We had a meeting, and all of us felt that you were the very person who would be able to talk her into returning.'

Fintan took a gulp of the whisky.

'So – no pressure, then,' he said.

'Well,' Edith said with a beseeching smile, 'it's just that you have made such an impression on her, and of course you are the perfect mediator, not being in either camp.'

'I can try,' Fintan said, not sounding convinced.

'Isn't she coming to a performance next week? Perhaps you could have a drink afterwards.'

They sipped the whisky quietly. Edith liked to drink good Scotch malt, and always decanted it and served it in crystal glasses. One had to have standards, after all.

Fintan was sad that Sally had left. The timing was dreadful, what with the opening night and that. He had meant to call her, but hadn't. But he also thought Sally needed to have some space, and he remembered what she had said about wanting more for herself than just cleaning. He had grown enormously fond of her in the short time he'd stayed at Marlborough Road. She was refreshing and down to earth, and he liked her lack of sophistication. The world of opera

119

could be bitchy and highly competitive. As in many other professions, the petty jealousies got to him now and again. He'd call Sally tomorrow.

17

Sally had been down to the offices of Maids to Order and had had a very unsatisfactory meeting with Miss Maybeth Weston. It seemed Bertha was right on the nail. Sally would be expected both to clean and to supervise. Not at all what she had been told when Maybeth had first offered her the job. She pointed this out to Maybeth, who was busy trying to deflect her questions by offering her three peach jump suits in 'medium'. They looked like rejects from Guantanamo.

'Well, honey, this is just a temporary situation. I sincerely hope that eventually you will be touring our client dwellings and checking they are cleaned to perfection, but until we have enough recruits, we would hope, in the interests of company harmony, you would agree to do some of the cleaning. You will still be paid at the rate we agreed.'

Sally left in a rage. She would take the job and meanwhile look for another. What choice did she have? She felt she had queered her pitch regarding Marlborough Road. She just didn't have the nerve to crawl back there and say she had made a mistake. She rode home on the bike feeling hollow and stupid. It wasn't the one incident with Charlie that had forced her decision. It was the certain knowledge that he would keep coming back. After they had split up, he used to come to the house each time he was drunk (every night) and make a scene. He'd wait for her outside her work as well, making a holy show of himself. She had had to take out a restraining order. It only stopped when he'd gone to jail.

Fintan finally got hold of Sally. She was taken aback to hear from him. He had never called her before. It took her a minute to find her voice.

'Is everything okay?'

'Well, apart from the fact that you've left us.'

'Ach, Fintan, it's too complicated . . .' She trailed off. What was there to say really?

'I have some good news and some bad news . . . Which first?'

'Good.'

'Well, you've won Evie's ballot – the trip to Crete, remember? The bad news is it was the ticket with both our names on, but I'd really love you to have it. I'm not sure when I would be free to go, and I know you'd love Crete. I've been there twice, it's wonderful.'

Sally couldn't think of a single thing to say. She was still stunned by the fact that he'd called. Eventually she managed 'How are they all?'

'Well, no point in lying. Everyone is very upset, and hoping fervently they can persuade you to change your mind.'

'I can't now, Fintan, even if I wanted to. I'm too far into this other thing, and I couldn't face them all.'

'Is it because of the drunken fellow?'

'Well I suppose that was why I left on Friday, and now I feel I can't go back. But before that . . . I was beginning to feel taken for granted. And I had been offered the other job

122

– the supervisor one. So I . . . I couldn't face explaining all about him to everyone.'

'You know him?'

There was no point in pretending. 'Yes, he's my ex-husband; we've been separated for ten years.' There, she had said it out loud. What would Fintan think of her now?

'I had a feeling it was. It was patently a good idea to get rid of him. Has he bothered you since?'

'No, and I'm hoping he'll go away off to London soon.' She hoped Fintan would assume Charlie was just over on holiday or something. She couldn't face telling him every single detail just now.

'It must have been extremely upsetting for you, but you must understand that no one here blames *you* for his behaviour.'

Sally said nothing. She was trying to stay composed.

'I think they all thought it was a bit of a laugh really.'

'I didn't.' Sally sounded on the verge of tears.

'Of course not. I'm sorry, Sally; I didn't mean to upset you.'

'You haven't.'

There was another awkward pause.

'Look, if the new job doesn't work out . . .' He trailed off.

'Fintan, please don't tell them just yet that it was my ex-husband. I would be mortified. I never lied about him, but I never really told them about him either.'

'Don't worry, I won't.'

They chatted aimlessly for a few more minutes. Fintan asked if she still intended to use her tickets for the opera. She said she did, but he had a strong feeling she would either not show up, or cancel at the last minute. He hung up feeling he had achieved little.

Edith arrived home exhausted from Ellen's and found Fintan ensconced in the kitchen. He was cooking something that smelled delicious.

'Dinner will be ready in half an hour; why don't you go and have a nice restful bath?'

She didn't need to be told again. She practically ran upstairs. Fintan's interest in her health touched her, and she realised that the only other soul who'd shown so much concern for her had been Sally. If truth be told, she thought ruefully, she had not appreciated her enough when she had had her.

Fintan had been shopping earlier. There was a good farmers' market in Belfast, and an excellent Asian supermarket, both within walking distance. He decided to try a bouillabaisse. He pointedly did not include Otis in the pot. Otis never seemed to replace any of the food he ate. He was out somewhere, and judging by the smell permeating the kitchen, he had fried up half the contents of the fridge before he left.

When she came downstairs, Edith's sole task was to lay the table in the dining room. This she did with great relish, giving Fintan the history of the cutlery and the napkins and all her pet theories on entertaining. The meal was superb. He had bought some good bottles of Meursault, which he had chilled, and after a few glasses Edith was behaving as if she was on a date.

'Well, Fintan, this is so lovely, we could be in a five star restaurant. What a delicious meal.'

'I enjoy cooking, and I enjoy the company of beautiful women.'

Edith positively dimpled at this, but Fintan wasn't lying. She did look lovely. She was contented, happy and eating good food. He was so glad he had made the effort. He resolved to cook for her again soon.

'You know, Fintan, I haven't felt so relaxed in months.'

'Well that's hardly surprising, Edith, you've had a lot to bear . . . what with Ellen and all that.'

'Yes, poor Ellen. Still, Fintan, she did enjoy her widowhood.'

'Oh?' Fintan was intrigued. Had Edith had too much to drink? 'Enjoyed her widowhood?' he echoed.

'Oh yes, she had had such a happy marriage too; she and Derek seemed so close, so we were all surprised. Most people expected her to go to bits.'

'But she didn't?'

'No, she coped remarkably well. She gave up bridge, which she claimed she had never liked. She took to playing golf, and most surprisingly she changed their very comfortable car for a snazzy sports car of all things.'

'I think I like the sound of Ellen.'

'Yes, she would like you too, Fintan. She loves handsome men. I even heard a few rumours of close friendships in her last few years of good health.'

'Good for her!' Fintan roared approvingly.

Edith smiled. 'Yes, I was a bit taken aback at the time, but I must say I'm glad now. We never know the moment, do we, Fintan?'

18

Saffron was overwhelmed. She had no one to turn to with her problems. Until recently she had regarded Trevor as her best friend. She reflected sombrely on Shakespeare's apt words: 'When sorrows come, they come not single spies, But in battalions.'

Two more babies, *two more babies*, what a terrifying thought. She hoped they couldn't feel her panic in the womb. It might transmit bad vibes to the poor darlings, and she didn't want them coming out nervous wrecks. And Trevor? She hadn't expected him to be thrilled, but whilst being reverential enough to her, and coming home dutifully on time, he had been flat and unenthusiastic. She thought he had seemed overwhelmed by the pregnancy. He wasn't home yet, and he'd been out late last night as well. He had some sort of business engagement – a legal meeting. It had taken her ages to get Posy to bed and read her story. When she finally got into bed herself, she was wrecked and tearful.

If Sally had still been around, she could have talked it over with her. She felt sad; she missed Sally shockingly. Marlborough Road was not the same without her. Posy missed her too –

she had asked about her several times last week – and Simon had even offered to give Iggy to the zoo if it would help bring Sally back to them. She shifted in bed, trying to get comfortable. She was alarmed at how fast her tummy was growing. It seemed that now, their existence having been acknowledged, the twins had decided to stretch and push out. She was also hungry all the time, and far too exhausted to cook. They had all become rather rather dependent on pizza and even, heaven forbid, chips and vegeburgers for the children. This was making her feel incredibly guilty and inadequate. Posy had been exceptionally difficult all week, as if she realised that her days as the baby were numbered, and Evie had been so busy with her school project she hadn't been available to help out. Saffron, who was normally quiet and placid and answered all her children's questions with infinite patience, had taken to fending them off with the first answer that came into her head. She allowed them virtually unlimited access to the TV. Neither of the children could quite believe their luck, and Simon had asked her a few times if she was feeling well.

It was well after midnight when Trevor came in. He smelled of drink, so she lay and pretended to be asleep. Two minutes after he got into bed, he began snoring loudly. Saffron realised that it had been some weeks since he had been amorous with her. Perhaps her pregnancy was putting him off, though it hadn't with the other two; quite the opposite, in fact. Maybe she should make the first move? She snuggled closer to him and nuzzled the back of his neck. Trevor was a light sleeper and normally he would have responded to her at once, but he muttered and moved away, and Saffron realised that he was simply pretending to be asleep. She felt hurt and rejected. What was happening to them?

19

Sally left for her new job on Monday morning with a heavy heart. Maybeth was effusive in her greetings, then handed her a checklist, and three addresses. One of them, the last on the list, had one maid short. Since they were only being paid for three hours, Sally might need to give the woman a hand, but hopefully when they had the full quota of staff this wouldn't be usual. Sally set off on her bike, taking careful note of the mileage; she was to be reimbursed for that. The first two houses were okay. She didn't have much to do, just point out a few things to the maids that needed redoing, and show one of them how to polish the big stainless-steel fridge with a drop of baby oil on kitchen roll to make it shine. She left her to finish the job even though she was tempted to do it herself because the woman was going so slowly. Two speeds she had: dead slow and stop.

The third job was up the Malone Road. Sally experienced a bit of a pang as she drove past her usual turn-off for Marlborough Road, but that was natural enough, she reckoned. She needed to get over herself, as Evie was fond of telling Clare. The house was in a gated street. It was a massive double-fronted Victorian with a long driveway. A large black shiny 4x4 was parked outside the front door. Sally smiled as she remembered Clare and Saffron's rants about what they would like to do to the sort of people who drove these destroyers of the planet. She rang the doorbell. The owner of the house was home. She opened the door to Sally and swept her with a supercilious glance. She was a young woman in her early thirties, very made up, Barbie doll type. She was wearing perfectly coordinated gym gear.

'I'm Sally O'Neill from Maids to Order,' Sally said.

'Oh, and about time. I take it you are the other cleaner? I have been on the phone twice to Miss Weston,' she snapped.

Sally opened her mouth to reply but the words didn't come; the woman's rudeness had taken her breath away. She indicated for Sally to follow her into the kitchen.

'I usually have two women come, and I'd need three today to make up for this one.' She nodded towards a shapeless woman of about fifty who was slowly drying a bowl at the sink. 'This is Molly; she has been doing the kitchen for the last two hours. I think you are *almost* finished, aren't you?' she said acidly.

Sally smiled at the cleaner, and said to the young woman, 'Sorry, I didn't catch your name?'

'I'm Rosamund Henderson; I prefer it if you call me *Mrs* Henderson,' she said abruptly. 'Can you follow me? I need to show you the bedrooms. I want you to change the beds and vacuum and dust. This way, please.'

Sally followed her up a large carpeted central staircase. Paintings adorned the walls. It was painted all soft pastels. It was obvious no money had been spared in the decoration. Mrs Henderson opened the door into what was obviously the master bedroom. She nodded towards a door leading off it.

'This is the en suite, it needs cleaning, and then you can hoover and dust the room and change the bed.' The fresh bed linen was sitting in a neat pile on the bed. 'The dirty linen goes in this basket and is taken straight down to the laundry room off the kitchen.'

'Cleaning materials?' Sally kept her voice sharp to match, but inside she was churning with humiliation.

'Downstairs in the utility room off the kitchen.'

'Vacuum cleaner?'

'We have central vacuuming, so you just plug this hose into the wall.' She indicated a long tube lying on the ground, and a flap thing on the wall. 'I am already late for the gym.' She glanced at her watch. 'I'll be back in two hours. Ask Molly if you need anything. I've already explained everything to her more than once. With luck maybe some of it has gone in.' And off she swept.

Sally heard the front door slam and the car start up. She went back down to the kitchen; Molly was putting away the bowls. She smiled half-heartedly at Sally. She looked dejected.

'I was here last week as well. She's full of herself, that one. Nothing to do all day, you see, the kids at school and the husband out making the money. It would make you sick. The last firm I worked for seemed to specialise in cleaning houses for grumpy wee girls who married up. They've a lot to learn as far as manners go.'

'You can say that again. I'll not be talked to like that by the likes of her. I'll finish whatever there is to be done today and that's it. I shouldn't even be cleaning, it's not part of my job description. I am normally a supervisor.'

'Oh? Do you know Bertha, then? I worked with her last week; isn't she a supervisor too?'

Sally nodded, stung. But Molly smiled at her, she wasn't being sarky.

'Sure just give me a shout if you need me. I'll be in the drawing room. She wants that big mirror cleaned; I may get on with it.'

'Well I suppose I'd better get upstairs and get the beds changed.'

Sally didn't know why she had been so pathetic as to drop the supervisor number on poor Molly. It had only made her feel like a sad git. And it was already only too obvious that her big, important title was meaningless anyway.

Otis had called Bronagh at work and she had agreed to go to QFT, the university film theatre, with him. She wasn't sure why she had agreed, and she certainly hadn't told anyone. The film was French, with subtitles. He said he really rated the director.

The foyer was buzzing, with lots of people talking at each other at the tops of their voices. They all appeared to know each other, or were pretending to at any rate. Bronagh looked nervously around for Otis. She had told him she would meet him here. She quickly spotted him standing at the bar. He was hard to miss; that carrot-coloured hair was like a beacon. He was with a couple of people around his own age. Taking a deep breath, she walked over to them. Otis appeared delighted to see her and introduced her to his friends. She spoke as quietly as she could in case her accent was too broad Belfast. She could tell they were giving her the once-over, wondering what she was doing with Otis. Hardly surprising; she was wondering herself. He asked her what she would like to drink, and she was about to ask for a vodka and Red Bull but then saw they were drinking wine, so she had a wee bottle of white wine. It was very strong and slightly sour, but she drank it anyway.

The film was okay, actually. She could follow it easily enough. Afterwards they had another drink in the bar. Otis chatted easily; you'd have thought he owned the place, he was that full of himself, but he was very nice to her, and kept patting her arm, in a fatherly way really. For a moment Bronagh wished she'd had a daddy when she was growing up, not some drunken jailbird who'd ruined her mother's life.

*

Sally came home to an empty house. Bronagh was out again tonight with some friends. She watched something useless on TV and tried not to think about the job. Maybe it had just been a bad day. It couldn't be like that all the time. She wondered where Bronagh was. She didn't usually go out much during the week. She had been acting a bit secretive recently, giving Sally evasive answers as to where she had been. Last night she had snapped off her mobile phone when Sally had come into her room.

'Bye! See you tomorrow night, then.'

'Who was that?' Sally had asked her. 'Tiffany?'

'Mmmm, yeah.'

'Where are you off to then, love? Anywhere nice?'

'Oh, nowhere special.'

Sally knew she was lying, and wondered why. But then she worked it out. Bronagh was off to see her father and didn't want to upset her feelings by letting her know. It did hurt, but part of her also understood. She had done her best for the child while she was growing up. Nonetheless, the cliché remained: girls always loved their daddies. When Bronagh had been a little girl she was the apple of Charlie's eye. She was almost eight when he was put away, and Sally had shielded her from his bad behaviour so that she would only remember the good times.

She lay awake waiting for Bronagh to come in. She didn't mean to be neurotic; she couldn't help herself. Finally she heard the front door.

'Bronagh, is that you, love? I'm still awake.'

Bronagh came into the bedroom. She looked flushed.

'Well, were you out anywhere nice?'

'No, I just went to the pictures with Tiffany.'

'Oh? What to see?'

'It was a French film; about school kids in a wee country village – it had subtitles.'

'And what did Tiffany make of that?'

132

'She wasn't that fussed on it, but I liked it. Mum, I'm really tired. I'll see you in the morning.' And she kissed Sally good night and went into her own bedroom.

Imagine her making up she was at a French film, and with Tiffany. As if! She was lying, of course. Tiffany had called the house looking for Bronagh at nine o'clock. She told Sally that Bronagh wasn't answering her mobile. Sally was convinced she'd been with her father. She wondered where Charlie had taken her. If it was anywhere local, Eileen would let her know. Sally normally wouldn't have minded, she would even have expected it, but coming on top of her new job, it was a bit much to take. She had looked after Bronagh alone all these years. Why should Charlie O'Neill just waltz back into their lives and ruin everything?

The only crack of light amidst the clouds in the following days was a text from Fintan asking how things were going. On impulse when she got home one evening she dialled Miss Black's. Her thoughts were in turmoil; she wasn't sure what she would say if Edith answered. As it happened, Otis did, and didn't recognise her voice.

'Is Fintan there?'

'Sure, man, hold on a sec.'

Fintan didn't have a performance every night. He had explained that the opera was in repertoire; it was running with *La Rondine* and he wasn't in both.

'Hello?'

'It's Sally.'

'Oh Sally, how lovely to hear from you. How are things?'

'I'm grand. I was wondering how Edith is?'

'Well, not any worse, but still looking frail. She misses you, of course. How is the new job going?'

'Ach, Fintan, I have to give this other thing a try. Sure they are probably too mad at me to want me back.'

'I should think they'd leap at the chance. Have you made your mind up about the opera?'

Sally didn't answer at once.

'You are coming?'

'Yes, if that's still okay.'

'Of course. The tickets will be in your name. Look, why don't we meet afterwards for a drink? Say the Crown bar?'

'Are you sure? Have you nobody else you need to see?'

'Absolutely not. It takes me ten minutes or so after the curtain comes down. I'll look forward to it.'

And before Sally could protest, he said his goodbyes and hung up.

20

Charlie O'Neill had been seething with indignation for over a week. He kept having action replays of the scene over at Sally's work. The indignity of falling over in the tree house, and then those patronising shits telling him to go quietly or they'd call the police . . . Who did they think they were? He knew what they were all right: smug bastards, with their fancy houses and posh voices.

He had been in the pub having a few drinks when the urge to see Sally had overwhelmed him. He had been trying to have a chat with her since he got out. Fuelled by Dutch courage, he had taken a cab to Marlborough Road. Bertha had told him she was at some fancy do over there. He had finished his six pack sitting in the tree house. From where he was, he could hear all of them high-falutin' types chatting away. They were laughing at the tops of their voices. And Sally was there too, right in the thick of it. He could still pick out her voice. All he wanted was a wee chat with his brown-eyed girl. That wasn't a lot to ask. Sally could at least have heard him out. He was hardly going to do her any harm.

It had been the same with Bronagh, his own wee daughter.

She wouldn't talk to him that day outside the hairdresser's. It was hurtful. You'd think she would love her daddy; all girls were supposed to love their daddies. Sally had probably poisoned her mind. He wasn't a bad man. He wasn't a real criminal; he'd just been unlucky all those years ago, when Bud Rafferty had had the bright idea of robbing the bookie's. He had been against the idea at first, but then Bud and Bottler McCann had talked him round. Why was he broke in the first place? Because he had spent most of his money in the bookie's – well, a bit in the pub too, but mainly the bookie's, and sure didn't everyone know that the races were rigged in their favour? For God's sake, you couldn't win if you tried. So it wasn't really robbing; all he and the lads were doing was getting their own money back. If it hadn't been for Bud bringing the bloody gun and that eejit of a teller having a weak heart and dying a week later, they'd all have been out in three years. And Sally should have known the entire gig was just to get a better life for her and the wee girl. He would have taken them all off to Disney World. That had been his dream, but try telling Sally that. Sure you couldn't win with women. You were on a hiding to nowhere. Everything you did annoyed them. He would take a run round to Sally's house now, he thought, and try to have a reasonable wee chat with her, make her see sense.

Bronagh was sitting in on her own; not that she'd be out tonight anyway. Tiffany usually called round most nights, but Tiffany had fallen out with her because she wouldn't admit she'd seen Otis again. Her ma had gone up to her granny and granda's. She usually made dinner for them on Tuesdays.

Tiffany would get over it. Bronagh had no intention of giving her all the dirt on Otis; she'd probably think Bronagh was off her head going out with the likes of him. 'That Mick Hucknall lookalike', Tiffany called him. But strangely, Bronagh had enjoyed the few dates she had been on with Otis. The guys she usually went out with had only one thing on their minds, but Otis hadn't tried to lay a hand on her yet, which was just as well. She didn't feel *that* way about him.

The doorbell rang. Probably Tiffany had decided it wasn't worth falling out over a man; their rows never lasted long. She opened the door and there stood Charlie.

'What do *you* want?'

'Ach, Bronagh love, that's no way to speak to your poor oul' daddy, now is it?' Charlie gave her his version of a winning smile. 'Is your mammy in?'

'No, she's up at my granny's.'

'Are you not going to ask me in?'

'All right, but you can't stay, my ma will be back at nine.'

Charlie followed her in, taking a good look round him as he did so.

'She has the place lovely, hasn't she? Very posh, looks like one of them places you'd see on the telly.'

'Hardly, it's a housing executive house.'

'What about a wee cup of tea?'

Bronagh hesitated, and then said, 'No, I don't think so.'

'Ach, love, don't be so hard on me.'

'Well okay then, but you'd better be quick. I don't want Mammy coming in on us.'

Bronagh pushed the button on the kettle and chucked a tea bag into a mug. She didn't ask Charlie to sit down, but he perched on one of the kitchen chairs anyway. He stared hard at her, and then when she met his glance looked away.

'You're looking lovely, Bronagh – honestly, you've turned into a gorgeous girl. I missed you when I was . . .' he looked awkward as he tried to find the right words, 'a guest of Queen Lizzie. I'd have loved the odd visit.'

'Well you should have thought about that before you robbed the bookie's. It wasn't easy for us, you know, on our own all those years, and Mammy working all the hours God sends.'

Bronagh glared at him. She was finding this very upsetting. But Charlie didn't respond; he just looked at her like he was going to cry. It was hard to resist his pleading look.

'I hear you're doing great at the hairdressing.'

'It's going okay.'

'You'll be opening your own salon next, what?'

'Aye, right. Where would I get the money for that?'

'Well maybe when I get myself settled, and get a wee job, I could help you out.'

'I can't wait.' She had recovered herself somewhat. 'Look you'd better finish your tea; my mammy will be back soon.'

'Can I see you again, love? Please?'

'I don't know . . .' She was about to say 'Daddy', but the word wouldn't come out. She walked to the door and opened it, and dejectedly Charlie left.

Bronagh was shaking. She wished she smoked, but Sally had done a good job on her. She had found her with cigarettes when she was thirteen, and had made her smoke an entire packet. It had put her off for life.

She couldn't get herself together after Charlie left. She felt so torn. She had forced herself to be cold and cruel, while a part of her badly wanted to hug him. She had felt so sorry for him tonight. He seemed such a lost soul. He was pale and a bit overweight, but you could still tell he'd once been a good-looking man. It was easier to hate your father when you didn't have to look into his eyes and do it.

When Sally came back in later, Bronagh didn't mention that Charlie had called round. Her mammy had enough to cope with. She looked tired and drawn. She told Bronagh that she was off to the opera next week, and was going to bring Eileen along for company.

'I hope she behaves herself.'

'You hope! How do you think I feel?'

138

'Why did you ask her then?'

'I had no one to go with, so I mentioned it to her. She wasn't keen at first, till she found out the tickets were free.'

To Sally's surprise, Bronagh said, 'I'll go with you.'

'You? To the opera? That's not like you.'

'What do you mean, not like me?'

'You know what I mean, love. You've never shown any interest in opera.'

'Neither have you, and I'm sure my auntie Eileen wouldn't know what opera was if it bit her in the neck.' She stopped and looked at Sally pointedly. 'What's wrong? Do you not want to take me?'

'Don't be silly, I'd love you to come. Sure you know our Eileen does my head in. I just didn't think it would be your cup of tea. It'll be great. I'm dying to hear Fintan sing, and he says it's one of the easier operas and has titles in English above the stage so we'll be able to understand it all.'

So it was settled. Bronagh would come to *Tosca*. Sally thought it was a lovely gesture on her daughter's part. She felt a lot cheerier about the trip to the opera now; she rarely went out anywhere with Bronagh these days. Maybe she'd buy something new to wear; she could always check with Clare how people dressed. And then she remembered: she couldn't ask Clare any more; she'd just have to guess.

21

The curtain came down and the audience rose as one to cheer. Bronagh and Sally were sitting in the front row of the dress circle and had had a great view of the whole show. Sally had forgotten completely her insecurities about her dress, and even Bronagh, who had been slightly fidgety at first, had been carried away by the whole drama. Fintan was right: the words had appeared along the top of the stage and had been ridiculously easy to follow. As for Fintan . . . Oh, his voice, what a beautiful voice he had, and how tortured he had seemed. Sally's heart was in her mouth listening to him. He sang like an angel, or how Sally supposed an angel would sing if given the chance. She couldn't remember feeling emotion of this sort before. She had a lump in her throat and the tears started when she heard the screams of him being tortured. And that awful twist at the end just as it looked like they could be together, when the awful Scarpia tricked Tosca with live bullets, and she loved Mario so much she leapt to her death. It was so romantic. Sally had been thrilled; yes, that was the word, thrilled.

At the first interval they had sat on, although most of the audience had made their way out to the bar, but then there was a second interval and so they got up to stretch their legs. Bronagh had bought them ice creams; the queue for the bar was ridiculous.

'I think you have to order drinks for the interval and then it's left on one of them wee shelves with your name on it.'

'Oh,' Sally said, impressed that Bronagh knew that; she didn't ask how. She just ate her ice cream and they made sure to get back to their seats as soon as the bell went. She had caught a glimpse of Miss Black and her silly old friend Isabelle coming out of the bar, and she wasn't ready to see her.

Bronagh agreed to go over to the Crown with her and leave the minute Fintan arrived. She had never met him, because he hadn't got around to using his voucher, preferring to leave his hair long for the show. The Crown bar was jammed full; it tended to be when there was a good show on at the opera house, and they were unsure where to sit. Suddenly Bronagh saw Otis sitting in one of the snugs, chatting earnestly with a couple of his mates. Her face paled, but luckily he hadn't seen her; she needed to get out fast.

'Mum, I feel a bit faint. Can we wait outside?'

Sally agreed – it was stuffy and noisy anyway – and they stood in Great Victoria Street and waited for Fintan. He wasn't long in coming. Sally made the introductions. He was most polite to Bronagh and delighted that she had enjoyed his performance so much. He was very modest about it, as Sally would have expected.

Sally didn't feel at all like going back into the Crown, so she said to Fintan, 'It's bunged in there; would you mind if we went somewhere else?'

He didn't mind at all; he always thought the place too smoky, and bad for his throat. They decided to walk to a wine bar round the corner, and after telling him once more how good she thought he had been and thanking him for the tickets, Bronagh made her excuses and left.

Fintan went up to the bar and came back with two glasses of white wine. He sat beside Sally and took a sip and smiled at her. He had just the slightest trace of eyeliner round his lashes – he obviously hadn't removed his make-up properly – but Sally thought it made him look even more appealing.

'It's so good to see you, Sally.'

She shifted in her seat. 'It's nice to see you too. I loved the opera. I didn't think I'd enjoy it so much.' She hoped she didn't sound too gushing.

'I'm so glad. It's a good one to start with. Now tell me all about the new job. How's it going? Nice people?'

Sally immediately thought of Rosamund from the big house. She wished the bitch could walk in and see Sally O'Neill now, sitting with the star of *Tosca*. She'd be sorry she'd treated her like dirt. She recollected herself. Fintan was waiting for an answer.

'Not nice people, to be honest, but I'm getting into the way of it. It's nothing like Marlborough Road. I think a lot of the people who use Maids to Order are people who don't want to have to deal with a cleaner, or ones who can't keep a cleaner.' She was quite sure Rosamund fell into the latter category. She related the story to Fintan.

'Oh, Sally! How awful for you. That is the height of bad manners. I hope you complained to your boss?'

'Sure what's the point? She wants the business and she doesn't have to listen to the likes of her, but if she asked me to go back there I wouldn't go.'

'You wouldn't think of going back to Marlborough Road? You are sorely missed.'

'I think I've burned my boats, Fintan.'

'Of course you haven't, not at all, but let's leave it for now. I think Clare is going to get a service in the meantime, and Patricia Thompson – is that her name? – she thinks her cleaner might take Saffron on temporarily. But it's really Edith I worry about.'

'Is she okay?'

'She seems frail, hasn't said much, but her sister looks to be on her last legs. She's still running up and down to Portadown, and of course I'm leaving in a few weeks. My next job is in Glasgow.'

Sally felt her heart plummet all the way to her toes. She'd forgotten Fintan wouldn't be here for ever. Her wine turned sour in her mouth, but she swallowed it anyway and wished for the ninetieth time that they had thrown away the key when they had locked Charlie O'Neill up.

They finished their drinks and then Fintan walked with her to the taxi rank and she went home. He had a performance the next evening and didn't want a late night. She wondered if she'd ever see him again. He hadn't mentioned the holiday to Crete, and Sally hadn't the nerve to introduce the subject herself, though it had been on the tip of her tongue. She'd enjoyed her evening very much; it had been a memorable one. She hoped with all her heart that it wouldn't be the last she'd see of Fintan Fanning.

22

Clare glared at the computer screen. It looked back blankly. She screwed up her eyes and challenged it. Think of a new thought on Maud, Maud Gonne. No, Maud was well and truly *gone* – she had lived up to her surname. She clicked on solitaire and tried not to weep at the aptness of the bloody game. Never mind Maud being gone; more to the point, Sally was gone and the kitchen looked like a food fight competition headquarters. Forget the kitchen, she told herself. Get over it. It is not my responsibility. I am more than a hausfrau. She was, wasn't she? She didn't crochet her own muesli, she didn't make patchwork quilts out of the children's old rugby shorts; why should she? For fuck's sake, she was a happening woman. She had her work. She had deadlines, quotas, images. Promises to keep and miles to et cetera, and Tony, the bastard, still wasn't home. He was supposed to have a day off today, having been in Dublin on business last night. The garden beckoned, the overflowing bins beckoned, plus the wonky light fittings that he alone could reach. The smoke alarm had no battery; they could be burned to a crisp in their beds for all he cared. Where was he? She would bet he'd gone straight into work to sort out a bit of paperwork. Jaysus, it was so unfair. He got away with murder. When she nagged him, the kids all took his side, even Anna, and Evie treated him as if he was the coolest dad on the planet.

She paused for a moment and let the froth of resentment stop bubbling through her addled brain. Logically she knew in her heart and soul that she had a lot to offer. No, she was not George Eliot or even Jane Austen, but in her own way she had gifts. Yes, gifts! She had a talent of sorts. She could write, she could teach. The students didn't fidget too much in her lectures, so why did she feel so swamped at present because her cleaning lady had left?

In her marriage she was the one with the showy degree, but despite that, for a long time she had assumed her biggest gift had been her ability to snare Tony and give birth to his children. Much as she loved them, they had recently developed the knack of making her feel that she was an inadequate mother and everything that went wrong was totally and completely her fault. At least Evie did. Clare tried desperately to think of something positive. And of course it was a no-brainer . . . at least she wasn't expecting twins. She'd go down to Saffron and have some of her vile fruit tea and her wonderful lemon cookies. That would do it.

Edith was tired. Her appointment with Brian Smedley was this afternoon at two o'clock. She had been wide awake listening to the radio since five forty-five. She listened with an earphone, out of courtesy to the house guest who slept directly above her . . . Fintan at present. Though if truth be told, there was something very comforting about a radio in the ear. It lulled one to sleep. It had to be talk; music didn't do it. Music excited her and made her feel like a participant. Voices were different; she could tune out voices, and besides, this rolling news on the World Service was an affront. It deserved to be tuned out;

145

whyever would one want to listen carefully? The quality of programming had dropped severely. Sometimes she changed to Radio Five in the middle of the night; she found the announcer, Rhod Sharp, soothing. He had a nice gentle Scottish burr, and a courteous and intelligent form of questioning, reminiscent of her late father.

She had better get up and have her bath. It was a sunny day and almost nine o'clock; she was wasting God's good weather, as her mother would have said. And there was the washing and ironing. She supposed she would have to tackle that herself, now there was no more Sally. She might pop along to Clare later and suggest they all have a go at luring Sally back. It had been two weeks now, surely long enough to make her point, whatever point she had intended making. Clare had made some vain attempt to get another woman, but it had proved fruitless and it looked like they would have to resort to agencies, and the thought of that made Edith shudder. Apparently you couldn't even be certain of getting the same person two weeks running. No, a pow-wow was definitely in order. Invigorated, she threw on her robe, went to the bathroom and drew her bath.

Saffron sat despairingly in her less than perfect kitchen, gazing in mild panic at her ever-increasing bump. Suddenly the back door opened and Clare came in.

'Hiya, what's up? Fancy some tea?'

'Oh no, I should be offering you, Clare. Sit down, let me put the kettle on.' Saffron waddled out of the chair – at least it felt like a waddle – and lifted the heavy kettle on to the Aga. 'Sorry about the state of the kitchen.'

'God, you should see mine. It's a midden.' Clare looked around her. Well, perhaps this was worse. 'Sure why don't we take it outside? It's a lovely day.'

Between them they carried biscuits, tea pot, cups and Posy

out to the garden. It really was a beautiful day, and so much nicer outdoors. Edith passed them, scurrying up the lane, and was hailed to join them.

'You have to see the funny side of it,' said Clare when the tea had been poured. 'Here we are sitting like the three witches trying to work up a spell to lure Sally back.'

Edith sipped her lemon and ginger tea carefully and nodded.

'She was at the opera last night, but I'm afraid I didn't spot her.'

'Oh?' Saffron's curiosity was piqued. 'I wonder who she was with.'

'Had I done, it would hardly have been appropriate to approach her. It was a full house, so many people there. I was with my friend Isabelle. What a performance. Fintan was mesmerising.'

Saffron nodded enthusiastically. 'Yes, Simon loved it. He went last week and thought Fintan was fantastic. Of course he was thrilled to know one of the cast.'

'And did you enjoy it?'

'Oh Edith, I didn't go. I couldn't face it. And Trevor was keen to take him. Simon said the Nelsons were there as well.'

Later that afternoon, as Sally drove off for her latest supervisory duties with a long list from Maybeth shoved into the pannier of her bike, Edith set off for her hospital appointment in a positive frame of mind. After all, she reasoned, Mr Smedley the surgeon had been reassuring on her last visit. She had had a colonoscopy and he had spotted a polyp and removed it.

'We'll send this off and see what the lab makes of it. Now, I don't want you worrying yourself needlessly. How should I put this, Edith? At our age the cell growth slows down, so even if it were malignant it might be easy enough to contain.'

It had been kind of him to say 'our age' – she knew she was at least ten years older than he – but he was a kind man and she played bridge with his wife. She had consulted him privately; she could easily afford it, so why not leave the National Health to those not as fortunate as herself? She had noticed him at the opera last night with Betty, his wife, and he had given her a cheery smile. That surely was a good sign. She wondered if Fintan had managed to meet up with Sally and have a chat with her as planned. He had been home quite late. She had heard him, but had resisted the temptation to get up and quiz him. He was still in his room now, probably exhausted from his performance last night. Edith had thought him wonderful as Cavaradossi and was very pleased indeed to let Isabelle, who could be such a snob, know that he was a house guest of hers. Perhaps Fintan would have a coffee with her on her return from hospital, if he was around.

She thought it would be quicker to walk to the hospital; the traffic was a nuisance at this time of day. She strode briskly through the park, noting how well kept the flowerbeds were; the rhododendrons and azaleas were in full bloom too, and the palm house sparkled in the sun. They were very lucky to have such an asset on their doorstep, so to speak. Life was worth living, though poor Ellen wouldn't have much longer now. Edith swallowed the lump in her throat; there was no point in being maudlin. Ellen wouldn't want her to be. She had made all her arrangements to be admitted to the hospice without the slightest hint of sentiment or self-pity; she was admirable, an example to all.

After arriving at the hospital, Edith only had to wait a few minutes before she was shown into Dr Smedley's office.

'Ah, Edith! That was a wonderful production of *Tosca*, wasn't it?' Brian Smedley sat back in his chair and regarded Edith levelly.

'Yes indeed. Fintan Fanning happens to be staying with me at present: a truly lovely person, such a gentleman.' Edith smiled proudly. The doctor looked suitably impressed.

148

'Oh, he was very good indeed, though I did have the honour of seeing Pavarotti perform the role some years back.'

Edith revised her opinion of Brian Smedley somewhat. She hadn't taken him for the boastful type.

'Now, Edith, I had a look at your lab results and I fear we might have a little problem.'

Why on earth did doctors always say *we*? Edith felt immediately nervous, but she tried to remain composed.

'What sort of problem?'

'It seems the polyp we removed from your bowel is malignant. I would like to operate and remove a small section of the intestine as soon as possible, and afterwards you will probably need chemotherapy.'

'My sister has bowel cancer; in fact she is dying from it.' Edith surprised herself at how unemotional she sounded. She had taken her cue from Mr Smedley. Inside she was paralysed with fear.

'Yes, that would fit in. Having a relative with bowel cancer doubles your chances of getting it, I'm afraid. But on the bright side, this looks containable. It seems we have caught it at an early stage, and the chance of a full recovery looks good. I would like to have you in next week, though, if you can organise that. Now, do you have anyone with you?'

Edith shook her head.

'Would you like to call someone?'

'No, it's all right, I'm fine.'

'I'm so very sorry, Edith, but I honestly think we have caught it in time. It won't be pleasant, because there is a chance of hair loss from the chemo, and you will have to take things very easy for a while, but with the right attitude I think we can beat this.'

He stood up and walked with her towards the door, patting her gently on the back as he led her out.

'I'm sorry,' he repeated, 'very sorry, but let's be positive.

Christine will be in touch as soon as we can organise a bed for you.'

Walking back through the park, Edith felt on the verge of tears. She looked again at the flowers and plants, this time with new meaning. Surely she didn't have to die yet, and leave all this wonderful profusion of colour? The sun shone almost mockingly at her, making the colours of the flowers brighter. No, she most certainly did not want to die yet. There was so much more for her to do. Heavens, she had planned to go to China next year with Isabelle. She hoped fervently that Mr Smedley was being straight with her, but then she had consulted him as soon as her symptoms had appeared; subconsciously she had realised they were similar to Ellen's, and Ellen had been careless, ignoring her weight loss for ages, pathetically feeling pleased that she was slimmer. It was only when she happened to mention a change in her bowel movements that she had listened to Edith's advice and gone to her doctor. Of course consequently her cancer had been very advanced when she finally went into hospital. Imagine, two sisters with the same illness within a year. It must be some defective gene, Edith thought. Her dear mother had died from cancer, although people didn't use the word so freely then. She wouldn't tell Ellen about hers; there was little point, though she would have to let her know she was going into hospital. She would think of some white lie to cover the reason.

All her life Edith had minded her feelings. Her father and mother had been pillars of the church, morally erect, controlled people; people who had little time for the untidiness of emotion. Even as small children Ellen and Edith were never allowed to laugh too much, or cry too much, or eat too much, or play too much. 'Too much of anything is a bad thing' was her mother's mantra. Edith could remember the occasional time when her father, coming home from his work and finding her alone, would hug her tightly and swing her round till she screamed with delight, but he would stop immediately and put her down with a gentle 'there, there' and a smile should her mother come in. Over the years the restraint had built so firmly into Edith's soul that she felt now that were she to give vent to it, and let the lid off, the outpouring of emotion would devour her.

She walked slowly down the lane, mulling over her news. She was in a state of mild shock, and so preoccupied she hardly noticed Lola, the McDonalds' dog, peeing on the lemon balm in her herb garden. She saw that Fintan was under the tree in the garden, doing his t'ai chi. She knew not to distract him, so she went into the kitchen and filled the kettle. She would make some tea and take it out into the garden, and chat with Fintan as soon as he finished. She considered telling him her news, but thought on balance she wouldn't. After all, although she was extremely fond of him and felt they had bonded, he was hardly a close friend. But then who was? Edith suddenly felt very lonely.

23

Trevor McNamara and Laura Nelson sat in one of the corner snugs in the Crown bar. It would not be overstating things to say that Trevor was not having a good time. For a start he felt very conspicuous; you could run into anyone here. But on the other hand it was usually so busy that there was also the chance of relative anonymity. Wordlessly, and with the same scary expression she'd been wearing for the past hour, Laura held out her glass. Trevor got up to buy her yet another gin and tonic. He ordered another glass of Guinness for himself. He had made the first one last over an hour; he needed to stay sober. As he steered through the noisy crowd back to the snug, he thought he caught a glimpse of Otis, Edith's loony red-headed lodger, with a girl of about seventeen. The girl glanced at him. She was a pretty young thing. It didn't surprise him in the slightest to see Otis with her; he'd always figured there was a touch of the perv about the man. Mind you, he was one to talk, considering the mess he'd got himself into. His heart was down in his boots at the very thought of it. How he had managed to get things to this state was beyond him. It was so random, as Evie might say.

Laura and Bill Nelson had lived in Marlborough Road for nearly seven years. They had been good neighbours, and their children played with the McNamaras' children. Trevor had always thought Laura an attractive woman. She was a barrister; he'd first noticed her in court, and they'd met at a drinks party the first Christmas after she and Bill had moved in. But tonight Trevor was here for one reason alone, and that was to tell her that he would never be able to see her again. Her outburst at the barbecue had been the final straw.

The affair – if that was the correct description – had begun a few months back, in April, at a cross-border law meeting in Dublin. They had met on the train on the way down – both were in first class. They had a drink and a chat and it seemed perfectly logical to share a taxi, since they were also, by chance, staying in the same hotel. Well, not really by chance, since all the Northern crowd were staying there. The dinner had put everyone in great form. They had served a simply wonderful standing rib roast with trimmings, and many bottles of good claret. Later on, back at the hotel, after a few rather excellent glasses of Calvados, Laura and Trevor had ended up being the last two guests in the residents' bar. They bantered a bit, talked about their children and exchanged the odd grumble about their respective spouses, although Laura seemed to have more gripes about Bill than he had with Saffron. Trevor thought her very attractive, easy company.

The barman was getting restless, but manners and regulations meant he had to stay up until they chose to retire. So since both rooms were equipped with minibars, and more drink tended to seem like a good idea at two a.m. when one had already had rather a lot, they had repaired to Laura's room. Trevor hadn't thought anything of it; that is, until they were actually in the room and Laura decided she would be more comfortable in a nightie. Well, a version of a nightie – it barely covered her and made her alarmingly more attractive than ever.

Before he could talk sternly to himself and tell himself that the last thing he needed was to behave like a reckless idiot, they were in bed together.

Laura Nelson was something else; Trevor had not experienced anything like this, even in his bachelor days. She appeared to have no sexual boundaries, and even though they had consumed vast quantities of drink, she kept him aroused for over two hours. He had left her room for his own in a state of sexual euphoria and passed out exhausted as soon as his head hit the pillow. The following morning there was a talk on European law in Trinity College during which he had barely been able to keep his eyes open or his throbbing head up. Throughout the tedious meeting, he had a sort of roll of fear in his gut when he thought of his romp with Laura last night, but he reasoned that she would feel the same. After all, they both had a lot to lose, and people behaved all kinds of silly ways when drink was taken. He tried to avoid her during the rest of the meeting, until his brain had processed things.

On the way back to Belfast, she sat opposite him. They couldn't discuss anything – the train was packed and the other seats were occupied – but she had, he thought, an extremely dangerous look about her. When she spoke there was a steeliness in her speech that he had never noticed before. That was when it hit him that this was not going to be brushed aside as a drunken escapade. He was right. Laura did not intend to let him off lightly. She was not going to be used. She told him this as soon as they were off the train and out of earshot of the other passengers. He was grateful at least that she had waited. They shared a taxi home, and during the ride she extracted a promise from him that they would meet for a drink during the next week.

Trevor carried his infidelity like a coating of lead in his heart; he was sure he would just blurt it out to Saffron. He desired absolution, but he also knew that was the most selfish thing to do, so he suffered quietly. Occasionally, though, unbidden thoughts of the sexual pleasure he had experienced with Laura drifted to the front of his mind and he had to concentrate on whatever task he was involved with to immediately banish the picture.

He didn't see Laura for the rest of that week, or the next. Perhaps she had wised up, he thought. Gradually he began to relax again and the intensity of the experience lessened. Life returned to its normal humdrum state. Saffron seemed a bit off form and not amorous, but this was a relief to him in a way. Then, out of the blue, Laura left a message asking him to meet her for a drink. He had to admire her nerve. He called her mobile and agreed to see her at a pub on the river, Cutter's Wharf. This particular venue tended to be frequented by a younger crowd, so he hoped they would not be spotted. He wasn't sure what to say to her. Perhaps he would just reassure her that he found her attractive and all that but point out that they were both married and that he'd prefer it if they reverted to their platonic friendship.

But as soon as he arrived, he realised he wasn't going to get away with any such thing. Laura had been waiting outside, sitting on a bench overlooking the river. It was a mild evening and most of the drinkers were outside, a noisy, rowdy lot. As soon as he approached her, Laura downed her drink in one and stood up.

'Let's get out of here,' she said, and led him briskly to a row of flats across the road from the pub. They were more like maisonettes – each had a regular tidy front garden. Laura walked to the door of one and opened it.

'Why are we here? Who owns this?' Trevor felt utterly out of his depth. 'I thought we were going to have a chat about . . . you know . .' His voice faltered.

Laura walked into a room, while Trevor stood frozen in the sort of living-cum-dining-room. For a full five minutes he literally couldn't move.

'Aren't you coming in?' she called out.

He went slowly into the room, and Laura was sprawled naked on the bed.

'No, Laura, we . . . I can't . . . I can't . . . Whose place is this?'

'It belongs to a friend; she's out for the evening.'

Trevor felt as if his legs were made of lead, but he was totally aroused too. Laura was tanned, trim, and oh God, she was so sexy.

'Look, this is crazy.'

'Only if they find out.'

'But we can't . . .'

'Don't you fancy me then?' she said.

Of course he did, but he was afraid too, and then suddenly he was undressing and in bed beside her. And of course it was thrilling and erotic and terrifying.

After that evening they had met for the occasional drink, nothing more, though he had a feeling she would have liked more. But there was no reason why they couldn't be friends; he enjoyed talking to her. She was refreshing. Lately he had begun to feel overwhelmed by both fatherhood and marriage. The relentless catering to the whims of the children had begun to irritate him. They were so demanding and energetic, and he was feeling anything but. Middle age had hit him with a vengeance. He wanted to have fun, but he was smothering in domestic bliss. He and Saffron had little or no social life beyond the lane. His thing with Laura gave him a little extra frisson, helped him cope with his chaotic home life.

His complaints about Saffron were minor, if somewhat disloyal. Laura was sympathetic; she found Bill infuriating at times. Trevor told her of his desire for a foreign holiday, and Saffron's unbending opposition. Her sojourn in India all those years ago seemed to have convinced her never to leave Ireland again.

'She feels air travel is ruining the children's legacy by destroying the environment. It really pisses me off.'

'I don't know why you don't just stand up to her. Where are you going on holiday this year?'

'Donegal again,' Trevor said glumly.

Each year, towards the end of July, they rented a house in Donegal. His suggested compromise, of renting a house somewhere like Italy or France, had been rejected yet again, and now all he could envision was three weeks of pure torture.

'I have suggested Club Med or even a gîte in France, you know. I mean, it might be fun to meet some new people and actually have a good time, see a bit of sunshine, drink some chilled rosé, that type of thing . . .'

When he had arrived tonight, he had his speech about how they needed to stop all this nonsense well rehearsed. But he had hardly sat down with the drinks when Laura presented him with a solution to his holiday woes.

'Why don't you and I go to the South of France for a week? You can tell Saffron you have a business meeting.'

'I can't, Laura, especially not now.'

'Well a weekend in Paris, then.'

'I can't. Saffron is pregnant, I can't leave her. It's totally out of the question.'

'I'm not asking you to leave her.'

'I know, but even for a few days. Look, Laura, I asked you here tonight to explain that I can't really see you again.'

'God, why are men such cowards?'

Trevor was on a damage limitation mission. He knew he was being a coward. It wasn't that he suddenly found Laura sexually unattractive, but surely Laura herself realised that it was all a big mistake and couldn't continue? Trevor had never been unfaithful to Saffron before. He loved her, and until recently had seen few faults in her. He wished he had never gone on the trip to Dublin in the first place. No one in Marlborough Road ever had affairs. Or did they?

'Does Saffron know about us?'

'Er, no, she has rather a lot on her plate at present, and I thought we had both sort of come to our senses.'

'I've asked Bill for a divorce.'

'Oh God, you haven't. Have you told him why?'

'Why . . . why?' Her lip curled contemptuously and she looked at him with utter distaste. Trevor had a feeling for a moment that he was in a movie – a surreal one at that.

'Don't flatter yourself, *Treasure*. This isn't to do with you. Although I think you should at least be honest about our fling. You don't deserve to get off scot-free. I didn't exactly do it all by myself.'

Trevor buried his head in his hands. There was nothing to say. They finished their drinks in silence.

Trevor finally poured Laura into a taxi and walked towards home. His head was spinning from the whole experience. He called Saffron as he walked, and let her know he was on his way. He'd told her he had had to have a drink with a legal colleague. At least it wasn't an outright lie. She was going to bed fairly early these nights, even though it was bright until late. The twins, Posy and the house with no Sally were proving too much for her.

I am a total bastard! Trevor repeated this to himself like a mantra. He hoped tonight had finally put the lid on things. Laura had Bill and her children to think about as well, even if she was sick of the whole business of motherhood and being a wife, and she hated her career.

As he walked down the back lane, he passed Evie and her strangely tattooed boyfriend on their way out for the night.

'Hi, Trevor! You'll not be popular coming home at this hour. Posy's just gone to bed.'

'I had a business meeting.'

'Aye, right!' called Evie.

God, she was getting very cheeky that one, but Trevor smiled anyway. He knew Saffron depended on her for babysitting, so he had no choice. Anyway, he liked her too.

'Laura Nelson is in our house right now and she's absolutely rinsed! She almost fell in our front door. You should drop in and help Mum and Dad out with her.'

'Ah, I won't bother, Evie; I'd better get on in now.'

Trevor's hand shook as he turned the key in the back door. Oh God, oh God, please, Laura, don't say anything to Tony and Clare. Please, oh please.

'Hi, sweetie!' he called out. 'I'm home.'

24

Mr Smedley was as good as his word. Within a week, Edith had a phone call from Christine, his secretary. They had a bed for her and she was to go in next Thursday evening; her operation would be on Friday morning. The time had come to make a few arrangements.

Ellen first: she was ensconced in the hospice and was getting wonderful care, and fortunately she had a few good friends who visited her daily. Before her own diagnosis Edith had been going three days a week at least to Portadown. Obviously this was now out of the question; she hoped Ellen could hold on till she herself was on her feet again. She pushed away the thought of Ellen dying without Edith beside her. It was too heartbreaking to contemplate. She decided to phone Ellen's best friend Marjorie, and tell her she was going in for something minor for a couple of days, and not to say anything to Ellen – explain it as a cold or something. Marjorie understood perfectly, and said she would call in more often.

'Try not to worry, Edith. You look after yourself. Ellen is so much stronger these last few days. Honestly, it's hard to take it in sometimes that she is . . . you know.'

Edith gave Marjorie her number and told her to phone in an emergency. With luck she wouldn't need to. She went to bed that night and slept reasonably well.

She saw Fintan next morning at breakfast. Otis wasn't around; she saw very little of him these days, but was too preoccupied to dwell on it.

'Fintan,' she began, 'I have to go into the hospital . . .' She stopped. This was difficult for her. But Fintan had misunderstood.

'How is Ellen?' He sounded concerned.

'She's very unwell, to be honest, though she's being very brave about it. But this is . . . it's . . . me; I have to go into the hospital on Thursday evening. I have to have a small operation.'

'Why Edith! Is everything all right?'

'Yes, it's just a routine op, nothing to worry about, but my surgeon thinks it can't wait.'

'Is there something I can do?'

'No, I'll be fine. I'll be out before you leave, so perhaps a few cups of tea in bed then would be nice.' Fintan sensed that whatever was wrong with Edith, she was not in a mood to discuss it at length.

'I am not quite sure how long I shall be in, but I shall telephone you after a couple of days.'

There, she thought, she hadn't really lied, just spared him some of the more personal details.

Fintan simply didn't believe Edith was telling him the whole truth. He recollected the card Sally had found in the drawer. It obviously had something to do with that. He couldn't say anything, of course, but he was saddened by her news.

'Edith, you've be so kind to me, and really made me feel I was staying with a friend, not a landlady. That has meant a lot to me. So if there is *anything* you want me to do, please tell me.'

161

'I'm sure I shall be fine.'

'May I visit?'

'But you are so busy.'

'Yes, but the opera is up and running now. I have much more free time.'

'Well perhaps on Sunday.'

'Right, Sunday it is. May I tell Clare and Saffron?'

'I don't want to worry them unduly; perhaps you could tell them if you run into them.' And she wrote down the ward and hospital.

On Friday afternoon, as Edith was prepped for her operation at Belfast's City Hospital, feeling lost and alone, Sally O'Neill was several miles away in County Down, thinking that she'd like to kill both Maybeth and Bertha McClure. She just wasn't sure of the preferred method of death, or which one she would like to kill first. She was going mad in this job; the balance of her mind must have been disturbed when she agreed to it. She was working as a maid yet again, in another big house, out in Cultra this time. This was Northern Ireland's 'Gold Coast'. Oh, there was money around here, little doubt about that. The last few weeks had opened Sally's eyes. She had always thought the Marlborough Road ones a wealthy lot, but they weren't in the same league as some of the people she had cleaned for since. Today she was in a modern house with the most beautiful long, elegant sofas in muted beiges. There were low glass tables, and leather and chrome chairs artfully placed throughout. Huge dramatic paintings of women with scowling angular faces covered the walls. The light fixtures were an array of gold discs that seemed to float in space, bathing the entrance hall in shimmering light, like perpetual sunshine. The hall was huge, as big as a normal room. She was polishing its wooden floor now, with a special machine. Then she had to clean the lights. The owner of the house,

162

yet another skinny, over-made-up girl, had told her before she drove off in her fancy sports car that they were all bought in Milan so she had to be extra careful dusting them. The place was making her nervous.

Mary, the other maid, was busy in the kitchen. It was gleaming stainless steel, and multiple Marys were reflected throughout: red, anxious and out of breath, polishing as if their lives depended on it. It was massive and looked like a restaurant kitchen, though one that hadn't been used. The entire house had seemed spotless when they had arrived. But they had stuck rigidly to the checklist, changing bed linen that looked as if it hadn't been slept on, dusting and vacuuming imaginary dust, and shining windows that looked as if they weren't there, so clean were they. They had been at it for three solid hours. Sally preferred dirt; there was something more satisfying about getting rid of it.

Suddenly something exploded in her head. She had had it. Enough was enough. If she had to sign on the dole on Monday morning she would do it. She was fed up to the back teeth with this awful job. She'd wanted to better herself, but this was worse than before!

'Mary!' she called to her fellow maid, who was still grinding away in the kitchen. 'Let's get out of here. I can give you a lift into town on the back of the bike. I think this place is clean enough.'

As they rode into Belfast past all the lofty mansions with their manicured lawns, Sally fumed. Maybeth Weston hadn't kept her part of the bargain, so Sally didn't feel obliged to keep hers. She'd look for something else; she was far too good for this sort of abuse. She would drive to the tacky headquarters of Maids to Order and tell Miss Maybeth where to put her job, *and* her peach-coloured jumpsuits. She was so pleased with this thought that she unconsciously speeded up, and it was only when she heard Mary's frightened squeak from the back of the bike that she caught herself on and slowed down. She couldn't afford to have an accident now. She had things to do.

When she arrived at the office, she handed her check sheets back. After looking through them, Maybeth smiled her false smile and addressed her in her bright fake voice.

'You know, Sally, that all our teams have almost completed their training in hygiene management. In a few weeks we will not strictly need you in a supervisory role. However, we are putting together a "dream team" of top maids like you who will only go to certain houses. I am sure you know the houses I'm speaking of . . . our wealthier clients.' Her fake grin widened. 'We need people we can truly depend upon for those clients. I thought you and Bertha would make a perfect team.'

Maybeth gazed at Sally confidently, as if she was bestowing some great honour on her. The condescending bitch! Sally couldn't believe her ears. Maybeth was completely moving the goalposts. And pairing her with Bertha, of all people! Sally's original attraction to this job had been purely the fact that she wouldn't be cleaning. She had put up with the fill-in days because there had always been some reason for it. Someone hadn't shown up, or it was a new job and there was no time to find extra maids. God! How Sally hated the term *maids*. It was so demeaning. She used to laugh at Edith introducing her to people as her housekeeper, but pretentious as that was, at least it wasn't insulting.

'We are getting paid today?' Sally asked.

'Yes, of course.' Maybeth opened a drawer and handed Sally an envelope, as if she was the Queen awarding her a gong. Sally took it.

'Thank you, Maybeth. I'm sorry to tell you that I won't be coming back. You'll have to find another partner for Bertha. I have decided that I have nothing left to give to Maids to Order.'

Maybeth's brightly glossed mouth opened wide, but before

164

she could utter a word, Sally turned on her heel and left the office.

She got on her bike with a light heart. Finally she was doing what she felt was right for Sally O'Neill.

25

On Saturday morning, Fintan decided to drop in on Clare. He would be gone soon, and Edith needed all the support she could get. He knew she could depend on her neighbours. It was odd, he mused, just how quickly he had become entangled in the lives of all these people. He would find it hard to leave.

When she saw Fintan pass the window, Clare wished she had bothered to run a comb through her hair. She heard him knock lightly on the back door and open it – she had unlocked it earlier to let Lola out.

'Coffee?' she called.

'Yes please.'

Clare wondered briefly why he had dropped in; she hadn't seen much of him these last few weeks. He was obviously quite a private person. Really, all they knew about him was his public face.

'We loved the show on Wednesday. You were amazing.'

'Thank you, we had a great audience, and of course Tosca is magnificent, as is Scarpia.'

Clare poured two cups of coffee and sat down at the table opposite him.

'I'm sure you are wondering why I'm here?'

'You don't need a reason. It's lovely to see you.'

'Edith is in hospital.'

'Oh my God, what happened?'

'Nothing serious – she told me she was going in for a routine operation.'

'She hasn't mentioned anything to me.' Clare looked taken aback.

'The trouble is, I don't believe her. I think she is downplaying it.'

'Do you know which hospital she is in?'

'The City Hospital. She wrote the ward number down for me.'

'That's very near here. Perhaps we should visit her this afternoon. When did she go in?'

'Thursday evening; apparently her operation was yesterday.'

'Oh poor Edith. I hope it is nothing serious. You know her sister Ellen is very ill?'

Fintan nodded.

'Look, I'll call the hospital and find out how she is.'

'Surely they wouldn't give that information out?'

'If you let me know the ward, I'll say I'm her niece or something. Maybe Bill Nelson could call; he works there.'

'No, I think we'll just keep it between us for now, though I'm sure you could tell Saffron. I said I'd visit on Sunday.'

Fintan finished his coffee and left, promising to leave in the details later. Clare would let Saffron know. But perhaps Fintan was right; she'd not tell the Nelsons. Laura had dropped in last week, outrageously drunk and behaving worse than Evie. They couldn't get rid of her. She had ranted on for over an hour, telling Tony and Clare how much she loathed Bill and how she was going to leave the fucking bastard as soon as possible. It had been highly embarrassing, and as luck would have it, it was one of the rare occasions when Clare and Tony had been

167

sitting alone, watching *Newsnight* and enjoying a glass of wine. Tony practically had to carry Laura back down the lane.

Edith toyed with her unappetising lunch. She didn't feel hungry. She hadn't slept a wink last night. Of course no one could in hospital. That was why they came round each night and offered sleeping pills. She had refused. She didn't want to get dependent. She was in a private room, but the door was left ajar and the place was a hive of activity, with phones ringing and bleeps going off. Mr Smedley had been in to see her early this morning before he left for the weekend and pronounced himself pleased with her operation. The prognosis looked good, he told her; they had managed to get all the affected part of the bowel, and she wouldn't miss a few inches, he joked, not with all those yards and yards of it. He was going to start her on chemotherapy purely as a precaution, but they would wait until she was up and on her feet first. She could barely walk today. Perhaps she would be feeling better tomorrow; she had the prospect of Fintan's visit to cheer her.

She had become greatly attached to Fintan; he really was a lovely man. She felt as if she had known him for ever. Otis, for all his way with words, was not exactly practical or dependable. She had begun to revise her opinion of Otis somewhat. Perhaps she had been too quick to allow him a room without a lease.

Earlier, with the help of a lovely young Filipino nurse, Edith had managed to place a call to the hospice to enquire about Ellen, and was told she was holding her own. She sent her love and asked if they would please tell her sister that she would visit next week. She felt sure Clare, or Trevor even, would be kind enough to drive her down once she was out of hospital. That would be in a few more days. There seemed to be no such thing as long stays in hospital any more, what with beds at a premium. Maybe tonight she would allow herself the indulgence of a sleeping pill; one could hardly get addicted in a matter of days.

As Edith lay there contemplating her life, with the racket in the corridor as background, her thoughts turned to Marlborough Road. How she missed her home and her neighbours, and Sally too.

26

For more than an hour, Sally had listened to an overwrought Bertha banging on about how she had ruined her chances of a brilliant career and turned her back on the chance of a lifetime. Sally had patiently explained that she didn't care to clean for clients such as Maybeth's. She'd rather starve.

'It's them ones over in Marlborough Road; sure they turned your head. Made you think you were something. Sure when did anyone over our way ever go to something like an opera?' Bertha's ugly red mug glared at her.

'I *am* something,' Sally said, in a voice that sounded a lot calmer than she felt. 'Bertha, why don't you listen? The reason I'm not going back to Maids to Order is *one*, I am not a maid, and *two*, I won't take orders from the likes of Maybeth's clients.'

Bertha roused herself to reply, but before she could, the phone rang. It was Fintan. Sally told him to please hang on one second.

'Excuse me, Bertha, would you mind going? I have to take this call.'

Bertha gathered her shapeless self up to go.

'You've got too big for yer boots, Sally O'Neill,' she said.

'Charlie's right, them oul' snobs have filled yer head full of rubbish.' And she stormed out, slamming the door as she went.

'Hello, Sally, I hope I'm not interrupting you?'

'No, it's just a friend leaving.' She wondered if he had heard Bertha. 'Is something up?' There was something about the tone of his voice that made her feel this was not a call for a cosy chat.

'Well I'm afraid there is. It's Edith; she's been admitted to hospital. She had an operation yesterday. She's told me it's merely routine, but I don't quite believe her.'

'Which hospital?'

'The City.'

'The City? Oh heavens, that card . . . I was worried it was more than a check-up. I should have asked her about it, but I didn't like to be nosy.' Sally had an odd sort of feeling in the pit of her stomach. She missed Edith Black, and the thought of something happening to her was not a pleasant one at all.

'She did say I could visit Sunday. Perhaps you'd like to come with me?'

'I'd love to, Fintan, but she's probably still mad at me for leaving her.'

'Oh Sally, don't be silly. I bet she'd love to see you. I'll phone tomorrow morning. We can meet and go together to the hospital.'

'That would be great. Whatever time suits.'

Sally put the phone down dejectedly. Poor Miss Black, she had abandoned her in her hour of need, and all for what? It was a good job Bertha had left. Sally would have been up for manslaughter.

Clare had had her shower and was just on her way out the back door when Saffron, accompanied by Posy and wearing a forlorn expression on her face, came in.

'Is something wrong?'

Clare watched helplessly as Saffron dissolved into tears, followed seconds later by Posy, who was obviously out in sympathy. She boiled the kettle and made a pot of strong tea, and poured Saffron a cup, which she drank without a word. Posy was bought off with a chocolate biscuit. Clare fed the dog and waited until Saffron was ready to talk.

'It's Trevor; I think he's having an affair!'

'Oh Saffron, I'm sure you're wrong! Trevor? It seems so unlikely.' She resisted the temptation to add that she couldn't imagine anyone having an affair with Trevor. He was hardly an attractive prospect; he didn't exactly score high in either the looks or the charm department.

'I hope I am, but he's been so different, even before he knew I was pregnant. I can't think of another reason why. There must be someone else.'

'But who on earth could it be? He's always home, unlike Tony!'

'Someone at his work? They did get a new secretary last month. He says she's nice, and she's probably very young.'

'But you're young!'

'I feel old and fat.'

'You're pregnant with twins.'

'I know, and he's resentful.'

'Saffron, this has all been quite a shock to Trevor, as well as to you. He's over fifty, probably thinks he can't cope. I think the whole thing has been too much for him. Have you asked him straight out?'

'No, I can't bear to. I'm afraid he'll admit it.' She seemed a lot calmer now. 'You see, he hasn't been coming home as much, not for lunch anyway, and he came in late last week and he had been drinking. And then with Sally leaving . . . well, the place is—'

'Saffron, I'm sorry things are a mess for you, but you need to know that Edith has gone into hospital.'

172

'Oh Clare, you must think me selfish, rabbiting on about my problems. When?'

'Thursday. Fintan just called in to tell me. She's having some routine operation, and obviously didn't want to bother anyone. Poor thing, what with Ellen so sick.'

'Oh heavens! We should go and see her.'

'Yes, but let's give her till tomorrow. We can walk round. Evie can mind Posy.'

They chatted generally after that, but Clare was intrigued with the idea of Trevor having it off with someone else. He wouldn't, surely? Saffron was at least twenty years younger than he was, and for all her eccentric dressing she was still awfully pretty, and kind too. But after Saffron, much calmed, had left, she suddenly had a flash: Laura Nelson – it couldn't be! But that scene at the barbecue when Saffron had announced her pregnancy? That was outrageous. And last week, when Laura had poured herself into Clare's kitchen full of the drink, she announced she had been out with a colleague. Would Trevor qualify? They were plying the same trade, and this place was a parish. It was none of her business, of course, but all the same she wondered whether, if she dropped in for a drink at the Nelsons', Laura might give herself away.

Next morning Clare sat in her kitchen, flicking listlessly through the pages of the *Observer*. Everyone else was still in bed. Evie had come in really late last night, and Clare could never sleep easily until she knew she was safely back at base. What was more, she had been drunk, dead drunk. Clare had heard her trying to open the front door for about five minutes, before she had thrown on a dressing gown and gone downstairs to let her in. Her eyes were glazed over and she was slurring her words, but Clare had resisted the temptation to bawl her out. Tony was fast asleep, of course. He could sleep through anything; besides, he figured one person worrying about the kids was enough.

173

'You're being ridiculous, love; you never worry whether Rory is in safely each night when he's in Edinburgh,' he had said before he fell asleep.

'Of course I do, I wonder constantly, but there's nothing I can do about it.'

'Evie is quite sensible; she'll be fine. Just get some sleep.'

But Clare had lain there fretting. She didn't like this Mikey much. Evie thought it was for snobbish reasons, of course, because he was a barman, but that had nothing to do with it, well not really. Clare just felt that someone with the same goals – exams, for instance, and a college education – would be a better example for her. Leaving aside his tattoos and piercings, which made her queasy, he appeared to spend most of his money on drink. You'd think working in a bar would put him off the stuff. There were so many articles in the papers about the perils of binge drinking. Evie's liver would be in a sling before she was twenty.

Saffron called in about two as promised. Trevor had offered to mind the children. Clare wondered if he had a guilty conscience. Just as well he had agreed to babysit; there was no sign of Evie yet. She was still in her pit, and Clare hadn't the energy yet for a stand-off. Tony was pootling in the garden, pretending to be a regular stay-at-home guy. All her rants made little impression on him. He'd hardly change now. He was just a workaholic, or a perfectionist as he preferred. She wished he'd apply a few of his standards to his marriage.

They walked round to the hospital. Saffron was huge, so they made slow progress. The twins were kicking like fury, she said. She had already chosen the names: Ariel and Calypso; from the latest scan it appeared they were having two girls.

Edith was on a surgical ward, in a side room. Clare thought she looked very poorly indeed; although she made the effort to sit up to talk, it was obvious to both women that she was quite weak. She was pleased they'd made the effort, but they

174

didn't stay long; they more or less said hello, left her some flowers and sidled out.

'Oh God, Saffron, she's looking terribly ill. What kind of surgery do you think she had?' Neither had liked to ask.

'I wonder if she has someone to look after her when she gets out?'

'I don't know. She made so little of it, saying it was routine, but a routine operation doesn't leave you looking like death.'

They had just reached the exit when they encountered Fintan and Sally, no less. All four regarded each other uncomfortably. Sally was most ill at ease. Fintan took charge of the situation.

'I take it you've been to see Edith? I've dragged Sally along.'

Clare nodded. 'She doesn't look a bit well, though she said it was nothing, just a small operation. We only stayed a minute.'

'Maybe we shouldn't go in, Fintan,' Sally said dubiously.

'No, I said I would come. We'll just pop our heads round the door to let her know we're thinking of her.'

Clare and Saffron left the hospital feeling uncomfortable. They were both wondering what exactly the relationship between Sally and Fintan was. Neither spoke for the first few minutes. Finally Clare couldn't contain herself.

'You know, Saffron, I'm just raging with Sally. After all those years she keeps in touch with Fintan and not us, and leaving that pathetic note . . . She should be ashamed of herself.'

Sally felt sick to her stomach. It hadn't occurred to her that she might meet anyone else from Marlborough Road, though she realised now that had been very silly of her. She wasn't at all sure any more she wanted to see Edith. It seemed a bit cheeky, to visit her after all that had transpired. She said as much to Fintan, but he brushed her protests aside.

'Look, Sally, stop worrying. You've come all this way. We'll literally just say hello. I can pop back later if needs be.'

He knocked politely on the door and heard a weak 'Come in.'

Edith looked up at her second lot of visitors in ten minutes. Really, people were very kind, but she wasn't in great form for them. Then she realised Sally was with Fintan, and felt a deep surge of contentment. She suddenly realised everything was going to be fine.

'Oh Sally,' she said, 'you've come back to me! How lovely.'

Sally looked at Miss Black lying there, looking in deep need of her, and to her own surprise she found herself nodding.

'Yes, as soon as you're out of hospital, I'll be there to look after you.'

Edith nodded and lay back in her bed.

'How very kind of you, Sally. Yes, I look forward to that. It takes a weight off my mind. You know, I'm feeling better already.'

Fintan left a *Sunday Telegraph* and a plant beside the bed. Sally added her box of chocolates, dark chocolates, which she knew Edith preferred. They left and made their way down to the lobby.

Sally didn't know what had come over her. She had found herself just agreeing to Edith's statement, acting from pure instinct, and now she was feeling somewhat apprehensive.

'Gosh, Fintan, I don't know what happened there, just agreeing like that to come back.'

'Admit it, Sally, you hate the new job and you miss them nearly as much as they do you.'

'As a matter of fact, I gave in my notice on Friday.'

'Well, what perfect timing.'

'But what about Charlie? What if he shows up again?'

'That's the least of your worries. I honestly don't think they give a stuff about Charlie.'

'I don't know that I'm ready to just go back to things the way they were.'

'I understand completely. Look, why not just see Edith

through her convalescence, and then if you feel like going back to Saffron and Clare, you can decide when would suit you, and how often. Remember what we talked about before? You sounded keen on the idea of doing some studying. Get a prospectus for classes in the autumn. There's nothing to stop you doing both.'

'I'm not sure, Fintan. It's been years since I studied. My brain doesn't work.'

'Do something easy to start with.'

'Such as?'

'I don't know – what interests you?'

'Well, I like paintings, and English.'

'Art appreciation maybe, that type of thing?'

'But perhaps I should think about business studies, or computer studies. You need that for everything these days. I could run my own cleaning company, give Maids to Order a run for their money.' She started warming to the idea, imagining Maybeth's face. Then reality struck. 'I do need to make some money.'

'We all do . . .' Fintan paused. 'Sally, I don't mean to embarrass you, but I can help out . . .'

Sally turned bright red and immediately got flustered.

'Oh, no way, Fintan. I can manage. I have savings.'

He quickly changed the subject, seeing that he had indeed embarrassed her, and they walked to where she had parked the bike and parted.

Clare and Saffron walked back chatting nineteen to the dozen about Sally and Fintan. They had both been gobsmacked at seeing Sally.

'You know, Clare, she wasn't in touch with Edith,' Saffron ventured. 'Maybe Fintan is still keeping in touch with *her*. She did look really embarrassed.'

'Yes, so she should.'

'I wonder if there's anything going on between them.'

'Hardly. I mean, I don't want to sound like a snob, but he's a well-known opera singer, and she's, well, a cleaner.'

As she said the words Clare thought that she did indeed sound snobbish, but it was a fact. They were an unlikely combination. She had wondered when she first met him whether Fintan was gay, but she had dismissed the idea quickly. He was definitely straight. She had good strong gaydar. She prided herself on it.

'Poor Sally, it probably upset her meeting us like that. I might phone her tonight, and tell her we'd still like to be friends.'

'Yes, you're right, Saffron. We should keep up the connection. She was part of all our lives for so long.'

'She might even come back to Edith to help her convalesce.'

'Yes, we should ask Fintan to suggest that to her.'

27

When Clare arrived back, Tony was still in the garden. She went to tell him about Edith. Evie finally got out of bed at almost three o'clock. One look at her made Clare mad as hell.

'I have had enough of your behaviour, Evie; last night was the final straw.'

'What behaviour? You nearly knocked me over, pulling the door open like that, and then slamming it shut in Mikey's face ...'

'Mikey wasn't even there. I heard you fumbling with the key for ages; you were absolutely drunk.'

'I was not drunk. I only had a few vodkas. Anyway, you can talk! You can hardly get in our back door for wine bottles.'

'That is not the point! When we were your age we did not drink. Anyway, I've had enough. You are not leaving this house for the rest of the week.'

'No way! I'd rather be in prison than in this dump. I'm thinking of moving out anyway and moving in with Mikey.'

'Yes, why don't you? He looks like he'd be just the right one for you, a tattooed layabout. He'd certainly keep you in the style to which you're accustomed.'

'He isn't a layabout!'

'I just hope if you are up to anything you are using condoms.'

Evie was outraged. This was so unfair. She'd hardly even kissed Mikey, let alone had sex with him. Her mother was a hateful old bitch.

'Oh thanks a lot for trusting me, Mum. It must be great to have a slag for a daughter. Maybe I will move in with him and have a baby and then I could be a teenage mum. That would really give you something to bang on about.'

Clare was sure her blood pressure was sky high. She stormed out the back door, aware that she was yet again losing control of the situation, and cornered Tony, who was sanding one of the garden seats and talking to Bill Nelson. She nodded to Bill.

'Tony, can you please come in here and talk to Evie at once. I have had enough of her!'

Tony sighed and shrugged his shoulders at Bill as if to say, women – all the same, eh?

'Clare love, why do you get yourself into such a state? What has she done now?'

'Well in case you haven't noticed, it is almost three o'clock and she is just this minute out of bed. She wasn't in till almost two last night and she was totally drunk. She is only sixteen, and she is your daughter as well.'

Tony went slowly into the house, not relishing for a minute a confrontation with Evie. Clare followed. Evie wasn't in the kitchen. Tony called upstairs to her. Anna answered.

'Evie has just gone out the front door, Dad. She slammed it really hard. She scared my hamsters.'

By dinner time there was still no sign of Evie. Clare had called her mobile repeatedly but had just got voicemail. Tony had also called and left a message, but whereas Clare was frantic, he was laid back.

180

'There's no point in getting yourself into a state. She'll come back when she's calmed down.'

'I hope you'll ground her for the rest of the week.'

'Yes, love. Look, we've been through this a dozen times. I'll have a chat with her about her behaviour.'

'A chat!'

'Here, have a glass of wine and relax.' Tony took a bottle from the fridge and opened it. 'Listen, why don't we barbecue? It's a lovely evening. Have you anything?'

Of course Clare had loads of stuff – she usually shopped on Saturdays – and so she occupied herself by making some marinades and a salad, trying not to think about all the things that could happen to a teenage girl alone in town, and attempting to convince herself that Evie would be home soon.

28

Evie totally hated all these run-ins with her mother. But her mum just whinged about everything she did. And she took all her bad moods out on Evie. Maybe she *had* been a bit drunk last night, but what was wrong with that? A lot of girls she knew got wrecked three days a week. Her mum so had an attitude problem. Evie thought it was because her dad worked so hard and obviously her mum felt she was just as smart as him. Evie was fed up listening to her go on about how she got the best degree and she needed to stretch her mind more. Who cared? She didn't pick on Rory; he seemed to be able to do what he liked, and of course Anna was the baby, so she was just a spoiled little brat. And she knew Mikey was regarded as not good enough, which infuriated her. Evie liked him – they were just pals really – but he was crazy about her, and couldn't do enough for her. He was very generous too; he wouldn't let her buy a drink. He had had a rotten life. His dad had left his mum when he was only six, and Mikey had hinted that he used to hit him and his older brother. His mum lived with some other guy now; Mikey didn't like him, and so he never saw her. He had left home at seventeen. He was different from all the boys at her school. They were all either boring swots or rugger buggers.

She phoned Mikey's mobile the minute she slammed the front door. When he answered, he sounded fairly wrecked. He had had a lot to drink last night too. She asked if he would meet her in the park. It was a lovely afternoon.

'Ach, Evie, I don't feel like moving. I'm knackered. Why don't you come round here?' he said.

Evie agreed, though to be honest, she didn't really care much for Mikey's place. She had only been there once before. It was a total kip, and smelly too. And all Mikey's friends were real dopers. They dropped E's and smoked pot. Evie didn't think pot was a bad drug; a lot of her friends had tried it, and it was practically legal. Mikey smoked it a lot. He had let her try it once, and it had made her head spin and her heart go too fast. She hadn't tried it since. She preferred vodka.

He opened the door to her looking as if he had slept in his clothes.

'My mum is so totally pissed off with me for last night.' She brushed past him, and he followed her in, rubbing his eyes. The place stank. 'I'm starving. Do you have anything to eat?'

She opened the fridge. There was a rotting lettuce, a jar of dried-out pasta sauce and some rancid bacon. She tried the cupboard. Great. Here she was starving, and all he had was two stale Pot Noodles and a rusting tin of chopped pork.

'Why don't we go out and get something?'

'It's Sunday.'

'So? People have to eat on Sundays. We don't have to go anywhere expensive. We could try the pizza place. It's open on Sundays.'

Mikey's best mate Andy was lying on the horrible stained brown sofa. Evie couldn't believe they were stuck indoors on a day like this, but then she herself had been in bed until half an hour ago.

'You go and have a shower; I'll wait.'

Mikey looked at her as if she was mad.

'Go on, it'll wake you up.'

Obediently, he did as he was told. She sat and watched TV with Andy, who was smoking a joint. She refused his offer to share it.

'I don't smoke,' she told him.

'Whatever. This is good stuff, though, it chills you. You seem majorly stressed to me. You should have a toke. Here.' He held it out to her. 'It'll relax you.'

He was right: she was stressed. She really hated all that stuff with her mum. It was so out of control.

'Well, maybe just one puff, then.'

Evie took the joint and tried to inhale. Almost immediately she began coughing like crazy. She went into the kitchen and looked for a clean glass to get a drink of water. Then she went back into the room, which she supposed doubled as Andy's bedroom. He handed her the joint and she had another go at it.

'Hold it in this time and swallow the smoke,' he ordered.

This time she didn't cough. She felt a bit floaty, but definitely more relaxed, and her head wasn't spinning. Pot smelled funny. Well, maybe it hid even worse smells, like boys' socks and stuff. Evie thought the smell of a house important. Clare liked scented candles and bunches of lilies. Marlborough Road always had a lovely smell of flowers and food.

Eventually Mikey came into the room, looking a lot better. His hair was wet.

'Let's go Evie. Later, man,' he said to Andy, who by now was totally chilled.

Part of Evie's plan in getting Mikey to take her out to eat was to waste time. She intended going home later, when they had all gone to bed, though she was beginning to doubt if she could manage that. She figured her mother wouldn't be feeling much like sleeping. She'd only been gone an hour and she had had five missed calls from home. She thought of phoning Rory, but then he was probably out with all his rugby mates doing his boy things, and he'd just tell her to go home anyway. But why should she go home and listen to her mother raving about how ungrateful and useless she was? She'd heard it all before. Maybe she'd stay at Mikey's tonight, even if it was a bit smelly there. He didn't exactly go in for fresh sheets, but she'd keep her clothes on. At least by tomorrow everyone would have calmed down. Deep down she felt this might not be quite the right plan, but she pushed her niggles to the back of her head.

They went to the pizza restaurant near the BBC. It was practically empty, except for a family and two other couples. One of them was Bronagh and Otis. Evie's jaw dropped. What was that all about? Surely Bronagh wasn't dating him? Bronagh looked a bit uncomfortable when she saw Evie. They acknowledged each other with a smile, but fortunately she and Otis were at a table for two. Mikey headed over to a seat by the window; he liked watching traffic. He was talking to someone on the phone.

'Right, mate, that sounds all right, we might be up for that. I'll phone you back.'

Evie waited for him to finish.

'That was Andy. He and his mate Brian are driving down to a gig outside Dublin, Oxegen; they have free tickets for the last two days. Some brilliant acts, d'ye fancy it? His other pal Jimmy's already there. They're leavin' now, back tomorrow night. They'll pick us up here.'

'No, I can't. I don't think Mum and Dad would let me go.'

'You know, Evie, you need to start doing things for yourself. They treat you like a kid; you're nearly seventeen.'

'I know, but they'd be dead upset. I was supposed to be grounded for a week.'

185

'Grounded for what? Going out with me? They don't think I'm good enough for you, isn't that it?'

Mikey sounded hurt, and bitter too, Evie thought. Perhaps she should go to the gig; after all, it was the school holidays, and it would put an end to her dilemma: she wouldn't have to face another bollocking from her mum and dad, at least not for a while. There was nothing worse than her mum's rage in surround sound. She didn't need it right now. The more she thought about going, the more it seemed like a good idea. She was strangely calm. Andy was right. Pot was okay really. She thought she'd text Rory and say she was fine and to tell the parents not to worry. She'd be back tomorrow night. Put a bit of space between them.

'Okay then, I'll go. You'll have to buy me a toothbrush, though.'

Mikey looked delighted. 'Brilliant. Jimmy has a tent set up and all. We can kip there.'

'Just one thing, is Andy driving?'

'No, he can't drive. His mate Brian is. It's okay, he's not into blow or drink. He's got his mum's car for the night.'

Evie went to the loo when she had finished eating. Bronagh was there too, fixing her make-up. She looked a bit put out to see Evie.

'It's not what you think,' she said. 'I'm not going out with him or anything. I mean, I have been out with him, but I don't fancy him. There's nothing going on. He's just nice to talk to and that. He knows all about poetry.'

Like Evie cared about poetry. But whatever, if Bronagh liked it.

'Don't worry, I think he's okay really, apart from his age. I thought he was going to be playing at Oxegen, y'know, the rock festival outside Dublin this weekend.'

'Oh yes, that one. I don't think it worked out.'

'We're going down tonight, just for the last acts. We're leaving in a few minutes, actually.' Evie suddenly felt very friendly towards Bronagh; maybe she reminded her of Sally. 'I wish your mum hadn't left us,' she blurted out. 'I really miss her, she was so good at calming my mum down.' And she started to cry.

Bronagh was a bit taken aback. Evie seemed such a together girl. Could she be stoned? Her eyes were red. Surely not? Maybe she'd had a few drinks, although Bronagh had noticed they had just ordered Cokes. She found a tissue and helped Evie dry her eyes and fix her make-up.

Once Evie had calmed down, she assured Bronagh she was fine. It was just that she had had a row at home, she said, and was not quite herself. Bronagh waited until she was sure Evie was all right, and then excused herself.

'Evie, honestly, I'd better go,' she said. 'Otis will be thinking I've climbed out the window. I'll give my mum your love.'

Bronagh and Otis watched Evie and Mikey leave. They had only had a pizza, which they appeared to have inhaled.

'How do you know them?' Otis asked.

'Evie gets her hair done in the salon.'

There was no point in letting him know her business. He still hadn't made the connection with Sally. Her mum had been telling her just last week that she missed everyone in Marlborough Road – everyone, that is, except Iggy McNamara, who was an iguana, and Miss Black's ginger lodger. Bronagh had said nothing. She wondered what exactly Otis had done to annoy Sally.

29

By eleven o'clock Clare was utterly distraught. She had been crying since Rory came home and showed her the text from Evie saying she would be back tomorrow night. Evie still wasn't answering her phone. Tony was doing his best to calm her.

'Clare love, she will be all right. There's no point getting yourself into a state. She says she will be home tomorrow.'

Despite his even tone, Tony was extremely worried too. He felt powerless. His inability to do anything about the situation was overlaid with a heavy dose of guilt. He realised now that he had been too dismissive of all those spats between Clare and Evie. He should have intervened earlier. He looked at his wife. She was the picture of misery: a competent, intelligent woman reduced to a weeping wreck. He hugged her close. He should have been able to protect them.

'This is what comes of leaving me on my own with the children so much. Children need a father; it gives them a sense of security.'

'Clare, it's not as if I have left home or I'm out on the town. I am working, for God's sake, providing the money so we can live in a house like this and have nice holidays!'

'Yes, but your work means far more to you than your family.'

'That's nonsense, and you know it.'

'You're never here.'

'I'm here now.'

'Yes, but we eat without you most nights. You should be here. Evie doesn't play you up the way she does me.'

'You shouldn't let her.'

'She pays no attention to anything I say. I have far too much to do. I run this house; I haven't got Sally any more. I am like a single mother with three kids, a dog and a demanding job. Anyway, you spoil Evie when you are here.'

'I spoil her?'

'Yes, you always take her side. You believe every single thing she says, her version of the truth. You never stick up for me. It's no wonder I lose my temper with her; she's impossible at times.'

Tony was flummoxed. He had never seen Clare quite so worked up, but there was no consoling her. He tried anyway.

'Clare sweetheart, please try not to fret. I have a feeling she'll be okay.'

'What do you mean, you have a feeling? I'm frightened she won't be. You should call the police and say she's under age. She could be passed out on drink and drugs for all we know. Someone else could have used her phone to text Rory.'

Rory came back into the room. He was feeling awful. His parents never had rows this bad. He tried to reassure Clare.

'Mum, I don't think someone else would have used her phone – how would they know who I was? And she doesn't even have me in under Rory; she has nicknames for everyone.'

'We should call the police,' Clare said stubbornly.

'Clare love, there's no point in going to the police. I don't think they would pay a lot of attention, unless she had been abducted.'

189

'She might well have been. Who is this Mikey anyway? All we know about him is that he's a barman with tattoos. We don't even know his surname.'

'It's Brown, I think.'

'Brown? That sounds like an alias.'

'Mum, please try to chill a bit. I'll go round to his flat now and see if they are there. They've probably just been in a bar in town.' By now Rory had phoned Evie dozens of times, but she wasn't taking his calls either. She was such a selfish brat at times. He'd choke her when she finally showed up. 'Don't worry, they're probably back by now. It's Sunday night. Everywhere closes early.' And Rory left.

Tony didn't know what possessed him to make his next move. He had come into the kitchen to make Clare some tea, and was standing beside the phone waiting for the kettle to boil. He was vaguely thinking it might be an idea to call Sarah, Clare's best friend. She could talk to her and try to calm her down. He pressed the first speed-dial button; *Sa*, it said, though the letters were worn. The phone was answered at once.

'Hello? Sarah?'

'Eh . . . no, this is Sally O'Neill speaking . . . Hello . . . Tony?'

Both of them were equally thrown.

'Sorry, Sally, I was trying to get Clare's friend Sarah . . . I must have pressed the wrong button.'

'No problem . . . I thought you were Bronagh.'

'Sally – Evie's run off . . .'

'What? When?'

Tony filled Sally in on the whole sorry saga.

'Oh God, no, that's terrible news. Poor Clare, I bet she's demented. Please phone me and let me know when she comes back. It doesn't matter how late. I won't sleep now worrying about her myself.'

Tony agreed, and then phoned Sarah, but got no response. Perhaps she was away for a few days.

Rory's visit to Mikey's place proved fruitless; there wasn't any response at all. It was after midnight when he returned. Tony persuaded Clare that even if she was upset, she'd be better in bed, and resting. It looked like they were all in for a sleepless night. Rory had got into Evie's page in Bebo and was checking out her mates. He began to call all the numbers from her last phone bill, but no one had heard from her. Periodically they dialled Mikey's place – to no avail.

At about one thirty, the phone rang. Even though no one was asleep, it was shocking. Everyone froze. It rang about three times. Clare cried out and Tony picked up the receiver.

'Tony? Sorry to ring so late, it's Sally. Bronagh has just come in. I was telling her about Evie, and she said she saw her earlier today, about three o'clock. She was with that boyfriend of hers, Mikey. She told Bronagh they were driving down to a festival outside Dublin called Oxegen.'

'Oh, Sally . . .'

'Bronagh says it's well patrolled and Evie said they were going with a few others.' Sally paused and then said, 'Eh . . . could I speak to Clare for a second?'

Tony handed over the phone, while relaying the news to Clare.

'Oh, Sally,' Clare wailed. 'It's all my fault. I lose my temper with her too quickly. Suppose something happens to her. I'll never forgive myself.' And she started sobbing.

Sally's heart went out to her. She couldn't bear to think of Bronagh running off. She waited till Clare had calmed down a bit.

'Would you like me to call in tomorrow afternoon? I'm going to see Miss Black in hospital about three; so I'll be over your way.' Her heart was in her mouth for the split second it took Clare to say:

'Oh Sally, that would be wonderful. I'd really love to see you.'

30

Throughout that long night, Clare's emotions ranged from panic to worry to fury and then back again. Lola, sensing upset, began a strange sort of high-pitched whining that was driving Tony bats. Normally it would have sent him up to the top of the house in an attempt to escape the noise and get some sleep, but he couldn't leave Clare. His exhortations for Lola to calm down were having no effect whatsoever, and it wouldn't be fair to the neighbours to put her out the back. He barely closed his eyes the entire night and went to work on Monday morning absolutely wrecked. He knew he probably should have stayed home with Clare, but he had an important meeting. He told Clare he would keep his phone on and would be home as soon as the meeting finished. He also told her, with a lot more conviction than he was feeling, that Evie would be back by dinner time. It didn't help. Clare didn't have any classes on a Monday, and housework, although it was piling up, seemed very low on her list of distractions. So at midday, partly to take her mind off things, she went to the hospital to see Edith.

Edith was looking much better and was sitting up reading the paper. Mr Smedley had told her she would be out in three days. She noticed that Clare seemed agitated, and managed with little difficulty to coax the story of Evie's flit out of her. She was very reassuring. She realised she didn't often see this vulnerable side of her neighbour, and liked Clare all the more for it. Being surrounded by achieving women in Marlborough Road wasn't always an easy cross for Edith to bear.

'Don't make it too hard for her to come back, otherwise you could scare her into staying away for longer than she intends.'

'Oh Edith, I couldn't bear it. Perhaps I should text her and say I am missing her and she won't be in any trouble if she comes home.' Clare sounded wretched.

'Yes, dear, I think that might do the trick.'

So Clare sat and sent off the message; laboriously, since despite the efforts of both Evie and Rory, she had not yet learnt to do predict text.

'And about the boy: try not to nag her. We all go through that stage, you know. I walked out with some most unsuitable young men in my time, by my parents reckoning, that is. You know I've often thought over the years that I would have been much happier had I not paid quite so much attention to their opinions. Perhaps I wouldn't be just a lonely old woman lying in hospital with no family to visit me.'

'Oh Edith, that's not true!'

'Well, dear, it is really. I know I have many friends in the lane, but delightful as they are, they are not family.' She smiled warmly at Clare. 'You know, I am awfully pleased that Sally is coming back to me. She's really the closest thing to family I have. I shall have to cherish her more this time. We can't have her running away again, can we?'

'She's coming back? When?' This was news to Clare.

'Well she said she'd be there for me as soon as I got out.'

Clare felt a sharp stab of jealousy.

'That's great, Edith. How did you manage to convince her?'

'I simply asked and she said yes. I know, it is so reassuring.'

'What about the other job?'

'I'm not sure. Perhaps she intends to do both.'

Clare tried to calm herself. Okay, Edith was sick, but after all, *she* had been Sally's first employer. Edith wouldn't even have had a cleaner if not for her. But she wisely said nothing more and changed the subject. Perhaps she could sound Sally out when she saw her this afternoon.

'I assume the operation was a success, Edith?'

Clare was curious about the nature of the operation, and was biting her tongue not to ask, but to her surprise, Edith told her briskly exactly what was wrong with her, and confided how bad things were with Ellen too. Clare offered to drive her down to see Ellen as soon as she was on her feet again. Poor old Edith; imagine having to cope with no family at all. Clare suddenly felt thankful for what she had. She decided she would try to sort things out with Evie and stop nagging Tony so much. Her own dissatisfaction was turning her into a whinger. Perhaps Tony was staying at work for a reason. She left the hospital feeling curiously uplifted, and a bit more confident that Evie would be back soon.

At three o'clock, Edith had her second visitor of the day. Sally knocked timidly on the door, peeked round, and was greeted with a friendly smile. She was looking very smart, not being in her working clothes.

'Ah, Sally, how lovely to see you! I was beginning to get bored. I would so love to have a radio; all they've got here is that ghastly TV. It is on twenty-four hours a day. I had to make a fuss to get it disconnected.'

Sally grinned. 'I see you're beginning to feel a bit better. Will I phone Fintan and ask him to bring you a radio?'

'Yes, what a good idea. The small transistor from the bathroom would be ideal. It would be so soothing to listen to Radio Four.'

194

'And are you comfortable otherwise? You're not in too much pain?'

'Oh no, whatever they're giving me seems to be doing the trick.'

Edith's voice, bled of its usual commanding tones, seemed to carry an extra warm quality to it. Sally felt welcomed; she smiled in return and placed a copy of *Homes and Gardens* down on the locker.

'I thought you maybe had enough chocolates.'

'Really, you shouldn't have bothered, but it's just what I need. I shall look forward to reading it.' Edith indicated a heavy, important-looking book by her bed. *Anna Karenina.* 'I'm afraid I haven't much felt in the mood to revisit Tolstoy.'

Her tone changed; she sounded almost anxious.

'Have you told your organisation you'll be working for me? I hope you haven't changed your mind.'

Sally reassured her that she would be there waiting when Edith was discharged. She told her she had left her new job and recounted the saga of Maids to Order, hamming it up a bit for Edith's benefit, and interspersing it with stories of the rudeness of the spoilt young things she had been working for this past month. She even did a passable imitation of the ghastly Maybeth, and Edith lay back and enjoyed all the gossip. It struck Sally that this was the most comfortable she had ever felt in Miss Black's presence in all the time she had known her. And she liked the feeling.

Sally's next stop was the suggested visit to Clare. She passed Simon on her way down the lane, and of course he hotfooted it up to tell Saffron she was there. Saffron had planned on calling down anyway. Trevor had just phoned to say he'd met Tony and that Evie was missing.

Sally sat down in the kitchen, keenly aware that she was in the visitor's role, but feeling welcome nonetheless.

'Would you like some tea?' Clare asked.

'That would be great.'

Clare busied herself setting out mugs. Camomile for her, and good strong afternoon tea for Sally. They had hardly had their first sip when Saffron and Posy arrived in the back door. Posy headed straight for Sally's knee and climbed up.

'Where Ebee?' Posy wanted to know at once. She still expected Sally to have the answer to everything.

'She'll be back soon,' Sally said, with a lot more conviction than she felt.

'You know I can't settle myself at all,' Clare confided. 'I took Edith's advice and sent her a text saying I just wanted her back and I wouldn't be cross, but she hasn't replied yet.'

'I'm sorry, I didn't even know she was away, Clare, or I would have been up earlier,' Saffron said anxiously. 'Trevor just phoned to tell me.'

'Well at least we knew where she was, thanks to Sally,' and Clare recounted the saga to Saffron.

'Gosh, I couldn't bear anything to happen to darling Evie; I do hope she knows how much we all love her. Don't we all love Evie, Posy?'

'Yes, I love Ebee.'

'They're all the same at that age. Sure Bronagh and I were at each other's throats for a couple of years. She'll settle down, Clare. She knows she's loved.'

Clare looked gratefully at Sally. 'Oh, I hope she does.'

'I suppose you've heard I'm coming back to Edith?'

'Yes, she told me earlier.'

'I must let Fintan know. I'll need a key. I sent mine back.'

'Are you in touch with him often, Sally?' Saffron couldn't resist imbuing the word *touch* with meaning.

'If you mean is there anything going on, well that's hardly likely, is it? He is a famous opera singer, after all, and I'm, well . . .' She trailed off. 'He's been very kind to me, and I suppose he seemed to just take me as he found me. Maybe it's easier to talk to people you don't know so well.'

Clare and Saffron immediately felt ashamed. They had always been just a wee bit aloof from Sally, but that was only to be expected. Their circumstances were poles apart. Both women liked having Sally in their lives, though. Each was dependent on her and was genuinely fond her. Of course it was easier for Fintan to just slide in and make a friend of her. He would be gone next week. Besides, Clare thought, there was just a hint of a project about his thing with her.

'How is the new job? Will there be a conflict between that and Edith?'

'I've left. I couldn't stand the way I was talked to.' She told yet again the story of Rosamund. The two women were hanging on her every word.

'Oh Sally, we were never that bad, were we?' Saffron said almost pleadingly.

'Well now, I would hardly have stayed ten years if you had been.'

'I suppose you wouldn't consider coming back here as well? Even for one day a week?' Clare crossed her fingers under the table.

'Yes, Clare, I'm sure I might be able to manage that, and of course to you too, Saffron. But let me just see to Edith this week. The other thing is . . .'

'Yes?' both women chorused.

'Well, I was thinking I might like to go back and study, get a few qualifications maybe.'

Clare cleared her throat. 'I've been thinking about that too. Fintan told me you were keen to catch up. I've checked the adult education prospectus at the tech. You are eligible to do an access course.'

'When would I have the time?'

'It's two evenings a week, and takes two years. You would

197

then be able to go on to university afterwards.' She handed Sally a page. 'It's all in here. I printed it off the web this morning.'

Sally felt light-headed.

'Have a read through. It's fairly straightforward; you're just the sort of candidate they're looking for.'

'Am I?'

'Yes, and of course I can't wait to help you with your choice of subjects.'

Just then Clare's phone beeped. It was a message from Evie: *Luv u mum very sorry for upsetting u on way home now.* Clare was almost crying with relief as she read it out to the other two women.

'Well,' Sally said, 'I suppose that makes two of us who are coming back.'

Posy couldn't understand what was going on when her very tubby mama and Ebee's mama suddenly started dancing with delight around the kitchen. But she thought she would join in anyway.

31

Evie turned her phone on. She had kept it off to prevent roaming charges over the border, which was why the message from her mother had only just beeped through. She read it a few times before she really took on board the fact that Clare was so frantic with worry that maybe she wouldn't get a bollocking if she went straight home. In truth, she was a bit worn out from it all. Her mother's plea convinced her that a prodigal return was in order. She texted back at once and said she was on her way home.

The concert should have been great, but she had felt strange because of the pot – and very frightened too. At times she felt her head wasn't attached to her body. It hadn't been a great experience. She and Mikey had argued because she didn't want to get in the same filthy sleeping bag as him, and he had called her a stuck-up bitch, although he apologised later. She had spent the entire night awake, wondering what on earth had possessed her to come along to the gig. She hadn't even enjoyed the bands, being as she was so overcome with guilt. She blamed her madcap decision on the fact that she had smoked the joint, but it hadn't really been that. She was just fed up having rows with her mum. She didn't know why they couldn't get along. Clare was cool really. She just exaggerated the importance of education.

Evie arrived home late afternoon. She didn't feel she could face a screaming match, so she avoided the front door and crept down the lane and in through the back door, but Clare saw her, and much to Evie's relief, with a whoop of delight simply took her in her arms and hugged her really tightly.

'Oh sweetheart, please don't do that again. I was so afraid something would happen to you. I'm so sorry I said those things to you. I honestly don't know what I would do without you.'

Evie couldn't believe she was getting off this lightly; it made her feel twice as guilty. Her mother looked wrecked as well, and on the verge of tears. Evie snuggled up to her. It felt good. Maybe her mum did love her after all. She expected her dad would have a 'wee chat' with her later when he got home from work, but she could handle that. She apologised to Clare about a hundred times and then went to have a very long bath. Rock concerts were too smelly.

When she came back down, her mum was in the mood to chat, and for once Evie was in the mood to listen.

'You know, darling, I'm just not managing my life very well. Perhaps I shouldn't have gone back to work when Anna started school.'

'But Mum, you love your work, you'd go bonkers here all day.'

'I know. It got so boring when Dad and I were out at a party or something, answering the endless "And what do you do?" with "Well I'm a stay-at-home mummy, actually, but I used to be a person."'

'I definitely want to have a career when I'm married.'

'I expect you'll have to work for those A levels then, won't you?' And they both laughed.

*

Clare felt more relaxed after her chat with Evie. She would indeed go bonkers stuck here all day. She had read and reread in the broadsheets the arguments each way, and had concluded that something in her remained unsatisfied without a career. She had a need to be defined. But of course, once she returned to lecturing, even though on a part-time basis, it had to be grafted on to full-time motherhood. This resulted in her becoming more discontented than ever. If truth be told, she was a bit lukewarm about her career. She knew she would never scale the dizzy heights now, even should she finish her long-overdue thesis. She had missed the boat. She watched enviously as younger, more ambitious colleagues soared past her, full of self-belief and vitality. But the money was useful; children were expensive. They could live well enough on Tony's salary, but hers afforded an extra security blanket. The upkeep of the house was a big expense – older houses always seemed to have something falling off or down – and of course the children going off to college would be quite a drain.

Tony drove home that evening having spent the day rethinking his own working practices. He did take on far too much, and being a civil servant, he was not paid any extra for it. The job expanded according to the amount of hours he was prepared to put in. He was effective, though, and got things done, but he found it difficult to delegate. He'd have to sort that out.

Clare was on her own in the kitchen making dinner when he got in. She had already phoned him to let him know Evie was back.

'She's in her room.'

'Maybe I'll just have a word with her before dinner, but I've been doing a bit of thinking, love, and I feel the house and the kids and your thesis is all just a bit much for you, and I know I don't help matters. You need a break. so I thought, since Evie and Rory are both here, that the two of us could fit in a long weekend somewhere nice. What do you think?'

'I'd love a break actually, and I suppose they could manage all right, especially now that Sally's coming back.'

'I'll check out some places, then. Maybe somewhere in Donegal.'

He was not relishing his proposed chat with Evie, but she had really crossed the line this time. Until she was in a position to keep herself, she'd have to obey the house rules. He and Clare had been very laid-back as parents, perhaps too liberal; that was part of the problem. Evie wasn't a bad girl really. She was just testing the boundaries, and the time had come to show her exactly where they began and ended.

32

Otis had a plan. The more he thought about it, the more it appealed to him. He would ask Bronagh to dinner. He would have the house to himself for one night before Edith came out of hospital. He had overheard Fintan tell someone on the phone that he was going down to Dublin overnight on Wednesday for some sort of a recital.

Otis had been a bit flummoxed to realise that he actually fancied Bronagh. He'd held back a bit, because she seemed to treat him as if he was her uncle or something. Last week he gave her a lift home and nearly kissed her as she was getting out of the car, but she had sort of shifted her cheek and it had ended up a half-hearted peck. He wasn't sure why he liked her; she was only a wee hairdresser.

Even though he'd be thirty-three on his next birthday, he'd only had one long-term relationship. She had upped and left him earlier this year. He wasn't that fussed. Women ended up bossing you about and looking for stuff. She had run off on him with some flash Harry, a guy who made his money selling insurance polices, or so she claimed. Otis thought he was probably a drug dealer. He sold the small semi they had shared, split the money with her, and left Portadown. It was a dump anyway, full of nothing but dour oul' gits, tacky roundabouts and Chinese restaurants. He had put his half of the money in the building society.

After she had cleared out, he decided to quit his teaching job. His heart had never been in it. The money was shite anyway and the headmaster was full of himself. Thought he knew it all. As for the parents, well, they were a constant source of irritation. Half of them were daft enough to think they'd produced a genius and were never done cornering him to ask about wee Jimmy's progress, and the other half seemed totally uninterested in what their kids were like. The latter were mostly from broken homes and behaved like savages. They paid absolutely no heed to Otis when they came to school. Otis figured they'd end up as paramilitaries, and hoped grimly that eventually they'd all shoot each other.

He decided on a move to Belfast to start his new life. He had certainly lucked out with Marlborough Road. Edith's sister Ellen knew Marjorie, his mother. She'd told Edith he was a poet, and Edith had offered to put him up. He let her think he was broke, so she went really easy on him with the rent and that. He used to get meals too, before that opera eejit moved in, then she transferred her affections.

When Bronagh agreed to come for dinner, his initial thought was to get a takeaway. Now he figured, since he would have the place to himself, possibly for the last time, that it might be better to cook for her. It would be much cheaper than a takeaway and she might be impressed enough that she'd be willing to go upstairs afterwards. The plan of action was to sort out a menu. He wasn't quite sure what sort of food she liked – they'd only had a pizza together till now – but he suspected she was just used to basic fare. Maybe he'd buy gammon steaks, and boil a few spuds. There was a packet or two of frozen peas in the freezer; Miss Black seemed to stockpile them. She was forever telling him they were as good as fresh ones. He'd noticed people put a slice of pineapple on top of gammon. He'd buy a tin; surely that would impress her – gammon with pineapple. Another thing, he'd not stint on the wine. He'd buy one each of red and white; there was an offer on round the corner, two bottles for eight pounds. He would get it early so the white would be cold, and there was some decanter thing he could put the red into, that would impress her. There was a bottle of sherry in the fridge. Sherry went off, so he'd be doing Edith a favour by finishing that. He'd use the silver too. It was a pity the wee cleaner hadn't been, for it looked in need of a polish, and even though he'd not been too struck on Sally, she was good at the polishing. But then he thought, sure it's far from silver Bronagh was reared, so he decided he'd use it as it was, and get out the crystal glasses while he was at it.

Bronagh was starting to feel slightly panicked. It was mental of her to accept Otis's invitation. Suppose somebody, like Evie for example, walked out of their house and saw her going into Miss Black's? What would she say? How could she explain it? Having a meal in Pizza Express was different from going to dinner. Would he have told Miss Black? There was a frightening thought. Just say Miss Black suddenly arrived home from hospital. Bronagh's granny had been sent home without warning last time. Sally had answered her enquiry about Edith earlier, telling her she would be home the day after tomorrow. Her mother seemed happier now she was going back to them all. Bronagh felt it just hastened the moment she would have to tell both Otis and Sally the truth; unless tonight was the last time she would see him. He told her he had lots of books he wanted to give her, and that he was cooking for her himself. No one had ever invited Bronagh to dinner before. She was looking forward to that bit; all the same she hoped he wouldn't cook anything too fancy. She had started to pretend that this was what things would have been like if Charlie had been someone cultured like Otis; she'd be going to him on weekends for a meal. Bronagh reckoned Otis was about thirty-five. Tiffany's dad was that age.

Otis straightened his clothes and took a last look around the dining room. He thought it all looked quite impressive. The table was one of those big mahogany ones and at first he had laid a place at either end of it, but then he thought that looked a wee bit pompous, not to mention too far apart, so he moved the place settings together. He had used the crystal wine glasses, and placed the candles in Miss Black's silver candelabra. He had managed to find two linen napkins, and as a final touch he had gone out to the garden and picked a small bunch of flowers, which he had arranged quite artistically, if he said so himself. Oh yes, he thought, she would be impressed; how could she fail to be? Sure wasn't she from west Belfast and what would she know about fancy tables and the like?

The doorbell rang, and there she was, smiling away and looking a wee bit bashful, but sure wasn't that why he liked her?

'Glad you could make it. Let me take your jacket; you go and sit down in the drawing room.' He nodded upstairs. 'We'll have a wee sherry first.'

Bronagh walked gingerly up the stairs. She remembered the drawing room was the one at the front. It was huge and old-fashioned, and all the walls were covered in paintings, scenes of mountains and lakes. There was one rather large one of some old fellow with a very stern look on his face; probably one of Miss Black's ancestors. There was some sort of classical music playing, and the overall effect was like a scene from a movie. She hovered in the middle of the room, unsure of what to do. A moment later, Otis bounced into the room and lifted a crystal decanter off a small table. There were two glasses sitting beside it. He filled them both. Bronagh was tempted to say that she didn't like sherry but she decided that wasn't a good idea; he had set it out so nicely. So she settled uneasily on one of the chairs and took the glass with a smile. She sipped slowly, for it was very sour, not a bit like the sherry Sally bought at Christmas; this was more like vinegar than wine. She decided to drink it all in one gulp, like medicine, then put her glass down on the little table beside her. Otis immediately poured her another one. Her heart sank. Maybe she should take this one a bit more slowly. She smiled at him again.

'Well,' she said, 'how is the poetry going?'

'Not bad, not bad at all. I've nearly finished the book. I'm hoping to hand it in to the publisher soon. I was thinking I might dedicate it to you.'

'That's really class; will you be able to buy it in the shops?'

'Oh definitely.' He didn't seem to want to go into detail. 'I've been cooking all day, so I hope you enjoy my efforts. Knock that sherry into you, and we'll go downstairs.'

Almost holding her nose, Bronagh tipped the second sherry down and followed him. Her head was reeling a bit. Funny, she had always thought that sherry was an old ladies' drink and not really alcohol. But Otis was knocking it back like there was no tomorrow.

They went into the dining room; it was an intimidating room, all dark and Victorian. Otis ushered her to her seat and made a fuss of opening her napkin for her. It was a large white linen one, not paper.

'Now you sit here, this is just the first course. How about a wee drop of wine to start?'

He poured quite a generous amount of white wine into her glass. He had two plates already laid on the table.

'We're having smoked salmon to begin. Do you like smoked salmon?'

Bronagh nodded. She'd had it before; it was raw, and you squeezed lemon on it. She took a bite. It wasn't bad actually. She washed it down with the wine. Otis sat opposite her. She noticed he practically inhaled his.

He poured her another glass of wine. Then he lifted both the plates, and scurried off into the kitchen. Bronagh was facing the window. It was still light, and she could see out into the back lane. There were children running up and down. She recognised one of them, as Anna McDonald. She had grown; she must be nearly eleven now.

Otis came back carrying two meals; he placed one in front of her with a flourish. It looked fairly unappetising: mashed potato, a huge heap of peas, and a bit of gammon, which looked raw. There was a ring of pineapple perched on top of it. Bronagh took a deep breath and another gulp of wine.

'Tuck in!' Otis said with a grin as he started to wolf his.

Bronagh realised that Otis had not got very good table manners; you would have thought he hadn't eaten for a week.

As Otis cleared away the plates, he declared that he was sure Bronagh wouldn't want to ruin her figure by having dessert. He hoped he'd guessed correctly, since he hadn't bothered to buy anything. Bronagh, having forced the gammon and rather a lot of the lumpy potatoes down, was feeling a wee bit queasy and agreed with alacrity.

'I wondered if you'd mind if I read you some of my latest poems?'

'Why not? Sure I'll sit here and you just bring them down.'

'Well I haven't printed them out yet, so they're still on the computer. That's in my room,' he added.

Bronagh was by now feeling quite drunk.

'Can't you remember them?'

'Ach, not every single word. I'd rather read them to you.'

'Could I have a cup of coffee first?' She thought she had better sober up before she went home.

Otis beamed at her and took her by the arm, leading her into the hall.

'No bother. I'll put the kettle on. Just come up and have a wee look first.'

Reluctantly Bronagh allowed him to guide her upstairs. She felt a bit apprehensive; she knew instinctively this wasn't a good idea, but her head was reeling and she couldn't quite summon the strength to protest. Otis couldn't resist a smirk as he led her upstairs. He hadn't had a decent shag in ages, and surely the drink would have loosened her up. He had invested enough time and energy in her; it was time for a little dividend. She probably fancied the knickers off him and was just playing hard to get.

'Here you are, Bronagh, this is my room,' he said, and he followed her in.

33

Otis scrolled down the few lines he had written. His room was very untidy, Bronagh thought, and somewhat stuffy; it smelled of stale smoke. She was feeling queasy. Otis coughed and cleared his throat.

'Listen, Bronagh, I wrote this especially for you.'

Bronagh tried to concentrate, but her head was spinning. The only chair was in front of the computer. She sat stiffly on the edge of the bed.

'It's a love poem.'

Bronagh felt like throwing up. She lay back on the bed in an effort to stave off the feeling; within seconds, Otis was practically on top of her and covering her with slobbery kisses. His hands were everywhere. Bronagh tried her best to push him off, but he was really strong.

'Ach, c'mon now, sure you must have realised that I fancy the knickers off you? I want to make love to you. I know how to please a girl.'

'No,' Bronagh cried. 'No, get off me! I don't want to, please just leave me alone.'

Otis's mood changed.

'What do you think you're up to, coming over here smiling and eating my food and drinking my wine? And now flinging yourself on the bed in that short skirt?'

He sounded half deranged. He was attempting to kiss her and tugging at her skirt. Bronagh sat up and tried with all her might to push him off, but he was so much stronger. He was holding her tightly by the wrist and he was scarily determined. Suddenly, before she could stop herself, she threw up all over him. Otis sprang up like a scalded cat.

'Ah, for fuck's sake, there was no call for that!'

Bronagh ran downstairs. She tried the front door, but it was locked, so she ran to the back and the key was in the lock. Her hand was shaking, but she managed to open the door and run out into the back lane. She was sobbing now, and still feeling sick, and so ashamed of herself. She straightened her clothes. Most of the vomit had landed on Otis, but she looked a sight. She suddenly remembered she had left her bag there, and her phone, but there was no way she was going back. She made it a few doors down the lane and then was violently sick again.

Evie walked Mikey to the back door. She had been looking after Posy and Simon, and had invited Mikey round to keep her company, as they hadn't seen each other since Oxegen, but now she wanted him gone before Trevor and Saffron got back. She was kissing him good night when she saw a girl staggering up the lane. She watched as the girl stopped at the Nelsons' back door and threw up. Suddenly she realised it was Bronagh.

'You go on, I'll call you later,' she said to Mikey.

Mikey shrugged. Sometimes Evie puzzled him, but then girls were like that. Anyway, he was dying for a smoke, so he shuffled up the lane. He glanced back to see Evie with her arm around the girl, talking earnestly.

Evie couldn't work out what had made Bronagh so upset.

She was crying her heart out. It had obviously been something fairly traumatic. Evie was at a loss what to do, so she just patted her on the back till she calmed down a little.

'Where were you? What happened?'

Bronagh shook her head; her voice came out in sobs.

'It doesn't matter, I'll be okay.' She dabbed round her eyes, and took a deep breath. 'Don't worry, Evie, I'm fine.'

'I'm babysitting for Trevor and Saffron. Why don't you come in here for a minute?'

'No, I'd rather not.'

'Look, the kids are in bed, and they won't be back for over half an hour.'

Bronagh let Evie lead her into the house. It was quiet. Evie went into the kitchen and poured her a glass of water.

'Here, maybe this will help.' She indicated a chair. 'Sit down.'

Bronagh obeyed.

'Can I call a taxi?' she asked.

'No, wait a bit, they come very quickly. Anyway, you need to stop being sick first.'

'I think I have.'

'What happened? Did you have too much to drink?'

Bronagh said nothing.

'Would you rather not talk about it?'

Bronagh nodded. 'I'm okay now.'

Suddenly Evie had an insight. 'You were with Otis, weren't you?'

Bronagh nodded, and then started to cry again.

'What did the bastard do to you? Oh no! He didn't?'

'No, no. I didn't let him, honestly. I ran away, but I've left my handbag there.'

'Do you want me to get my dad to go down to him?'

'No, please, please. It's my fault. I didn't fancy him or anything; I just thought he wanted someone to talk to about his poetry.'

'Aye, right, poetry, I don't think so. Sure he's a mad bastard.

What would he know about poetry? Look, you wait here, I won't be a minute. Don't worry, no one will come down.'

Bronagh sat and waited. Why on earth had she been so stupid? Why had she believed that Otis just wanted to teach her about poetry? Surely he knew that she had just thought of him as a father figure? She felt sick at the thought of him fumbling all over her, and tearing at her clothes. Sure he was not even a bit attractive or sexy. Why would he think she fancied him in the first place? She had never flirted with him or anything like that, had she? He had said that she had, but he was lying.

Evie marched purposefully down to number 29. She could see Otis in the kitchen, sitting at the table. She rapped the window loudly. He looked up, startled.

'Evie! What are you doing here?'

'Can you let me in, please?'

He swung the back door open and smiled broadly at her. After Bronagh left, he had had a quick shower and changed into a grubby tracksuit, but he still smelled strongly of sick.

'Well, Evie, this is an unexpected pleasure. What can I do for you?'

'Bronagh left her handbag in your bedroom. She's in my house, and my dad sent me down to get it, so can I have it, please?'

Otis paled. 'Is she okay? I think she got the wrong impression; I didn't mean to upset her. I mean, we'd just had such a great meal. I went to a lot of bother.'

'To upset her?'

'Is she upset?'

'Hello? Yes, she is! She's in absolute hysterics. I might have to call a doctor. So could you please go now and get me her bag?'

Otis disappeared upstairs in a flash and came back and handed the bag to Evie. Evie checked it for Bronagh's phone.

213

'I think she got the wrong end of the stick.'

'No, I don't think she did somehow.'

'Should I come up and apologise to her?'

'I don't think an apology would make much difference at this stage. You'll be lucky if my dad doesn't call the police.'

Otis looked as if he was about to faint. Evie turned on her heel and left. She was quite pleased with her performance. Serve the nasty bastard right.

When she got back, Bronagh was sitting quietly in the kitchen. She had obviously gone into the cloakroom and washed her face. She seemed more composed.

'Thanks very much, Evie. I need my phone to call Mum. She'll be wondering where I am.'

'Do you want to stay the night in my house? We have a spare room. I think the bed's made up.'

'No, I'd rather get home. Mum will be starting to worry. She doesn't know I was with Otis.' Bronagh pulled an anxious face. 'Evie, you won't tell anyone about this, will you?'

'Not if you don't want me to, but he shouldn't be allowed to get away with it.'

'Nothing really happened; I mean, like, you know . . .' Bronagh trailed off.

'Yes, but if you hadn't managed to run away, it might have. He's so old – and a ginger! No one in the lane likes him, but then no one likes Mikey, and he's young.'

Bronagh smiled. 'You can't win.'

Evie laughed. 'I know. Listen, I phoned the salon like you told me, and Jimmy is doing my streaks next week. I'm the last appointment. Do you want to go for a coffee after?'

'Yes, that would be nice. And Evie, thanks for sorting things out for me. It was really good of you.'

'Don't be silly. I just got your handbag – oh, and I told Otis my dad was thinking of calling the police.'

'Oh my God, you didn't! What did he say?'

'I didn't wait to hear, but I bet he's worried sick, and it serves him right, the disgusting pervert.'

As Bronagh left in her taxi, she was looking forward to going for coffee. Evie was great fun, nice, and dead ordinary. She suddenly felt really glad her mum was going back to work in Marlborough Road. It would be a perfect place as soon as Otis moved out, and somehow she had a feeling that wouldn't be too long.

34

Fintan had another job to go to after Belfast; a production in Glasgow of *Don Giovanni*. Rehearsals didn't start for three weeks. He planned, therefore, to stay an extra week with Edith; see her back on her feet, as it were. It would be relaxing to stay around and not have to rush off to work or rehearsals.

Edith was being discharged from hospital today. Clare had been up to the house yesterday before Fintan left for Dublin and selected a suitcase of clothes. She was picking Edith up after lunch, as soon as Mr Smedley had finished his ward round.

Fintan arrived back about nine thirty. Sally was coming at ten to give the place a good cleaning and make sure everything was to Edith's satisfaction. Clare had offered to cook a casserole and send it down, but Fintan thought a nice omelette might suit Edith better, and of course he could do that easily, so he suggested Clare do something next week, after he'd gone. Edith would need more support then.

The kitchen was a total disaster. Bloody Otis must have had a party. He called upstairs but got no reply. Otis had buggered off somewhere. Fintan didn't understand how Edith tolerated the man. He cursed him inwardly. He couldn't let Sally arrive back to this. He cleared a space and made a pot of coffee.

Sally arrived on the dot of ten, feeling more light-hearted than she had in weeks. She parked the bike smartly outside Edith's back door and came in to the smell of freshly ground coffee; Fintan had timed things perfectly. For a second she felt a bit embarrassed, but recovered quickly.

'I went to see Edith yesterday; she looked great, and she said she had good news from her surgeon.'

'Yes indeed. She'll just have to take it easy for a while. Sadly her sister has taken a turn for the worse. Her friend rang as I got in this morning, so I told her we'd try to bring Edith down to visit this weekend. I hope it doesn't upset her too much.'

'Poor old Edith. I know she's been expecting it, but it'll be hard for her when Ellen goes. She has no other family. God love her, she hasn't her sorrows to seek, has she?'

'No, she certainly does not. I'm afraid the kitchen is in a bit of a state. Otis must have had people in.' He indicated the pots and glasses. 'I'll give you a hand.'

'No, don't worry, I've coped with worse.'

'At least let me get all the dishes together.' He took a tray and went into the dining room, where the table was still full of dishes, two of everything. Obviously Otis had had a romantic dinner *à deux*. He'd used the best cutlery, silver and crystal.

Sally and Fintan worked in tandem until they had restored the ground floor to pristine condition. As they worked, Sally told him of her plans to take the access classes.

'I called the Belfast Institute and they've invited me to an open day tomorrow. Right enough, they sounded very friendly.'

'Good for you. I bet you'll make an excellent student.'

217

'Clare has said she'll help me to select subjects. Though you have to do the basics again.'

'Good, and you'll be able to combine it with working in Marlborough Road?'

'Yes, I think so. I'll know after I've been to see them, though this house is a breeze compared to the other two. God knows what Posy will have stuck on the walls, and Saffron, honestly, have you seen the size of the poor girl? She can hardly get about; those twins will be born walking. And I have to face Iggy the iguana again. I'm dreading the thought of that baggy oul' face staring back at me.'

Fintan threw back his head and laughed. 'Sally O'Neill, I don't believe for a single minute you are dreading any of it. If I'm not mistaken, you are positively looking forward to it all. Well?'

Sally laughed. He was right, of course, but she did feel a trifle apprehensive. It would take a while for her to settle back into the routine.

'Now,' he said, 'I'm afraid I have to go; I've an appointment in town. I'll maybe see you tomorrow morning.'

After he'd left, Sally washed her cup and Fintan's and put them away carefully in the cupboard. She would do Edith's bed next, and use her good Egyptian linen. Then she would cut some flowers from the garden. She wanted Edith to arrive home to a perfect room with everything in its place.

The idea of taking the classes had excited Sally. She was looking forward to the open day. If she could stick to her resolve and see it through, it would make a lot of difference to her life. It was just the sort of challenge she needed. The following morning at ten, she made her way to the tech and was shown into a room and asked to take a seat. There were three other women waiting. Two were about her own age, and one was possibly around fifty. A woman who told them she was one of the tutors popped her head round the door and said she'd be back in five minutes. She handed out some forms for them to fill in. Sally felt somewhat intimidated, but began to do as she'd been told. Then the older woman spoke.

'Heavens, this reminds me of being back at school waiting for the headmistress.'

The others laughed, and the ice was broken.

'I'm feeling a bit scared, actually. I have hardly had time to read a book since my last child was born, and she's sixteen now.'

Sally smiled back in solidarity and then the tutor returned. Her name was May. She was helpful and gave them some general information, then she showed them the library and the lecture theatres and fixed a day for enrolment. It was all surprisingly easy, at least that part. Sally still felt unnerved when she thought about actually getting down to it, but Joyce, the chatty woman, walked out to the car park with her and confided that she was feeling much the same.

'Oh,' she said when she saw Sally's bike. 'I'm impressed. I'd say you must be somewhat bohemian. You'll take to social studies like a duck to water.'

Sally left for Marlborough Road feeling gratified.

Things had been a little better in the McNamara household of late. Saffron had gradually come round to the idea of twins; they had always talked of having four children, and at least now she was getting off with just three pregnancies. Trevor seemed to have gone from belligerence and annoyance to stoicism. There had been a shift in their relationship.

Laura hadn't been around recently. She had taken the children on holiday to her parents. With her departure, Trevor's mood had lightened considerably. Bill planned to join the family for a few weeks before school went back. Trevor had chatted to him a few times in the lane and concluded that he knew nothing of his dalliance with Laura. Either that or he was a very good actor. Trevor had an uneasy feeling that it might all rear up again, but for now he was just mightily glad of the respite. If he could get to the end of the summer – better still, the pregnancy – with no further contact from Laura, well that would suit him just fine.

By about lunchtime both Saffron and Clare had separately found excuses to drop in to Edith's. Now that Sally was back in business, they were checking that she wouldn't run away and leave them again. To their immense satisfaction, she was bustling about Edith's house hell-bent on restoring it to its former glory. She indulged them when they arrived within minutes of each other by stopping for a quick cup of tea to catch up on the goings-on in the lane. Besides, she needed to consult with Clare about the arrangements to get Edith home from hospital.

'Oh, Sally, did you hear that the Nelsons are separating?' Clare settled down with her cup of tea.

Saffron looked at her amazed. 'Gosh, Clare, even I hadn't heard that.'

'Yes, apparently they're splitting up. Laura called me. She's spending the rest of the summer with her parents in Devon, and then when the law and school terms start again she'll come back. She says they'll probably put the house on the market.'

'Oh dear,' Saffron said, 'that's awfully sad, especially for the children. I thought they were quite happy.'

'To be honest, I thought something was up. She came into our house a few weeks ago absolutely plastered, and sat yacking on about men being bastards.'

'Well a lot of them are.' Sally had already finished her tea and was back bustling round.

'Trevor is friendly with her, I wonder if he knows about it.'

220

Saffron had a vague expression on her face. Immediately a look flashed between Sally and Clare, as if suddenly they both knew without a doubt that Trevor was somehow inextricably connected to this news.

'I was so looking forward to having her around after the twins are born, what with her experience.'

'Ach, Saffron, we'll all chip in with the twins. Sure it's only two of the one baby. You need to look after yourself and enjoy being the mother of two for these next few months.'

Sally took their cups, put them on the draining board and shooed them both out the door.

'I can't sit around chatting all day. I'll see you at nine tomorrow, Clare, and I'll be into you at lunchtime, Saffron.'

The two women left, but lingered outside in the lane.

'Gosh, Clare, that is fairly awful news about the Nelsons. It's so out of the blue. And selling the house – why?'

Clare shrugged; she had no idea. 'I expect they can't afford to run a house this size and another one as well.'

'Heavens, I do hope they don't sell to a property developer. He'd fill it with students. That would be all we need.'

'Stop, don't even go there. Maybe it'll not happen and they'll sort things out.'

'I hope so; it would be so awful for the poor children.'

Saffron walked home feeling inexpressibly sad, but also strangely relieved, and she didn't want to think why. She was very glad, however, that she hadn't voiced her suspicions about Trevor's friendly behaviour towards Laura; it would have served no purpose. Laura had always been a bit discontented with her lot in life. She had never liked Northern Ireland. Perhaps she'd be happier away from here.

There is a saying in Ireland, 'If you don't like the weather, just wait five minutes.' Trevor was mulling this over as he walked home in the pouring rain. He had left the car at home this morning, since the sun had been shining brightly. The down-pour had started seconds after he left the office. He had no umbrella and he was soaked. He looked longingly at each passing car, hoping one of them might be a neighbour, but no luck.

'Gosh, Dad, you're soaking,' Simon chirped when he arrived home.

'Full marks for observation, son.'

'Why you all wet, Daddy?' Posy was out of her high chair finally and perched on a little booster seat, being a big girl. They had all been waiting for Trevor to have family dinner.

Trevor softened. 'Because, sweetheart, it's raining very hard and Daddy had no umbrella.'

He went upstairs to change, and came down to a roast vegetable and couscous stew. Saffron had opened a bottle of wine (non-organic).

'I thought I would have a little with water. I think it's safe enough in the third trimester and I knew you could use a little glass, Treasure, when I saw the weather.'

Trevor felt mollified; sure he was just an old grump. He had a lot to be thankful for. Saffron was beautiful – pregnancy suited her – and the kids were full of chat. He began to relax and enjoy his meal. He was a lucky man to have all this.

They had just finished pudding when Bill Nelson arrived at the back door looking a bit dejected. Trevor felt an instant pang of nervousness, but sprang up immediately and offered him a glass of wine.

'No thanks – you don't have a beer, do you?'

'No problem. What would you like?' Trevor named three kinds of fancy beers.

'Oh, anything, whatever's cold.'

They sat down, and Saffron cleared the table and spirited the kids out of the kitchen. She felt Bill wanted a man-to-man chat, possibly about his upcoming separation. Really, it was too awful for words. She fervently hoped Clare had somehow got the wrong end of the stick. Poor Bill – or maybe it was poor Laura. Whatever, no doubt Trevor would tell her all later on.

Bill almost drained the bottle in one gulp. Trevor opened the fridge door, took out a second and handed it to him.

'Cheers. I suppose you've heard the news, mate?'

Trevor shook his head. His legs had turned to lead, and he felt his throat constrict. He quickly poured another glass of wine for himself, sat down again and tried to look composed and concerned. Women were so much better at this, he thought.

'Laura is leaving me. I suppose you can guess why?'

Trevor gazed mutely at Bill. He was literally petrified. The words wouldn't form.

'I know, mate, nothing to say really. I should have appreciated her when I had her.' He shook his head slowly. 'Twelve years we've been married, twelve years. It's hard to believe.'

Trevor's fingers tightened on the table. The room was spinning. He took a deep breath and another large sip.

'Bill, I'm really sorry, these things can—'

'Listen, Trevor, you're right, we all do crazy things. I don't know what possessed me – insanity, male menopause, vanity, and of course she was willing . . . such a tease, and young and foreign and hot.' He looked intently at Trevor.

What was he talking about?

'Puri . . . I hate the name Purificacion. Ironic, eh?'

'Oh yes, the au pair . . . You mean you . . . ?' Trevor spilled the words out.

Bill stammered on, glad to confess, unburden himself. Trevor was almost jealous. There was no absolution for him.

'Anyway,' Bill continued, 'I'm sure you get my drift . . . I know it's not politically correct to say this,' he added hurriedly, 'but believe me, coming out of the bathroom and dropping

223

her towel . . . things like that, you know. It drove me crazy. I was mad for her. She had me at her mercy.'

He bowed his head, as if to indicate the weight was too much. All that temptation had floored him. He had been blameless, like Trevor. For a minute neither man spoke, then Bill looked up, wanting only that Trevor understand. Trevor nodded furiously. Bill took the cue with gratitude.

'It's hard for men of our age – well, any age really – to resist someone like that.' He sighed. 'I should have, though. Laura came home last weekend . . . We were . . . you know . . . Seems she'd got an early flight. She . . . well, she fired her on the spot.'

Bill paused and drained the second bottle. He placed it on the table with a thump.

'Sorry to be drinking so much.' He gestured towards the fridge. 'May I?'

Trevor nodded wordlessly, concentrating on not passing out with relief.

'Anyway she's moved to stay with another Spanish girl, Puri has. I said I wouldn't see her again, but apparently Laura has decided our marriage was crap anyway. Can you believe it? Crap, that's the word she used.' He lowered his voice. 'Said I hadn't been any good in bed for years – I mean that hurt, that really hurt.'

Trevor reached across the table and patted Bill awkwardly on the hand.

'Women say things, Bill. I'm sure she didn't mean it. And are you sure it was just because of Puri?'

'Well, what else could it be?'

'And it was . . . just the once?'

'Yes, just the once . . . dreadful timing.'

'Yes, dreadful,' Trevor echoed.

Bill looked at him dolefully.

'I mean, I've been working too hard, and so has Laura. Puts a strain on things, but everything was fine. At least I thought so. Now she says she wants me out of the house by the time she and the kids come back from Devon.'

And to Trevor's utter horror, Bill put his head in his hands and began to sob.

35

Sally was hardly back to work when events in Marlborough Road suddenly speeded up. It was as if everything had been suspended until her return. Edith came home from hospital to a house that positively gleamed; even the searching rays of late summer sun could barely find specks of dust to float in them. On her first afternoon back, Otis announced he had bought a property nearby and would be moving into it at the end of the month. Edith didn't mind at all. In fact she found herself quite relieved at his announcement; though it was a great puzzle to her where on earth he had found the money to buy anything, let alone a house. She hoped he had done nothing illegal. Throughout his sojourn with her, he had constantly pleaded poverty. He had even missed the rent one month. Were it not for the fact that Marjorie, his mother, was so good to Ellen, she would have asked him to leave long ago.

Sally was especially delighted to be getting rid of him, hardly able to contain her glee. She had felt the house would never be clean with him in it. All that smoking in his room, and frying everything; he had even ruined the non-stick pan. But there was something else about him that unsettled her, though she couldn't quite put her finger on it. Still, good riddance, he was off soon. Meanwhile he was keeping a low profile, staying in his room on the rare occasions he was home.

Fintan had only a few days left until his departure, a real cause for sadness for both women. He was such an asset to Marlborough Road. What a pity Northern Ireland only staged operas a few times a year.

Fintan and Edith were having a cup of tea and a chat when he suddenly said to her, 'Edith, have you considered taking a break in the sun? A week somewhere before you begin the chemotherapy?'

'Why, Fintan, what a nice idea!' For a moment Edith thought he was asking her to accompany him, then quickly she understood that it was merely a suggestion.

'You know the holiday Sally won?'

'Yes, that was very lucky. She says you won it together.'

'Not really. Anyway, I don't think she will use it . . . Perhaps you could buy it from her? Would Isabelle go with you?'

'Oh, I don't wish to be unkind, Fintan, but Isabelle can be such a fussy old bore. I couldn't stand to be with her for a week. We went to Rome together once for a long weekend . . . she drove me crazy. More interested in the cats than the Colosseum.'

Edith didn't like cats; they peed on her plants and sprayed the tyres of her car.

Fintan smiled. An idea was forming.

'What about your going with Sally?'

Edith looked surprised.

'Going with Sally – me?'

'Yes, I expect Sally would be just the right person for you to go on holiday with. She's sensible and friendly . . .' He paused. He had to phrase this delicately. 'Years ago, Edith, someone of your class would have had a lady companion.'

'I couldn't suggest it to her; she'd think it strange . . .'

But Fintan was sure by the look on Edith's face that she was intrigued by the idea. And she hadn't said no. If Edith could get past the class thing, she would enjoy Crete with Sally. And it would be a good thing for Sally as well. It would give her a boost. They didn't have to stay welded together. Edith could take a few trips to museums and ruins; Sally could lie by the pool, maybe even take along a few of the books from her forthcoming English syllabus to read. He decided to leave Edith with the thought and changed the subject.

Edith was improving daily, though she was still weak. Clare drove her down to see Ellen twice, and then Edith's friend Isabelle volunteered for the job. She had known the Black sisters since childhood, so in a way it was more appropriate.

Ellen wouldn't be long for this world. Edith thanked her lucky stars she had heeded her own symptoms early. Mr Smedley had been most encouraging when he came round to discharge her, and even she knew doctors were reluctant to commit to anything these days, what with all the ghastly lawyers hounding them.

Even as she rationalised her own feelings about it, Edith knew that she was being terrifyingly unemotional about her illness, but she simply couldn't help herself. There was a guard, some kind of inner mechanism that made her do that. It stopped her giving way to the awful feeling of hopelessness and doom she knew was buried deep within her right now. At times she mentally compared it to a lid that pressed down and, as it did, snuffed out her true feelings about Ellen's imminent death and her own mortality. If she allowed the lid to open even a crack, she would find herself washed out in the tide.

At the end of her first week of recuperation, Edith was still feeling a little bit frail. Sally was coming today, so she sensibly decided to stay in bed. She had been to see Ellen the day before. She spent almost three hours at the hospice and it had taken a lot out of her. She didn't think her sister would last the week.

Sally brought her lunch on a tray, fixed beautifully. It held a plate with two triangular sandwiches filled with ham, cheese and thinly sliced tomato, a piece of shortcake, and a pot of tea (Earl Grey). Edith was most appreciative. The dynamic between the two women had shifted considerably since Edith's illness and Sally's return. It was now much more in the nature of friendship and mutual respect than a mistress/maid situation.

That was mainly down to Fintan, reflected Edith. He had made an immediate friend of Sally, and this had somehow permitted Edith to break through her class prejudices. Being ill, and counting her blessings and finding Sally at the top of the list, had put the seal on it. Certainly attitudes had shifted on both sides: previously Sally only cleaned Edith's bedroom when it was empty. This new-found intimacy also made Edith brave enough to heed Fintan's suggestion.

'That holiday you won a while back, Sally. Have you decided when you are going?'

'Ach, don't worry about that. I won't be taking any time off. I don't think I'll use it.'

'But what an awful pity. Could some of your family not avail themselves of it?'

'Well there's a chance Bronagh would go with a friend, but she's not that keen. I've offered it to my sisters as well but nobody's interested. Half of it belongs to Fintan, though. He might be able to use it when his next opera finishes.'

'Could you not find a friend to go with?'

'Well to be honest, not really. Anyhow, it only covers flights and hotel. I wouldn't be much use at finding places to eat somewhere like that, not knowing the language or anything.'

'Well, Sally, I have a suggestion to make. I wonder if you would consider my coming with you? I could go to look at the museums and ruins and you could rest by the pool. I think a break in the sun might be the very ticket for me.'

Sally was speechless. Six months ago she would have thought the suggestion outrageous – in fact Edith would never have made it – but improbably, it now sounded a perfectly reasonable idea.

'Don't answer now, think about it overnight. I expect we'd have to go in late September. The sun is more bearable then.'

Sally finished cleaning and took the tray down, leaving Edith to have a nap. Funny the way things turn out, she thought.

Ellen died the following weekend. Edith went to Portadown for the funeral and stayed a few days to sort things out. It was wretchedly sad, even if it had been expected. Edith allowed herself the luxury of tears, but those few outward drops only kept the pain in check. She would do most of her grieving in private, alone in bed, where she fought against a dull ache of loss and a deep sense of regret that she had always rationed or curtailed her hugs for Ellen. She vowed that she would change; she would start to show more affection. Perhaps like the child in the story of the Snow Queen, she too could thaw. Her neighbours – whom she also counted as friends – could and would be her role models. Previously she had lamented their lack of control, tutted inwardly over the abundance of affection and indulgence they displayed to their children. Perhaps from now on she would strive to become more like them. And Sally, who was being so solicitous of her; she would try to be more affectionate to Sally. Edith knew that if her attitude relaxed, Sally would respond. That was logical. And there was something else she could do for Sally. The thought of it made her positively gleeful. Perhaps she would get a chance to be Fairy Godmother sooner than she had thought. Ellen had been very thorough; most of her worldly goods were left to Age Concern, with a few of the family things set aside for Edith and some nieces and nephews on her late husband's side to choose from. Ellen had been very well off. She had left the bulk of her money to the hospice, but even so there was a sizeable legacy for her sister. Edith, who was not short of money thanks to an adequate pension and careful management over the years, suddenly went from comfortably off to rich.

Sally arrived for work promptly at nine o'clock on Tuesday morning. Edith was in the kitchen reading the paper. Emboldened by her new approach to life, she looked up.

'You have yet to give me an answer about Crete, Sally.'

Sally looked slightly disconcerted.

'I'm sorry, Miss Black.'

'Edith, Sally, please call me Edith.'

'Edith then. I suppose I put it out of my head.'

The opposite was true. Sally had thought of nothing else since Edith had made the suggestion, but she felt overwhelmed by the idea. Imagine Sally O'Neill going off to Crete with Edith Black. She was sure she couldn't cope. Suppose she hated the odd food? She had never tasted Greek food before. Goodness, she hardly even liked Chinese. She preferred to be able to make out what she was eating, and all that jumbled-up stuff confused her. What if Edith wanted to go to fancy restaurants? And there was another, even bigger reason, and that was the money issue. Sally managed her money well, but by the time she had paid the bills, there wasn't a lot left. Even if Edith paid her for the other ticket, it wasn't rightly Sally's; it was Fintan's, so she couldn't accept any money.

She said that to Edith.

'Oh, nonsense, it was Fintan who suggested I use it. I must admit it hadn't occurred to me. But I think it's an awfully good idea.'

Sally couldn't think of anything to say. She didn't want to

harp on about the money. Maybe she could manage it. She had some savings. But Edith had obviously read her mind.

'Sally, I know you might be worried about the financial side of things, but Greece is awfully cheap compared to here, and eating out is very reasonable.'

Sally hesitated. Here was an opportunity she might never get again. Maybe she could bring a couple of the novels Clare had given her to read. She could always talk to Edith about them. Bronagh was old enough to stay on her own, and if she put her mind to it, she could manage the financial side all right. Sure wouldn't she be buying groceries anyway if she was at home?

'Maybe I should drop into the travel agent's tomorrow on my way over. We'd need to check they have vacancies for whatever week we choose.'

'That would be wonderful, Sally. Oh, isn't it fun to have something to look forward to?'

And Edith sat back contentedly. Yes, this was the first step on the road to the new Edith.

On her way out, Sally met Fintan walking down the lane.

'I see you put Edith up to going on holiday with me.'

Fintan laughed. 'Well, there was no point in letting the trip go to waste, now was there? Never look a gift horse in the mouth.'

'Do you think it will be okay – me going off with her? I mean, we're so different.'

'Yes, you are, but you respect each other, and I think you both need the break. I wish I was coming along.'

Sally smiled, and thought how nice it would be if Fintan did accompany them on holiday. But of course she said nothing.

'I'm calling into the travel agent's tomorrow to see what dates are available.'

'Good. That's great news. Let me know how you get on.'

★

Sally arrived at the McNamaras' in a cloud of emotion, and even the presence of Iggy in the kitchen couldn't dampen her good spirits. Saffron, though, was not to know this. She hauled herself out of the chair when she saw Sally arrive.

'Oh Sally, please don't worry about Iggy, he's just here for a minute to say goodbye.'

Iggy sat immobile on top of the plate rack over the Aga, his heavy-lidded eyes fixed on Saffron and Sally.

'What do you mean, goodbye?'

'He's going. Simon and I have had a long chat about this, and since Simon will be going to school, and the twins will be arriving soon, there'll be no one to look after the poor old thing. So we've agreed that Iggy needs to go to a new home. We advertised at the reptile shop and we've found him a new owner, someone highly recommended. He phoned last night. He sounded a very friendly person, and he already has two other iguanas. He'll be here to pick him up at two. Isn't that great?' Saffron looked at her for approval.

'I hope it isn't on my account you're getting rid of him. I have put up with him for three years now.'

'Of course not, Sally, I promise.'

She lowered her voice, as if Iggy could hear what she was saying.

'To be honest, Trevor can't stand him either, and I don't feel as inclined to clean up after him, what with the pregnancy and that. Besides, Simon is so looking forward to going to school, and feels Iggy would miss him dreadfully if he left him alone all day.'

'Well I can't say I won't be glad, as long as Simon doesn't grieve for him. I remember Bronagh took it badly when the cat died.'

But as Iggy surveyed her from the top of the Aga while she cleaned the kitchen, Sally couldn't help feeling triumphant. She wouldn't have to gaze at that baggy oul' face again, and she was sure he'd be happy in his new home; sure weren't there two wee friends there for him to pal around with? Yes, life was on the up.

After dinner that evening, Sally called Edith and said she would definitely go to Crete.

'Oh Sally, I'm so glad. We'll have a wonderful time. Fintan assures me it's his favourite part of Greece.'

The following morning she was at the door of the travel agent's as soon as it opened. She handed over the voucher Evie had given her, and got all the details and a list of available dates. The last week of September was their preference. The girl looked up the predicted weather on the internet and told her it would be about seventy-five degrees during the day and a bit cooler in the evening. They could have two single rooms for a supplement of thirty pounds each, although Edith had told her she fancied an upgrade, which she would pay for. Sally felt that arrangement was essential; there was no question of sharing a room. She would be too embarrassed, and she felt sure Edith would want her privacy. The hotel looked lovely. It had a large swimming pool, and was very modern; probably not to Edith's taste, but it was near some Minoan ruins, which definitely were. The girl put that particular week on hold, and printed all the details out. She gave Sally a card with her direct line and told her to call when they had decided for sure. She would need passport numbers and the room supplements.

Sally drove to Marlborough Road feeling excited. She'd nip in to see Edith after she'd finished at the McNamaras' and they could sort it all out then.

There was just one more thing she needed to do to make the week perfect. She had heard from Eileen that Charlie was going off to Coventry in a week's time. He had two brothers there and one of them had offered him a job. She couldn't wait. She needed to talk to him before he left, though. She waited till Bronagh and Tiffany were settled watching a film and went upstairs. She found the piece of paper Eileen had given her and dialled the number on it.

'Hello, Charlie? It's Sally.'

'Ach, Sally, it's great to hear from you. What can I do for you, love?'

'You can come to the solicitor with me on Monday morning. I want a divorce.'

36

Sally and Edith saw Fintan off on Friday. The taxi that took him to George Best City Airport left behind two women with heavy hearts. The truth was, both of them were more than a bit in love with him. He had brought a lot of pleasure and a new focus to their lives. He left in a flurry of hugs and promises to stay in touch, and talked of getting back to visit at the beginning of October, when he finished in *Don Giovanni*.

Clare and Tony were going away too, finally getting off for their weekend break. Tony had booked a five-star country house in Donegal. The food was highly recommended and it was supposed to be luxurious. There was a spa as well. Clare had reckoned she was seriously in need of pampering. The snag was that it was a long drive.

Rory and Evie had promised to look after Anna and Lola the dog. Anna would spend a lot of the time at the McNamaras' anyway, though she had made Clare promise she could eat her meals at home. Poor Anna, she wanted to be a vegetarian really. How could she not, with Simon's constant proselytising? However, the truth was, she didn't like vegetables much. To calm Clare's nerves, Sally agreed to come in on Friday as well as Monday morning. If there was one thing Clare needed to do, it was relax.

It was Rory's idea to have the party. He had a barbecue in mind. That way, everyone could bring their own food and drink. He thought he would invite all of his mates, who, now term had finished, had descended on their parents to live off them during the summer months. But Evie was not going to let him get away with that. No way. If Rory was having a party, then she was inviting her friends as well.

'*Your* friends? Like Mikey and all his druggie buddies? I don't think so.'

'Well you're not having a party then. Mum will kill you if she finds out, and how on earth will you keep the house tidy?'

'It's a barbecue, stupid! Everyone will be outside.'

'Yes, but they need to be indoors to use the bathroom.'

'They can go in the bushes.'

'Get real! That is the most ridiculous thing I've ever heard. Just say the kids are around. Anna. Simon. Posy.'

'Well I'll tell them to use the downstairs cloakroom.'

'Aye, right, and pee all over the floor.'

'I don't pee all over the floor.'

'Yes you do. Mum is always giving off about it.'

'Sally's coming on the Monday morning.'

'So? You would expect Sally to mop up a smelly toilet? And what if Mum and Dad come home early? You'll never get away with it. You'll have to tell them.'

'I'll have the party on the Friday night; that way I have all weekend to clean up.'

'Rory, are you listening to me? You had better tell Mum and Dad. You can't expect people in the lane not to notice you all outside.'

So Rory was on his best behaviour for a few days, and then over dinner the night before Tony and Clare were due to go, he told them that he had asked a few friends round tomorrow night. Would that be all right?

'Please? Mum, Dad, honestly – you know them all. Sam, Ali, Smithy, Jules? Please? Look, it'll be okay, we'll mainly be outside.'

Clare and Tony exchanged looks.

'Listen, mate, this break is so that your mother can unwind. She can't be worrying about the house, and I don't want to be coming back to Armageddon.'

'Dad, I promise . . . Look, I've been working all summer, and I passed all my exams with no re-sits and you promised me something for that. Please? I swear we'll behave.'

'Well maybe this once, but definitely outside. And don't let it go on too late, and make sure you keep the noise down.'

'And Rory darling, don't forget poor Edith's not long out of hospital and Saffron's pregnant. She needs to rest. You won't let things get out of control, will you?'

'No, honestly. I promise, Mum.'

'Well okay then. But make sure Anna isn't up too late, and remember to feed Lola.'

Clare tended to give in easily to her only son.

So it was agreed. Of course Evie, after a mixture of threats and persuasion, got Rory to allow her to invite a few of her girlfriends. Mikey could come along later. He worked on Friday nights. She thought she might invite Bronagh as well, although she was aware that Bronagh might feel a bit out of place. Rory's friends were real rugby types, and had no idea how to behave with girls when they were drinking. They were so immature. She phoned Bronagh to ask her. Bronagh seemed pleased to hear from her, but was doubtful about the party.

'My mum would wonder how we even knew each other.'

'Don't be silly, we've always known each other.'

'Yes, but . . . you know what I mean.'

'She knows I go to the salon for my streaks.'

'You've never said anything about . . . you know?'

'No, of course not. I promised you.'

'Thanks . . . Mum says he's moving out.'

'I know. They are all delighted round here to get rid of him. My mum says even Miss Black will be glad to see the back of him.'

Bronagh said tentatively that she would consider coming. 'I'll phone you and let you know for sure.'

'You can bring a friend if you like.'

'No, I don't know anyone who would fit in.'

'Thanks!'

'You know what I mean, Evie.'

'I know. Rory has already called Mikey and his mates freaks. If you do come, just come by yourself, and come early. I'll be on my own; Mikey won't be here till the bar closes.'

Sally was pleased to hear Evie had invited Bronagh.

'Ach, that was nice of her. I'm glad you've made friends with Evie. I told you they're not bad kids; just a wee bit spoiled. Rory's a lovely boy, so he is.'

Bronagh said nothing. She was tempted by the invite, but surely Sally of all people knew it wouldn't be easy for her.

'You should go, you might meet somebody nice. You have to aim high, Bronagh pet. Do better than me, and find a man who can keep you.'

'For starters, I'm never, ever getting married, and I'll be able to keep myself. I'm going to open my own salon, and drive a Porsche like Alan.'

'Would you not go along even for an hour?'

'I'll see how I feel on Friday.'

They left it at that. Sally hoped Bronagh wasn't ashamed of her being a cleaner. She had never said anything to that effect to Sally, or acted as if she minded, but the young ones were so self-conscious about status, and more aware of what was available in life than she had ever been as a child. When Sally was growing up, no one round where she lived had anything. Posh people were rarely encountered, and the only time she had felt inadequate was when she went to the grammar school. Bronagh had been to Belfast's only girls' comprehensive, but had chosen to leave at sixteen to do hairdressing. No role models, as Clare would say. It was just taken for granted that Evie and Rory and their friends would go to 'uni', as they called it, whether they were clever or not. It was indeed a different world.

On Friday morning before setting off for Donegal, Tony popped into the office to sign a few urgent letters. It was now almost noon and he hadn't come back. Clare had got herself into a state.

'Mum, you need to take a chill pill. You know Dad is always late,' said Evie helpfully.

'Yes,' snapped Clare, 'I do, unfortunately, but we have a long drive ahead of us, and I will be furious if we don't arrive in time for dinner; it's included in the price. The last thing we need is to be caught in the rush-hour traffic.'

Eventually Tony pulled up in front of a small crowd of onlookers who were trying to pacify Clare. As usual she had flitted from rage, to panic that something might have happened to him, and then back to rage as soon as she saw the car approach.

Tony went into the kitchen, muttering apologetically and started to gather up the bags. He was about to remark on the amount of luggage but thought better of it. Watched by Sally, Evie, Simon and Anna, he carefully loaded the bags into the boot and kissed Anna and Evie goodbye whilst dutifully listening to a tirade from Clare about her having to do his packing yet again. Clare twittered about the kitchen. Now that they were actually ready to go, she couldn't leave.

'Calm down,' said Sally. 'You'll not enjoy the drive. Here, don't forget your handbag.'

'You're right, Sally, we'd better go. Anna, be a good girl for Saffron, won't you? And Evie, please tell Rory not to overdo it tonight. I've asked Trevor to pop down to check on things.'

'Thanks a lot, Mum! It's for young people, not OAPs or randoms like Trevor.'

Tony started the engine. This was so bloody typical. He'd almost broken the sound barrier on the way home, and now Clare was doing her usual fussing.

'Right, we're leaving!' he yelled.

Finally the Saab wound its way back up the lane with Clare slumped in the passenger seat, and Sally, the children and the stray neighbours peeled off to their various tasks with a collective sigh of relief.

Sally hoped Clare would really unwind; she had been on wires all summer. She had to concede that at times Clare had a right to be infuriated with Tony. Sally hadn't laid eyes on him since she had come back. He rarely left that office of his, though what on earth he found to do there day and night she didn't know. Any dealings she had had with the Civil Service had given her the impression that they just spent the time thinking up ways to annoy people by inventing complicated forms to fill in. As she took the satisfyingly dry washing in from the line, she glanced up at the sky. It looked a bit iffy. She hoped the weather was going to hold, so at least the kids would have a dry night for their barbecue.

37

The layout of the Marlborough Road back lane prevented total privacy for any of the gardens, as they were situated on the other side of the lane from the houses. Some people had created their own space by constructing conservatories that shielded the garden from the general view – as in Miss Black's case – but others, like the McDonalds, had simply gone for the open-plan garden.

Rory and Evie's guests mostly knew to come down the back through the gates at the top. That evening, as they passed Saffron's kitchen window, she saw that they all carried large parcels of drink from the off-licence. She hoped that they wouldn't be too rowdy a bunch, for there seemed to be an awful lot of them, and she hoped too that it wouldn't go on all night. Her bedroom was at the back of the house, and sound carried.

It was early evening, summer was waning, and dusk was earlier. Simon and Anna were out roaming round like the free-range children they were. It was a safe environment, and the older ones were good to them. Saffron thought she'd give them till nine o'clock then get them in for bed. Anna was spending the night at the McNamaras', as were the extended hamster family.

Evie and Rory had borrowed garden furniture from a few of the houses to add to their own. Evie had also bought plastic cups, though most of the guests were drinking beer out of bottles. Earlier, on his way to work, Mikey had dropped in and, winking heavily at Evie, handed her a bag of 'brownies'.

'No, Mikey, don't be ridiculous. None of Rory's friends take drugs.'

'They're hardly drugs – there's only a wee bit of pot in them.'

'Well just take them away. Dad would go crazy if we did that in the house.'

'But I'm already late for work; I can't bring them into the bar.'

'Right!' Evie took them and shoved them into a cupboard. 'You can get them when you come back.'

By eight o'clock Rory had the barbecue ready and was cooking sausages, chops and steak; anything his mates had managed to purloin from home. This was Rory at his best, wise-cracking with all his old school friends. Most were off at different universities now, but when they met up in the holidays they reverted to schoolboy behaviour. They were still at that stage boys go through when affection is expressed with a mock punch. Evie thought them all too immature for words, and they were two years older than she was as well. Mikey and his gang didn't behave like that, but then they were different, they weren't students. Mikey was the only one in his flat in full-time employment.

Evie had invited three of her girlfriends, but was still hoping Bronagh would come too. She saw Bronagh as a sort of project. Even a week or so since the incident, she couldn't for the life of her work out why Bronagh had even gone near the dreaded Otis. She must have no self-confidence. Evie thought her very pretty – even if she wore too much make-up, and her earrings were too big. She did have a slightly pronounced Belfast accent, but she was a warm, friendly girl, and after all, her mother was almost part of Evie's family. She'd give Bronagh till nine, and then she'd call her to check if she was coming.

The barbecue was in full swing when the heavens opened. Chaos ensued, as the by now large crowd decanted themselves into the McDonalds' freshly cleaned kitchen. Evie and Rory exchanged a look of anguish. They knew they would be unable to relax for the rest of the evening – a fairly accurate guess as things turned out.

The din was deafening; the kitchen had the lowest ceiling in the house and was already starting to look trashed. Rory hoped fervently the rain would cease. He had been in and out to the barbecue in the downpour, and was getting fed up.

The girls, at least those who were Evie's friends, had made their way into the living room, and settled down for a running commentary on Rory's mates: who was fit and who wasn't. Evie just thought that all Rory's friends were morons, since they still roamed in a pack and acted like eejits when confronted with a bunch of girls.

The doorbell rang, and Evie went to get it. Bronagh stood on the doorstep looking apprehensive.

'Brilliant,' Evie exclaimed. 'I'm really glad you came. I hope there's some food left.'

'Well I've eaten already. I wasn't going to come, and then Mum said she'd pay for a taxi over.'

'Great. C'mon, I'll introduce you to my friends.'

Bronagh followed Evie into the room and was introduced to the gang. Her hair was pale blonde with a pink fringe, which drew admiring comments. The other girls were still at school and the rules did not permit multicoloured hair.

While the girls chatted and drank their alcopops and vodkas in the living room, the boys gradually loosened their inhibi-

244

tions in the kitchen. Mikey drifted in after midnight. The decibels had climbed, and even Rory was starting to relax. As yet, no one had made the connection between the heightened euphoria they were all starting to feel, and the bag of brownies Rory's friend Robbie had found earlier in a cupboard and handed out. Mikey had a bottle of vodka with him, and this too was liberally distributed.

Bronagh alone remained sober. She was on her way to the bathroom when she noticed a bedroom door wide open and one of the boys passed out on the bed.

'Evie,' she called downstairs, 'there's someone lying on your mum's bed, looks in a pretty bad way.'

Evie disentangled herself from Mikey and ran upstairs. She was drunk, but not as much as some. She took one look at the prostrate body and ran down in a fury to get Rory.

'Rory, that moron of a friend of yours is upstairs lying on Mum's bed and groaning!'

'Which moron?'

'Robbie.'

'Is Orla not with him?'

'No, she's pulled Johnny and they're outside.'

'In the rain?'

'It's stopped raining.'

'Evie, just leave him. He'll be fine.'

'He won't be fine. We'd better call him a taxi.'

Rory went upstairs to check things out for himself, wondering why his head was spinning so much; he'd only been drinking beer. Besides, with policing his friends all night, he thought he had remained reasonably sober. Robbie was sprawled unconscious across the newly laundered bedclothes. His shoes had left large mud stains on the duvet cover. Rory gave him a shake and was rewarded by a low moan.

'Evie, he's passed out. We'd better leave him till he wakes up. A taxi wouldn't take him.'

'Well he can't stay there.'

Evie summoned help, and several rather drunken young revellers attempted to move Robbie off the bed. Suddenly he lifted his head upright, fixed his mouth into a wide O shape, and threw up all over the bed, the carpet and the magazine rack, Rory's jeans and shoes and anyone within three feet of him.

'Why did you invite this stupid eejit? I knew this would happen. He always gets wasted. Mum and Dad will be furious. We promised them there'd be no bother.'

'I'll clean it up in the morning, we can wash the sheets.'

'Right, well that's it! I'm telling everyone to leave now. The party is over.'

While Rory went and got a cloth and the vacuum cleaner, Evie flounced out of the room and stormed down the stairs.

'Out! Out! Now!' she screamed. 'Everybody leave!'

She seemed hysterical. A few people shrugged and started to move.

Bronagh had been sitting in the living room feeling somewhat overwhelmed. This was the first party of this kind she had ever been to; in a private house, that is. None of her mates lived in anything big enough to throw a party. She had been at drunken gatherings before, in clubs and that, but even she had been kind of surprised to see how out of it most of the boys here were. She wondered had they been taking anything else. When Evie finally stopped shrieking and attempting to push people out the door, she went over to her, touched her on the arm and tentatively suggested this, and then wondered immediately if she had put her foot in it. But Evie didn't seem upset by the question. She shook her head.

'No way, Rory's friends are totally straight; they don't even smoke dope . . . Oh my God.'

She shot out of the room like an arrow and into the kitchen. Bronagh followed. Evie pulled open a cupboard door beside the Aga.

246

'Shit, shit, shit!' She glared at the already dwindling group of boys who remained in the kitchen. Some had already left after hearing the fracas upstairs. 'Did anyone here eat the brownies?'

Blank stares all round.

'They were in this cupboard.'

'Do you mean those wee chocolate buns?' Sam, Rory's best pal, asked her, words slurring, eyes rolling round in his head. 'Aye, we had those hours ago. They were class.'

'Aaaah! No wonder everyone's wasted! Why didn't I just throw them in the bin? Oh Bronagh, just say someone has taken an overdose? What'll I do?'

'I'm not exactly sure, but I don't think you can overdose on pot, though it would probably be better not to drink. No one is driving, are they?'

'No, absolutely not.'

'Well then, they'll just sleep it off probably.'

Mikey sauntered in then, vodka bottle in one hand, a lump of hash in the other. With a smirk he asked the group casually, 'Does anyone want to skin up?'

He was totally unprepared for Evie's reaction. She let out a loud roar, and despite her slight frame managed to push him bodily towards the front door and out on to the street before anyone could reply. He was too stunned – or stoned – to protest.

'Don't come back here!' she screamed after him. 'You've ruined everything!'

'Listen, I'd better call a taxi,' Bronagh suggested.

'No, it takes ages on a Friday night. Why don't you stay with me? Jennie's dad is picking all the others up at one. Please, Bronagh?'

Bronagh looked at Evie and immediately felt sorry for her. She was just a kid really. It had all been too much.

'Right, I'll text Mum and say I'm staying. She checks her

phone if she wakes up and I'm not in. Now, Rory, you collect up the bottles and Evie and myself will load the dishwasher. Then we'll all go to bed.'

Rory and Evie looked at each other in utter relief, thankful that someone was taking charge. The party had not worked out remotely as planned and they both felt somewhat defeated by events. Evie was so glad she had invited Bronagh. Eighteen-year-old girls were so much more sensible than boys of that age.

38

Sally listened carefully, trying to keep a straight face, as Evie explained how Rory had managed to break the vacuum cleaner. She had arrived first thing Monday morning to a surprisingly clean house; albeit with a rather unpleasant smell of sick mingling with Clare's best Jo Malone candles. Clare and Tony were due back at lunchtime.

'Hmm,' she had remarked, 'funny smell round here.'

'Oh Sally, it was awful. Someone threw up all over Mum and Dad's room and Rory tried to vacuum it up, and then he vacuumed a sock to clean out the hose, and then the sock got stuck in the hose and he tried to get it out with a wire coat hanger. And then the coat hanger got stuck—'

'And don't tell me – he's punctured the hose?'

'Yes, in six places.'

'Your mammy's lovely purple cleaner; and she only bought that new last year.'

'Did Bronagh tell you what happened?'

'She mentioned yiz had had a wee bit of bother.'

Bronagh had been surprisingly unforthcoming about the party, except to say she had enjoyed herself. Sally hadn't pressed her. She was quietly pleased that Bronagh and Evie seemed to be making friends. It would be good for Bronagh to widen her social circle, and good for Evie to know people who weren't indulged and middle class.

They were on the landing outside Clare and Tony's bedroom. It looked like a votive shrine. Evie had lined up every candle in the house and placed them around the room.

'Oh Sally, it really stinks. Do you think Mum will notice?'

They both knew that Clare had a nose like a bloodhound. There was no way she wouldn't register the smell.

'I would say so; sure it would knock you out of the house. I'll have a go at it with baking soda, and if you explain nicely, she won't be too hard on you. She'll need to know about her Dyson, though.'

'Oh Sally, I hope you're right.'

Sally did her best with the carpet, and with wide-open windows the smell faded. The vacuum cleaner was beyond repair. When she turned it on, it had the effect of wafting the smell of sick all over the house. She gave up and borrowed Saffron's. As she was leaving it back, she saw Tony drive in and park. Clare got out of the car. They both looked relaxed.

'Oh Sally, we had a lovely time. The place is gorgeous, and the food was lovely. I only wish we could have stayed for the rest of the week, though I did miss my baby,' she said, suddenly seeing Anna, who had raced out when she heard the car. Anna threw her arms round her mother. Tony unloaded the bags. Sally followed the small procession into the kitchen, which was as neat as a pin.

'Did you bring me anything, Mum?' said Anna.

'I might have. Just give us time to get in the door. I have to have a cup of tea.'

Evie was in the kitchen alone, Rory having gone off to work.

'I'll put the kettle on,' she said, and rushed to do it. 'Did you have a good time?'

'Yes, darling, absolutely lovely. Gosh, we should go away more often,' said Clare, amused by Evie's sudden helpfulness. 'Oh, how did your barbecue go, sweetie?'

'It rained, I mean really poured, and we had to come in, and . . .'

Evie looked at Sally expectantly.

'Well, Clare, there was a wee bit of a problem with the vacuum cleaner.'

'The vacuum cleaner? But it's hardly a year old.'

'Well, some wee lad who was at the party was sick, and Rory tried to vacuum it.'

'Vacuum sick? You're not serious?'

Tony walked back into the kitchen just then, having taken the bags upstairs.

'Has someone been sick in our bedroom? Unless, Clare, those expensive candles of yours are rancid. The smell is fairly overpowering.'

'Oh Dad, I'm really sorry!' Evie burst into tears.

'It doesn't matter, love,' said Clare, giving her a hug. 'These things happen at parties.'

Sally looked at Tony in surprise. 'You should take that woman away a bit more often.'

It was not just the relief of her mother's being so under-standing that prompted Evie's tears. Bronagh had stayed in her room on Friday night and they had chatted well into the early hours of Saturday morning. Slowly she had come to the conclusion that Mikey was the wrong boy for her. She had known that all along, but somehow having someone her own age disapprove of his liking for drugs clarified things.

The following night she had met up with him and broken off the relationship. She could have dumped him by phone, so his reaction, which was bitter and included calling her a spoilt

251

middle-class bitch, threw her. It also had the effect of making her even more determined to stick to her guns. She assessed her situation. She had been dossing all year and her marks were down. She determined to work harder next year and pass all her A levels. She suddenly saw with great clarity that she wanted to go to university and make something of her life. Perhaps if she did well in her exams she would take a gap year first, as Rory had done, but that was a long way away. She didn't say any of this to her parents; even she realised that it was time for action, not words.

39

The last few months had been a whirlwind for Sally: Charlie getting out of jail, her starting and finishing at Maids to Order, leaving and going back to Marlborough Road. At times she had thought her life was rushing wildly out of control, but now suddenly the storm had passed and she had a focus again.

She was looking forward to her holiday, and afterwards to going to college. She had taken Clare's advice and bought a few classic books. They were only a pound each – imagine! When she had been at school, books were expensive. She was forever making excuses when she came in without the money for a new textbook. Comparatively, these paperbacks were so cheap. She got the titles Clare had suggested, and then added *Wuthering Heights*, *Emma* and *Oliver Twist*; all books she had read while at school and loved. She wasn't that struck on TV anyway; she had always enjoyed reading and never given up on it. But like many others, she was fond of the new chick lit and crime. Not any more; she was on the road to self-improvement.

She persuaded Bronagh to do Edith's hair. Otis had snaffled the original free voucher, but Bronagh said Miss Black could come to the salon on Wednesday evening. It would give her a boost. She was making a steady recovery, but she had been through a lot. First her operation, and then Ellen dying; and she had a week of chemotherapy ahead of her before the trip.

Fintan had been as good as his word and phoned both Edith and Sally to tell them he was settled in Glasgow. He had borrowed a friend's flat in the West End and was managing nicely, though he missed Marlborough Road. He was keen to hear all the details of the forthcoming trip to Crete, and his enthusiasm was adding to Sally's anticipation.

The others in the salon were giving Bronagh funny looks; Miss Edith Black was not by any stretch of the imagination their usual type of client. She had phoned for an appointment and arrived on the dot, announcing loudly that she was a client of Bronagh's. Then she had proceeded to tell all within earshot what a pretty girl Bronagh had turned out. Bronagh was glad she had dyed her hair back to her own natural brown this week. She smiled weakly as Edith filled Alan in on their connection.

'I have known Bronagh since she was a little girl, so I am prepared to put myself in her safe hands. Her mother and I are off to visit the Minoan ruins together in a matter of weeks.'

Alan nodded in a knowing way, though he hadn't an idea what she was gurning on about. Still, she sounded well-spoken, a potential regular, and he was impressed in spite of himself.

Edith explained carefully to Bronagh that she merely wanted a trim, though she was persuaded to have her hair shampooed first, a job Bronagh did not trust to Jimmy, but did herself. She then conditioned Miss Black's surprisingly long, thick white hair and was now carefully trimming the ends. Edith chatted away at the top of her voice as if she thought Bronagh was a bit hard of hearing. She seemed oblivious to the fact that the entire salon was listening, even above the hairdryers.

'Oh yes, Bronagh, your mother is a national treasure, so competent. I can't think how we would manage our lives without her.'

Bronagh put Miss Black's hair into a French pleat. She thought it looked great, very elegant. She had used a tinted shampoo, which had taken the yellowish tinge out of it. She held the mirror so Miss Black could see the back.

'Oh, that looks wonderful, Bronagh. Aren't you very clever?' She fumbled for her purse and produced a few pound coins, pressing them into Bronagh's hand as if it was a fortune. 'Thank you so much, and please do give Sally any more free vouchers if you get them. I'm very pleased with this.'

And she patted her head approvingly, had a final glance in the mirror and swished out of the door of the salon.

Sally and Charlie met in the solicitor's office. Sally was delighted her solicitor was a woman; Charlie was indignant and demanded to see 'the boss'. It was embarrassing. Their decree nisi was a formality anyway. In Northern Ireland you had to prove you had been apart for five years to get a divorce; well, since Charlie had been locked up for more than that, it wasn't much of a problem. Sally had got a legal separation about six years ago; it was necessary in order for her to get housing benefit. Her wages weren't enough to cover her rent.

In the days following her phone call to Charlie, the more Sally thought about it, the more convinced she became that now was the right time to get a divorce. She was, in a sense, beginning a new life, and perhaps it was better to start it as a single woman. Besides, it would in a way be a deterrent to Charlie. At least he could be sure that she meant it when she said she would never have him back. It also might speed his journey across the water.

Yesterday, when she had spoken to him to remind him that they were meeting the solicitor, he had seemed reluctant.

'I thought maybe you were ringing me up to say you wanted me back.'

'Charlie, that's not going to happen.'

'I've paid my dues, Sally.'

'I know, but sure we weren't even living together when you were put away.'

'Put away! You make it sound like I was a dog or something.'

'You know rightly what I mean.'

'Did Bronagh tell you I had a wee chat with her?'

Sally's heart sank. So she had been right about Bronagh seeing him. She wished her daughter had felt able to confide in her. But she didn't want Charlie knowing that.

'Yes, I think she mentioned it.'

'She'd like us back together.'

'Well Bronagh of all people should know that's just a fantasy. I need to move on, Charlie, and so do you.'

'We're getting on, Sally; neither of us is a spring chicken.'

'You speak for yourself!' Sally was forty-two, young enough to start again. Sure she was younger than Madonna, for God's sake. 'I want a divorce, Charlie, and I can get it with or without your permission.'

He had agreed to the meeting then.

The solicitor said they would get legal aid and it was just a matter of signing a few forms; there wasn't much in the way of worldly goods. The contents of Sally's house had all been bought and paid for by her, and the house, until she could get the money to buy it, remained the property of the housing executive. So Charlie was due half of nothing.

They filled in several forms. The woman told them the divorce papers would be mailed out to them.

Despite everything, Sally was sad as she left the office. Charlie lingered. He seemed unwilling to walk away. He touched her awkwardly on the sleeve.

'I'm dead sorry it all had to end, Sally. We were a great wee couple at first.'

'I know, but that was a long time ago, Charlie. It's all water under the bridge.'

She was sounding a lot harder than she felt, because she was gutted by it all really. It had been a while since she'd had any illusions, but they had started their marriage with so much hope. She had really meant it to be 'till death us do part'. For all his flaws, she was sure he had too. Still, it hadn't been all bad: they had produced Bronagh.

'I'm sure Bronagh will stay in touch with you.'

'I'd like that, but she seems to think it would upset you.'

'Charlie, I would be more than happy if she kept in touch. She's eighteen now, and whatever has happened between us, you're still her father. Sure isn't she the image of you?'

Charlie's expression softened, and he smiled for the first time that morning.

'D'ye think so?'

Sally took a look into his lovely blue eyes, ignoring the beer belly and the receding hairline.

'Yes, of course I do, I'll tell her to give you a ring.'

When they parted, Sally got on her bike and drove in the direction of Marlborough Road. Her face was wet with tears.

Bronagh got up to clear the plates. Sally had been sitting throughout dinner wondering how to broach the subject of Charlie and the divorce. The last thing she wanted to do was to make Bronagh feel guilty. It wasn't as if she wanted to wring a confession out of her. Who could blame her for wanting to see her own father?

'I saw your daddy today, this morning actually.'

'Oh?'

'We're getting divorced; we had to sign the papers.'

'Well, Mammy, it'll not make the *Irish News*, will it?'

257

'No, I just thought you'd like to know that it's official, legal, whatever. That's all.'

'Okay. I hardly thought you'd be getting back together.'

'Bronagh love, I just want to tell you that I don't mind if you go out with your daddy now and again. I know he's off to work in Coventry with Tommy any day now.'

'Why would I go out with him?'

'I just thought . . .' Sally trailed off uncomfortably.

'He came round here once; you were at my granny's. I didn't let him stay. That's the only time I've talked to him.'

'Oh . . . ?'

'You needn't believe me if you don't want to.'

And Bronagh rushed from the kitchen and upstairs. Sally waited a second and then followed. Bronagh was lying on her bed sobbing her heart out. Sally hugged her.

'There, love, there, I didn't mean to hurt your feelings. It's just that one of those nights you said you were out with Tiffany, well, she called looking for you.'

Bronagh sat up and stopped crying. She really didn't want to tell Sally about Otis. There was no point now, and in truth she was a bit ashamed of it all. Viewed from this distance, it had been a big mistake. She wasn't sure what she had been hoping for in going out with him; certainly not romance; maybe the chance to make her way a bit in the realms of culture. Even though the relationship, such as it was, had been a disaster in the end, she'd enjoyed going to different places and wouldn't be afraid to try new things next time, and in a way it had helped strengthen her friendship with Evie too.

Sally was waiting for her to say something, but she decided there was little point in explaining. It would be better for her mother not to know. She trusted Evie and Tiffany not to say anything.

'I was going out with a boy and Tiffany didn't like him,

258

that's all. I didn't really think you would like him either. Anyway, it's over now and I'm okay.'

'Are you sure?'

'Yes, Mammy, I'm sure.'

Sally decided not to quiz her any further. Whatever had happened was done with anyway.

40

Marlborough Road was calming down, in a manner of speaking. The birds still sang, Lola still barked, but summer was definitely drawing to a close. The trees were slightly less lush. The conkers were hardening on the chestnut trees. There were a few late-blooming roses, but the apples were on the trees, and since it had been such a hot summer, the blackberries were ripening early on the brambles in Saffron's garden. Sally hoped fervently that she wouldn't take one of her mad notions for jam. The thought of all those big messy pans made her shudder. It hardly seemed possible that the kids would all be going back to school next week.

The first week of September, Edith was going back into hospital for her chemotherapy treatment. She was being very positive about it, although naturally enough this was all on the surface. She had discussed it with Clare and Saffron and with her friend Isabelle, and of course she had talked things over with Sally. Sally planned to call in on her every day on the way home from Marlborough Road, and assured her that she would have the house shipshape for her return. Not that there was anyone there to blight the perfection of number

29; without any lodgers, the place was astonishingly quiet.

Sally wasn't sure if the quiet suited the house any more. In her mind, Fintan had changed the dynamic of the place for good. He had added pizzazz to the quiet Victorian house, and it didn't seem to want to settle back down. Another lodger had been due to arrive mid-September, but Edith had cried off because of her illness. She would participate in the programme again come spring.

Sally herself was focusing on the fact that, like the children, she too was going back to school. After all these years she would be a student again. Her heart was in her mouth at the thought of it, but she was also looking forward to it. She had bought some pens and notepads and couldn't contain her excitement at the idea of having lectures. She would miss two nights because of the holiday. Her tutor, May, had been very understanding when she explained she was going off for the week with a friend who would be recuperating from chemo. She told her she would catch up easily.

Bronagh was impressed by the fact that her mother had actually got around to enrolling in the classes. Sally's sister Eileen, however, seemed to find the idea odd, and said so to Bronagh.

'Your mother's getting some rare ideas, doing her GCSEs at her age. She always said she couldn't wait to leave school. I don't know how she can be bothered going back.'

'She had to leave school early. Granny and Granda needed the money. She was the oldest.'

'I know she's the oldest, but why on earth would she want to go back and learn now?'

'Maybe because she wants to make something of herself, Eileen. I mean, there's more to life than drinking in bars, you know.'

Eileen, affronted at Bronagh's cheek, was for once lost for words. Bronagh was grimly satisfied at having snapped at her aunt; she was glad Sally was nothing like Eileen. She was beginning to appreciate her mother more than ever, realising how solid a support she had been all her life. It couldn't have been easy for her to get herself over to south Belfast every working day for the past ten years and clean houses. She deserved a chance now to do something for herself. It would be brilliant that Sally had somewhere interesting to go two nights a week; maybe she'd even make a few new friends, or meet someone else. And having reacquainted herself with Charlie, Bronagh was even more convinced that her mother was doing the right thing. If they had ever had anything in common, those two, Charlie's behaviour had put paid to it. Bronagh would keep in touch with him, though. He was still her da after all. Maybe if she ever got married he could give her away, she thought wryly.

Saffron was impossibly large, and could hardly get about. Sally noted that Trevor seemed back to his old adoring self. He was living on his nerves, though, winging it on a daily basis. Each day that passed uneventfully, without the prospect of Laura looming in front of him, he took as a blessing. He arrived home from work on time each day, and thanked the gods that Saffron was having an uneventful if taxing pregnancy.

Since his emotional evening at the McNamaras', Bill Nelson had rarely been seen around, though his car went up the lane each morning at eight on the dot. Neither Laura nor the children had reappeared. A For Sale sign had gone up on the house, and there was much speculation about what it would fetch; property prices in the area had soared. The break-up was a considerable source of speculation. Patricia Thompson, who was closer to Laura than either Clare or Saffron, told Clare that things hadn't been good between the couple for quite a few years. It appeared that having the twins had done for them. Laura had tried her best to combine motherhood and her job with only a series of au pairs for support. But the twins, as Sally had always observed, were not the easiest, and Bill had rarely been at home while they were small. Laura had been nagging at him for ages to move to England to be near her parents, and getting nowhere. Clare repeated all this to Sally and Edith, but both agreed not to pass on to Saffron the bit about the twins — it was better she was kept in the dark about that particular detail.

On Monday morning, Clare and Sally took Edith to the hospital for her treatment. She would be there for a few days. In line with her new attitude, she allowed them to fuss over her and agreed readily to any proposed visits. Sally had insisted she buy herself some new nighties, a pair of slippers, and a lovely pink silk dressing gown, which Edith thought was positively frivolous. She had been about to complain at the expense when Sally silenced her by assuring her that she would get many years' wear out of it. This thought in itself cheered her up.

'You're right, Sally,' she said. 'I'll just have to live long enough to wear it out!'

Edith was really enjoying the relief of dispensing with the stiff upper lip. If people wanted to make a fuss of her, well then, she would let them. It was only a matter of learning not to say no at once. She would obey her instincts of course; at this stage in her life she didn't want to turn into some maudlin old cow. She had had an aunt, a sister of her mother's, who went that way in later years. It was most embarrassing for her parents. However, the other side of Aunt Maud's 'condition' was that she became very affectionate towards Edith and Ellen. The two girls had liked that part.

Edith thought that she and Sally might even have some fun on this forthcoming holiday. She was looking forward it. Clare had given her an up-to-date book on Crete to take into hospital. She would concentrate on that and just find a way to cope with the ghastly chemotherapy. She'd be at home for two full weeks after her treatment, and with luck would be back to normal before they left for Crete. After all, as Mr Smedley said, this was a 'belt and braces' approach; he was just being extra sure. At any rate, she felt extremely optimistic.

There was little anyone could do to make chemotherapy a pleasant experience, but Sally was determined Edith would get through it with the minimum of unpleasantness. She had worked out a game plan. She would make sure Edith ate no hospital food, so each day she dutifully picked up a little package lovingly prepared by Clare and brought it up to the hospital. Clare was such a good cook, and made delicate little sandwiches and sent small jars of French yoghurt and flasks of beautiful homemade soup. Edith was ecstatic in her appreciation. She looked forward to Sally's visits, and despite the unpleasantness of the drip, she was holding out bravely. Saffron had loaded her up with herbal remedies as a protection against hair loss, but she had further treatment to come on her return from holiday, and was aware her lovely thick hair might be affected. She had chosen a rather elegant wig just in case. But she might be lucky. She was taking each day at a time, the thought of the Greek sunshine determinedly in her thoughts.

41

Sally brought Edith's suitcase down from the cupboard at the top of the house. She and Clare were helping her pack for the holiday. Sally had ironed every item carefully and was folding them into the suitcase. She had Edith's shoes all polished and in lovely cloth drawstring bags, her underwear packed in silk envelopes with zips. The two of them were off tomorrow, and there was an air of excitement in the gathering.

'I'm so jealous. I wish I was going with you,' Clare said.

'Oh Clare, you're hardly back from France and you told me you had a wonderful time.' Saffron looked a bit rueful. 'Trevor says we're following your example next year; no more wilds of Donegal for him. He has visions of pastis before supper, and divine Provençal wine to drink, sitting on our terrace overlooking the lavender fields, or endless rows of strong, erect sunflowers.'

'Good, you'll love it. Perhaps we could have a magical mystery tour from the lane to Provence.' Clare shuddered inwardly at the thought of spending a summer holiday with four extra children and two vegetarians, but she knew it was just chat. It would never come to pass; Tony would put his foot down.

Saffron smiled benignly, now and then readjusting her bulk. Her belly was huge, and any excitement caused the twins to somersault and twist around inside her. Their movements were visible to all. Posy spent a lot of her time these days addressing her mother's bump, telling the two wee babies in there that they could play with her dolly and watch Pingu if they would just hurry up and come out. Even Edith, who had never been involved in the pregnancies of any of the women in the lane, was fascinated by the whole process, so the packing was quite a long-drawn-out affair. Eventually the case was ready and Clare and Saffron left.

Sally busied about, setting things right. The flight tomorrow was at a respectable time. The plan was that Sally would come over to Edith's and Trevor would drive them to the airport. She herself would finish packing tonight. It was all done really; she had been putting things in her suitcase for a week now. She had only to close it.

She was on her way out the back door when Edith called her back.

'Sally, there's something I want to say to you before we leave. Please sit down.'

Sally put her crash helmet on the kitchen table and pulled out a chair. She felt apprehensive; for a brief instant it flashed across her mind that Edith was going to say she had changed her mind about the holiday. It was all a bit unreal anyway, too good to be true.

'Sally, I have been doing a lot of thinking whilst in hospital, and I have decided to let you know that I had intended leaving you quite a large sum of money when I die.'

'Ach, Miss Black . . . I mean Edith, sure didn't the surgeon say you were great? It'll be a long time till you go.'

'Precisely. I aim to be around for quite some time. So I have been having a rethink. Ellen has unexpectedly left me an extremely large amount in her will. I have no immediate need

266

of it, so you may as well have your legacy now. It's possible that I could live to be a hundred – a lot of women do these days.'

Sally was dumbfounded. Had she heard correctly? Edith Black was going to give her a large sum of money?

Edith sat across from her with a smile on her face, waiting for her to speak.

'Well, what do you think?'

'Edith, I couldn't . . .'

'Yes you most certainly could, but assuming you accept, there are two conditions that I will expect you to adhere to. We'll have my solicitor draw us up a proper contract.'

'Two conditions?'

'Yes. Firstly, I want you to use the money to buy your house.'

Here she paused and took a deep breath.

'And the second is this, and I am very aware that this is a selfish stipulation: I want you to continue working for me as long as you are physically able. Now what do you think?'

Sally wasn't sure what she was thinking. She was dumb-struck.

'I know it's rather sudden, announcing it like this. I was going to tell you while we were away, and then I thought it better to let you know now. That way you could perhaps enjoy the holiday more, not having money worries, and perhaps you and I could treat ourselves a bit as well.'

'Edith, it's really kind of you, but I'm not sure if I can accept it.'

'Nonsense, of course you can. As I said, I have had lots of time to think whilst in hospital, and there's an old saying – I'm almost certain I heard it from you – "There are no pockets in a shroud."'

'You probably did. My mammy says that a lot.'

'And your mother is right. You know, my sister Ellen enjoyed her life and still managed to leave a considerable estate. I feel

267

I should follow her example. I have more than enough money to enjoy whatever is left of my time. I don't have expensive tastes, so it seems entirely logical to share some of my good fortune with you. Now what do you say? If all goes well in Crete, this need not be the last of our trips.'

Sally felt her emotions surge up, and before she could think about it, she went over to Edith, threw her arms around her and gave her a big hug. Edith, although slightly taken aback, found she liked the hug very much. She patted Sally on the back, and realised that the younger woman was on the verge of tears.

'Oh Edith, I just don't know what to say.'

'Well how about "thank you" and "I agree"?'

'Thank you very much . . . and yes, I agree.'

42

Later that evening, just as Sally was putting the final touches to her packing, separating the things that could go as hand luggage from those that had to be checked in, the phone rang. It was Fintan. He often phoned to find out how Edith was and to see what was happening on Marlborough Road. His voice sounded warm and friendly.

'I hope I'm not calling too late. I just wanted to say *au revoir.*'

Sally felt a warm glow. His voice really affected her. As far as she was concerned, it would never be too late for him to call.

'No, Fintan, not at all. I never go to bed early. It's lovely to hear from you. I'm finishing off my packing.'

'Good. I hope you and Edith will have a fantastic holiday in Agios Nikolaos. You'll love it. I've given Edith the names of a few good restaurants.'

Agios Nikolaos was the name of the town in Crete where Sally and Edith would be staying. Sally wasn't sure of the correct pronunciation; even Edith pronounced it differently each time, and made a joke of it by saying: 'It's all Greek to me.' Over the last few weeks Sally had taken to looking at the pictures of the town in the book Clare had given Edith, and of course in the holiday brochure too. It was a harbour town, and their hotel was one of the prettier ones, overlooking a lake. In the pictures it looked lovely.

'I spoke to Edith earlier, and she told me you had everything packed for her. You're very good to her.'

'Well she's very good to me. I enjoy doing it anyway.'

She was tempted to tell Fintan about Edith planning to give her the money for her house, but decided not to. It hadn't happened yet. She wondered if Edith had told him, but he didn't mention it, so Sally supposed she hadn't.

They talked about Edith's health, and Fintan said he'd try to get to Belfast soon for a long weekend. He'd been offered a job in Dublin in October and could just take the train up. He was off work all this week and was sorting out his flat in London. It had been months since he'd been in permanent residence.

'You wouldn't approve of the mess, Sally,' he laughed. 'You'd have all the rubbish in a bag ready to go out.'

After a few more minutes of chat about the lane and how Clare and Saffron and the others were keeping, he wished her a safe flight and said he'd talk to her very soon.

Sally put down the phone feeling unsettled. She knew she was being ridiculous, but Fintan's remark about her clearing out his rubbish had upset her. That was all he saw her as really, a cleaning lady. She quickly dismissed the thought. Sure he was just teasing, and hadn't she told him often enough about her desire to throw all the rubbish out of Saffron's or Clare's? That was all he meant. She had been up to high doh all evening anyway. She could think of little else but Edith's intention to buy her home for her. She walked around the house thinking how lovely it would be not to have to pay rent any more. This would all belong to her.

Bronagh came in shortly after Fintan's call, and assured her mother for the hundredth time that she would be able to manage fine on her own.

'Mum, I'll be grand. You just go off and enjoy yourself. I bet you'll have a fantastic time.'

'I hope so. Miss Black is going to hire a car. We're going to see some important ruins, and she says there's lovely wee fishing villages we can drive to. She doesn't like the sun. I hope she won't mind if I lie by the pool a wee bit; I'm so pasty-looking these days.'

'Mum, will you stop obsessing? You told me she said she didn't mind if you spent the entire holiday by the pool.'

'I know, but she's maybe just being polite. I'm sure she'll want somebody to go with her to look at the ruins. I don't know a thing about Greek ruins, but I suppose they'll tell you everything when you get there. Clare says it's just a lot of interesting stories about Greek heroes and that. It's called Knossos.'

She pronounced it *Konossos*. They both started laughing.

'I think that's how you say it.'

'I hope you get good weather, that's the main thing.'

'Oh, Clare has checked the forecast. It's supposed to be sunny all week.'

'Well then, what are you yacking on about? Just go and enjoy yourself.'

Next morning Sally arrived over at Edith's with her case. There was virtually a crowd there to see them off. Clare and Saffron fussed round making sure they had passports and tickets and that toothpaste and the various cosmetics were in see-through bags. Sally hoped Saffron wouldn't unexpectedly have the twins while they were gone; she appeared to have got bigger overnight. Posy had made Edith a 'Have a Lovely Holiday' card; at least that was what she said it was. Sally thought it looked like a drawing of Iggy the iguana.

Trevor was as prompt as any taxi and very chatty on the drive to the airport. He got them there with hours to spare. Sally was a bit apprehensive about the flight; she wondered what on earth she would find to talk about to Edith for almost five hours, but she needn't have worried. Edith seemed to want to talk about growing up in Belfast, and how things had changed so much since her youth, and Sally wasn't bored at all. Edith had lived in the terrace all her life, and she chatted about the various families who had come and gone over the years. The current residents had mostly been there for the last twenty years. There would be some competition for the Nelsons' place, since houses in Marlborough Road didn't make it on to the market very often.

She asked Sally about where she lived, and Sally told her. It seemed like a different world.

'You know, once you own the house, you can always sell it and move. You don't seem to like living over that part of town.'

That was true: Sally didn't, although things had been a lot better since the Troubles had ended. Most of the people who lived in her area had been there all their lives. And her parents were nearby. That had been a godsend when Bronagh was young; it meant that the child had somewhere to go after school when Sally was working.

She was glad Edith had brought up the subject of the house again. It reassured her that she hadn't just dreamt it all. They chatted happily about the holiday. Edith seemed to take flying in her stride, but then she had travelled quite a bit. Sally hadn't flown much in her life; about six times, she worked out. It was a bit bumpy going over the Alps, and Sally had to suppress her fear. She was glad when they landed safely and she could relax. Edith had dozed off during the last part of the flight. It was tiring for her, but at least they would be in their hotel in about an hour, and they could go to bed early. There was a coach organised, but Edith had decided they would take a taxi.

'By the time they have everyone rounded up, we could be in our beds,' she declared.

They had been served dinner on the plane; it wasn't great, but it would do them for tonight. It was ten o'clock local time when they stepped out on to the tarmac. Darkness had fallen, but even so the air was balmy. Sally felt bleary-eyed and concerned about Edith, who looked exhausted. They made their way in a straggle through passport control and to the baggage reclaim. With luck they would get a taxi quickly. At least they had the euros and no worries about currency. The first time Sally had been abroad was to Spain, and she had spent the entire time trying to work out prices in pesetas. She thought the euro a great idea.

She found a trolley and loaded the bags on to it, and pushed it through into the arrivals lounge. The signs for taxis were in English and Greek, and they were just about to head in that direction when Edith's phone rang.

The mobile phone was a recent acquisition of Edith's. She had bought it when Ellen was dying, so she could be contacted at any time. Sally thought it was hilarious watching her use it. She didn't seem to realise that it wasn't connected to anything, and appeared to have the idea that it was necessary to speak up and enunciate very loudly while on it.

Sally hoped nothing was wrong. She had planned to text Bronagh when she got to the hotel, so she couldn't even understand why Edith had switched her phone on. Unless she had forgotten to turn it off in the first place, though that seemed most unlike her.

Sally stopped beside her and made a show of fixing the luggage in case Edith thought she was eavesdropping.

'There's no one there,' Edith said with some annoyance. 'It's just a text saying I can use my phone here. Honestly, as if I didn't already check that.'

Suddenly Sally felt a tap on her shoulder. She turned round

abruptly and almost fainted when she saw Fintan standing in front of them with a wide grin on his face.

'Oh my God, Fintan, what are you doing here?'

She turned to Edith, thinking that she must have known, but Edith was also looking at Fintan as if she had seen a ghost.

'Heavens, Fintan . . . you're here?'

'Yes, sorry it had to be such a surprise, but I wasn't sure of my timetable until yesterday.'

'But I talked to you last night!' Sally exclaimed.

'I know, I know. I booked the flight two days ago on impulse. It's easy to get one at this time of year . . . I got in two hours ago from London. I had intended to tell you when I called last night, then decided it would be better to surprise you both . . . I mean, you might have dissuaded me from coming.'

'As if we would,' Edith replied. 'It's just delightful to see you here.'

The two women looked at each other with a mixture of pleasure and confusion, both obviously thrilled that he had appeared. Sally relinquished the trolley to him and Edith took his arm, and the three of them walked towards the exit.

'I know we're going to have a really perfect week.' And Edith smiled blissfully at Sally, who nodded mutely, feeling absurdly happy, as if she was in a dream.

'Good, that's settled then,' Fintan said happily. 'Now, ladies, I've already hired a car, and it's waiting outside. I have been thinking for the last week – ever since I found out I was free – that I couldn't leave two lovely ladies like you for an entire week without an escort. So here I am to offer my services as a guide. After all, I know my way around here, and you both need to be handled with care.'

The two women smiled in agreement and allowed him to manoeuvre the laden trolley expertly towards the exit. It looked like the holiday had got off to a flying start.

When Fintan had loaded the car and was heading out of

the airport towards Agios Nikolaos, Sally and Edith began to relax. The windows were down and the balmy night air with the fragrant whiff of wild oregano drifted around them.

'You know, ladies,' Fintan said with a smile in his voice, 'I've never missed anywhere as much as I have Marlborough Road.'

Sally immediately thought of the For Sale sign that had gone up on the Nelsons' house just yesterday. She could hardly mention that, could she? But Edith didn't miss a beat.

'Well, Fintan,' she said quickly, 'I think we have a house coming on the market very soon. I could always mention your name to the residents' committee . . .'

Your Cheatin' Heart

by Annie McCartney

A novel of sex, drugs and rock 'n' roll

When twenty-one-year-old Maggie Lennon leaves
Northern Ireland to work for the summer in America,
what she finds is the weird and wonderful world of
Chattanooga, Tennessee; a job as an all-night DJ for
Radio WA1A radio; a boss called Zollie D Follie; and
a best friend, Sharla Emma-Lea Ayn, who introduces
her to sex, drugs and rock 'n' roll. Soon she's mingling
with pop stars including Buford 'BigBoy' McConnell,
falling in love with Nate, whose family own half of
Tennessee, and partying with the in crowd.

But then the bubble bursts. Her love life crash lands
and the drugs don't work any more. Pretty soon
Maggie's standing with a gun in her hand, Buford's
girlfriend Sue Lynne is lying on the floor and the
police are on their way . . .

'A rollicking, no-punches-pulled take about love, lust
and romantic crash-landings' *Woman's Own*

'Maggie Lennon dives into life with a delicious
fervour' Stella Duffy

978 0 7515 3593 8

All I Want is You

by Martina Reilly

Poppy Furlong has the dream life – gorgeous home,
loving husband and a five-year-old son she adores.
Then overnight she loses it all – her home, gym
membership, expensive car, regular trips to the beauty
salon – because her husband's business partner has
disappeared with the company profits.

As she attempts to rebuild her family, Poppy leaves
Dublin for the suburbs. There she acquires a mother-
in-law from hell, a father she hardly knows, a new job,
a new friend, a better insight into parenting, and a
new life. Will it match up to the old one? Or might
it just be better?

'Hard to put down, laugh-out-loud funny . . . perfect
holiday reading' *Woman's Way*

'A compelling, heart-wrenching tale that will keep you
riveted till the end' Collette Caddle

978 0 7515 3790 1

Wish Upon a Star

by Martina Reilly

It's hard for Lucy, being the sister of super-model Tracy Gleeson. It's hard because Tracy is gorgeous and Lucy feels distinctly average; Tracy is famous and Lucy works as a receptionist in a vet's clinic; Tracy has just landed a part in a major Hollywood movie and all Lucy has ever wanted to do is act.

Worse that that, however, is the fact that Lucy almost had it all – only she fell pregnant and is now a single mum living in a tiny house with Fianne, her daughter. While she loves her child with all her heart, she didn't quite imagine her life would feel over at the age of twenty-eight.

And now, Fianne wants to get to know her father – only Lucy never told him that she was pregnant. So, against the advice of her best friends and her doom-laden mother, Lucy begins the search to trace the boy she has tried so hard to forget . . .

'A cracking read – warm, splutter-out-your-tea funny, and unputdownable. I loved it' Sarah Webb

978 0 7515 3863 2

Wedded Blitz

by Martina Reilly

Warring spouses, embarrassing parents and the battle of the hairdressing salons . . .

When Jane married Jim, she thought it was for ever. But now there are cracks in their marriage that they just can't seem to fix. When Jim announces he's moving out, Jane is left to pick up the pieces of their family life. And then her mother decides to visit . . .

Determined to remain upbeat, Jane decides to make a real success of her work, only to discover that Cutting Edge, the hairdressing empire, is opening a shop only yards away from her own humble salon. With the staff in uproar and their customers deserting them in droves, Jane decides to play Cutting Edge at their own game.

Then life deals Jane and Jim one dreadful blow, past hurts rush to the surface, and they are forced to confront what drove them apart in the first place . . .

'Clever, frank and funny' *Bella*

978 0 7515 3845 8

Other bestselling titles available by mail: